Never Let H

Book Three

CW00524861

es

Please return/renew this item by the last date shown
on this label, or on your self-service receipt.

To renew this item, visit **www.librarieswest.org.uk**,
use the LibrariesWest app, or contact your library.

Your borrower number and PIN are required.

LibrariesWest

1 3 1788622 4

To my family, my readers, and everyone who has supported me while I worked on my No Escape series

Felicity

1

On some level I knew I was dreaming, but still I tossed and turned, tangling myself up in my sheets, my vision filled with the image of the rose on my windscreen. *Wake up,* I told myself. *Wake up, now!* I couldn't wake up, but my nightmare began to change, shifting to the memory of the house where Jay had kept me prisoner in Tatchley. I grabbed at my wrist, trying to free myself, listening intently for the sounds I knew would come next. Footsteps. Quiet at first, then louder as Jay approached the top of the stairs. My heart started to pound as he drew back the lock on the outside of my bedroom door. *This isn't real,* I told myself. *Wake up. Wake up now!*

But then a thought struck me. Perhaps it *was* real. Perhaps my escape from Jay had been the dream and I'd never really left this room. I clawed frantically at my wrist, screaming as my nails scraped the cold metal handcuff. 'No!' I screeched at the top of my lungs, and I carried on screaming as I woke up, because I couldn't remember where I was or that I was safe.

'Felicity,' a voice was saying. 'Felicity, stop. You're okay. You're okay.'

I was still making sounds. I was still scratching. The nightmare clung to me and I couldn't get out of it.

'Fliss,' the voice continued, its tone strong yet soothing. Gentle hands touched my arms, but I still didn't understand so I hit out wildly. 'It's me,' the voice said. 'It's Scott. You're at home. You're safe. The children are safe. Nobody else is here.'

'Scott,' I said slowly. He turned on his bedside light and I put my hands over my face because I was so frustrated and disappointed with myself for getting taken in by these nightmares. Scott didn't say anything; instead he started stroking my hair. Gradually I moved my hands away from my eyes and let his face come into view, and the sight of him filled me with a fresh surge of relief. His face was open, calm – the face of a man I loved, not the face of the monster Jay had turned out to be. Scott reached down to kiss my forehead and his stubbly beard prickled me. 'That was a bad one, wasn't it?' he said.

I nodded but didn't reply.

'You've made your wrist bleed.'

I turned my head to look at my arm but as I did our bedroom door opened, revealing two sleepy-looking boys. 'Mummy?' said Leo, hugging his cuddly toy dinosaur tightly, while Dennis just stared at me with his eyes huge, fiddling with the hem of his pyjama top and looking like he might start to cry.

Scott was instantly out of bed, putting an arm around each of the boys. 'Mummy just had a bad dream,' he told Leo. Then he turned to Dennis, who said, 'Flissty has too many bad dreams. Why does she scream all the time?'

Scott started to try to explain, and I pulled myself together and got out of bed to cuddle Leo. 'Did I wake you up?' I asked.

'Yeah.'

'I'm sorry, sweetie.'

'Why are you scared?'

'I'm not scared.'

He pushed me away, a gesture that tore at my heart, and he moved closer to Scott again. 'Daddy, stories,' he said. Scott looked round at me sympathetically. It had become a bit of routine: my nightmares would make me scream and wake up the boys, who would then expect to be read several stories by Scott before they would go back to sleep. '*I'll* read you a story,' I said, and was greeted by two small, frightened-looking faces. 'Okay, you go with Daddy then.'

After they had disappeared upstairs, I sat back down on the bed and crossed my legs. It was unfortunate that the sounds from our room carried so easily to the boys up in their attic bedroom – it seemed that at least fifty per cent of the time I would end up waking them. I sighed and looked at my blood-streaked wrist. All of us had had a lot to deal with in the past months, especially as we'd also moved to our new house.

When Scott came back into our bedroom, he lay down quietly beside me.

'Did they settle okay?' I asked him.

'Eventually.'

'I can't believe I'm doing this to them,' I said. 'They're scared of me.'

'They're not scared of you. And they're not angry with you either. Once we were upstairs they both asked if you were okay. They wanted to come back down and cuddle you, but I said you might have gone back to sleep. Leo said, "Poor Mummy."'

'I don't want to be "poor Mummy". *I'm* supposed to be looking after *him*.'

Scott was silent for a time, then he said, 'I am so angry with Vicky. I don't think I'll ever forgive her for putting that rose on your car.'

I looked away from him, a dull ache in my stomach. Even now I was sickened by the thought that Vicky wanted to hurt and scare me badly enough to do such a hateful thing, but I said, 'We have to try.'

Scott propped himself up on his elbow and looked at me with a mixture of astonishment and admiration. 'I don't know how you can not want to kill her.'

'I'm too exhausted to be angry any more.'

'We lost our baby because of her.'

Fresh pain bloomed inside me at his mention of it, but I refused to give in to anger. 'We can't blame her for that. Blaming her makes it feel even worse. I don't want to believe she's pleased I've lost the baby, or that she would want something like that to happen.'

'But do you *really* think the stress of believing Jay had found you and Leo didn't contribute?'

'I don't know!' I said, frustrated by his question. 'Why does somebody have to be to blame? We don't know why it happened. It just... it just did!'

His face softened and he stroked my cheek. 'I'm sorry. I didn't mean to go on at you. I'm sure you're right that what she did had no bearing on us losing the baby. I just... I feel like this is my fault. You'd never have crossed paths with Vicky otherwise, would you?'

'No, I wouldn't. But if it was a choice between having you and Dennis and putting up with Vicky, or being alone, you know which I would choose.'

He sighed. 'You don't deserve all this. She doesn't even seem sorry for what she did. All she's sorry for is that she got caught.'

I didn't answer. I didn't want to think about it, or talk about it. I wanted to forget it had ever happened. But Vicky's "prank" – as she'd called it to justify her actions – had cost me dearly, there was no doubt about that. I hated her for it, but despite my disgust at her actions I had to admit, when the police had discovered it was her, relief had won out over anger. I was just so glad that it hadn't been Jay.

Scott

2

'How are you holding up?' Martin asked, as he followed Scott into the living room of the new house. Although they'd been there a few months now, there was still a cardboard box in the corner yet to be unpacked, and squares of various paint samples on the wall.

'Felicity's getting there,' Scott said. 'She's managing to go to work again now, but I have to drive her there and back. She's doing well, though. She's trying to come off her anxiety medication.'

'That's good,' Martin said, 'but I asked how *you* are doing?'

Scott was taken aback by the question. He never spent much time thinking about himself, just trying to stay strong for Felicity. After finding the rose, she'd had a complete breakdown, and though the police had quickly found a witness who'd seen Vicky placing the flower on Felicity's car, the damage had already been done. Felicity was crushed, and though she was beginning to show signs of recovery, he had to watch her struggle every day. He admired her courage in carrying on at all; her efforts in trying to get through the day were like those of somebody trying to put together a broken glass with their bare hands – everything she did looked painful, and the pieces never quite seemed to fit.

Scott realised that Martin was still waiting for him to answer. What should he say? He didn't even know how he was doing; he just carried on and tried not to think at all. 'Okay, I guess,' he said weakly.

'Really?' Martin said. 'Because I've barely seen you recently. I know you've been doing up the house, and that there's been a lot to deal with, but you've never even properly explained what happened that affected Felicity so badly.'

Scott quickly tried to summarise – the rose, Vicky, the fact he'd told Vicky that Tim was going to split up with her before he died.

'Do you think that's why she did it?' Martin asked. 'She was trying to get revenge on you for telling her the truth about Tim?'

'I think so. She's been weird about the thing with the rose; she says it was a prank, but… I mean, it's not the kind of thing you play a prank on somebody about–'

'We did hide underwear under her and Tim's bed to try to split them up, remember.'

Scott sighed. He did remember, all too well. 'I know,' he said, 'and believe me, she has brought that up more than once, saying that what she did with the rose was no worse than what we did with that stupid lacy underwear, and maybe she's right. I don't know. The thing with the rose, though, it just seems… twisted. Sick. She said she didn't realise it would be so upsetting for Fliss, and I know she didn't realise the full extent of what Jay had done, but I'd told her Jay was a rapist. I said he was violent. How much worse did it have to be before she realised it wasn't an appropriate topic for a *joke*?'

Martin was silent. 'I don't know what to say,' he told Scott eventually. 'It's so messed up. So that's all she ever said, that it was a prank?'

'Kind of.' Scott thought back to the arguments he'd had with Vicky about it. 'It kept changing. She seemed almost like she was annoyed we were so angry with her to begin with, like there was something more to it. Then she was acting like it was all a big joke, or like Felicity deserved it.'

'Well, if there's one good thing to take from this, it's that at least it *wasn't* Jay.'

'I still worry about him. A lot. Much more than I let on to Fliss.'

'Perhaps you should get away from here for a day,' Martin suggested. 'Get a change of scenery.'

Scott didn't answer straight away. It certainly sounded tempting. It had been a while since he'd done any rock climbing, and he was starting to miss it. 'I don't know,' he said when he finally spoke. 'I'm still concerned about Felicity. It's not that she needs me with her every second of the day, but I prefer to be somewhere close by. So that I can come quickly if anything happens.'

'You can't do that for the rest of your life,' Martin said, 'and Felicity wouldn't want you to, either. She's not like Vicky – she doesn't want you to be at her beck and call.'

'She might not want it to be like that, but even she admits she needs it at the moment. Look, I'll mention it to her. But I can't promise anything.'

...

'What were you and Martin talking about?' Felicity asked sleepily, woken up by him getting into bed.

'I was just telling him about Vicky, and about how you are.'

She turned her lamp on and Scott sat down beside her. 'What did you say about how I am?'

'I told him the truth. It doesn't help to lie to people, and nobody thinks any the worse of you for having a tough time.'

'It makes me so embarrassed. I don't want to just be "the woman with the violent ex". I don't want everyone to think I'm nothing but a bag of nerves who jumps at every shadow. Even though that is who I am half the time.'

He smiled at her reassuringly. 'Nobody thinks that. You don't have to be ashamed of how you're feeling at the moment.'

'I just want things to be normal.'

'Well, on that note,' Scott said, 'Martin reckons I need a change of scenery.'

'I was thinking you hadn't climbed anything in a while,' she said, 'unless you count going up a ladder to clean out the gutters.'

Scott laughed. 'Well, we wouldn't do anything too major, just go somewhere for a day. Probably quite a long day, but–'

'It's fine,' she said. 'Honestly. I know you're worried that as soon as you leave Vicky will do something, or... or Jay is suddenly going to turn up, but I was on my own for two years before I met you. I can do it. And I've made a decision. From tomorrow I'm going to start driving myself to and from work again.'

He nodded. 'Okay.'

'I get so obsessed with the idea that Jay is following me, but I'm being ridiculous. I'm imagining it because I let Vicky get inside my head and it threw me back into the past again, but it's not real. It's all in my head.'

'Well, if you do want to talk any more about what went on with Jay, whether it's with me or with a… professional, you know that you can.'

She gave a small smile, without warmth. 'I told you I tried that before. I can't… I can't talk about it. Not any more than I have already. Not any details.'

'If you were able to say more of it out loud, perhaps those memories wouldn't have so much power. Perhaps they wouldn't come back to you as nightmares.'

'I'm doing my best,' she said. 'Maybe I'll be able to open up, eventually. But in the meantime, of course you should get out of Alstercombe for a day. Go and enjoy yourself. If I get in a pickle, I'll call Natasha.'

Scott was instantly reassured. His sister had been an absolute rock through their turbulent few months, looking after Leo and Dennis when necessary, bringing them meals straight after the rose incident, when they had both been too stressed to even think about food, let alone cook it.

'There's something else I've been thinking about too,' Felicity said. 'I want to do a barbecue for everyone, when the weather warms up. For Natasha and for all your friends and family, to say thank you for their support.'

'That's a great idea.'

She looped her arms around his neck. 'I love you,' she told him. 'And we're going to get through all of this. We've got through the worst already – now things can only get better.'

11

Jay

3

Twisted uncomfortably on the sofa, his shoulders hunched, Jay swiped through picture after picture of Felicity and Leo on his phone. He had lots now – none of them very good, always taken from a distance, but he obsessed over them, staring at her face, agonising over how to get her back.

It had been months since he'd found her – since the day outside the dentist's, when he had watched her. He'd been on such a high that day, but something had gone wrong since then. She'd stopped showing up to work, and he'd seen a police car parked outside the flat she shared with Scott. It had scared him off for weeks, and though he now felt safe enough to visit Alstercombe regularly again, he was unnerved by the fact Scott drove her everywhere, and the way she looked when she made her way from his car into the dentist's, huddled into herself, sometimes glancing over her shoulder, like she was scared of the whole world. They'd moved house too, though if they'd done it to throw him off the scent, it hadn't worked. All he'd had to do was follow her home from work one day to discover her new address.

'What are you looking at?' Stephanie asked. He glanced up sharply. She was sitting in the armchair near the fireplace, watching TV, while he'd had his eyes glued to his phone for the last half hour or so. 'Nothing,' he told her.

She watched him a moment longer. 'I think I'm going to go to bed,' she said.

'I'll be up soon.'

She nodded and made her way slowly out of the room. He rolled his eyes. Stephanie and Felicity were both so fucking miserable all the time. It was draining just to look at them;

Stephanie moping around the house like half her mind was missing, Felicity twitchy and nervous, like a frightened little mouse.

'What made you so scared?' he whispered to her face on his phone screen. 'Did you see me? Did somebody else see me?'

A wave of anger swept through him. It was only after his meeting with Vicky that Felicity had started acting weird. He threw his phone down onto the sofa. Vicky. If that woman had done anything to jeopardise his chances of getting Felicity back, he'd break her fucking neck.

Calm down. Keep a clear head.

It was too risky to try to approach Vicky and ask her what she had done, though he'd been tempted many times. His best bet was to carry on with what he had been doing so far; watching, waiting, being cautious. It was testing his patience to its limits, but if that's what he had to do then that's what he had to do. And he'd do anything for Felicity, even if she showed no sign of appreciating it.

...

Stephanie didn't acknowledge him when he got into bed beside her, though she was still awake.

'When are you going to snap out of this?' he asked her. 'I've told you over and over and fucking over how sorry I am. I wasn't in my right mind when I hurt you. I've never done anything like that to you before, have I?'

She was silent.

'Well, answer me.'

'No,' she whispered.

'And have I done it again since?'

Again there was no sound from her.

'Have I?'

'Please stop, Jason.'

'Have I ever hurt you again since?' he pressed her.

'No.'

'Then stop with this... I don't even know what it is you're doing. Acting like a victim. If anything, you should be flattered I wanted you so much that I lost control. I mean, you are my girlfriend for fuck's sake, would you rather I'd gone and shagged someone else that night?'

'I'm tired. I need to get some sleep.'

'Whatever,' he said. 'I'm tired too. Tired of trying to get you to be reasonable.'

Suddenly, she turned the light on and sat up. 'Why don't you tell me what you're spending all your time doing, then? Do you really still expect me to believe that you're going to turn those old friends of yours in to the police? That you're spending all these hours, weeks, *months,* gathering some sort of *intelligence* on them?'

'Steph—'

'I don't know who you are. I don't know what you're doing. I let you stay here, even after what you did, because I loved you, and because I wasn't sure I could cope with being on my own. But you know what? Now, I'm not sure I can cope with you being *here.*'

Jay stared at her – he hadn't seen this much life in her for a long time. She looked truly furious. But if her anger had surprised him, her next words worried him deeply. 'I don't love you any more, Jason,' she said. 'I want you to get out of my house. I want you to leave.'

Stephanie

4

Her heart was pounding. She'd taken a big risk confronting Jason like that, but she couldn't take any more. When he'd first come back to the house after he'd hurt her, handing her a huge bunch of flowers and telling her how much he loved her, part of her had wanted to let him back into her heart. He'd apologised over and over for what he'd done, for raping her – not that he'd ever used that word – but nothing he could ever say or do would make the memory of that night go away. It was as if a fog had lifted, and her illusions about him had fallen away. Now she saw him for what he really was. The bloodstained clothes, his mood swings and hot temper, the time spent away from the house, the way he was keeping hidden. Even though she didn't know exactly what it was he was involved with, she simply couldn't keep fooling herself that he was a reformed character, and she couldn't let him drag her down with him.

'Did you hear me?' she said. 'This is my house. I let you stay here because I thought you were a good man who'd just gone down the wrong path in life. I believed that you were trying to make amends. But I don't believe that any more, and now you need to get out.'

'Where the fuck is this coming from?' he said. 'You were fine five minutes ago.'

'I was not fine five minutes ago. I haven't been "fine" for a long time now, Jason, and if you really did love me, or care about me, you would have realised that.'

'I do… love you, Steph. Please…' He was genuinely worried now. There was something approaching panic in his blue-grey eyes. She took a good look at him. She tried to see past his odd disguise – the jet-black hair that didn't suit him at all, the glasses, the naff, ugly clothes. What a contrast to when she first saw him at the wildfowl reserve. He'd been a little dishevelled, but so charming. And he'd looked so good; his hair its natural sandy shade, his clothes fashionable, nicely fitted and showing off the shape of his body. He'd smiled at her, listened to her, and she'd been so excited by the fact that he was showing interest, since no one had really seemed interested in her before. Now, she could barely remember that man, or what she'd seen in him beyond his looks.

'Why have you never let me take any photos of you?' she asked.

'What?'

'Photos. I've wanted to take pictures of you, of us together, like normal people do–'

'I told you why!' Jason said. 'I'm worried if stuff like that gets online I'll be found. And anyway, why would I want you to have a picture of me when I look like such a twat?'

'Don't try to distract me,' she said. 'And yes, I believe you don't want photos of you to turn up online. But I also think you're scared I'll do a reverse image search.'

He raised an eyebrow. 'I don't even know what the hell you're talking about.'

'Really? So if I did a search with a photo of your face, you wouldn't be worried about what might come up?'

He shifted his position a little, but he didn't appear overly concerned. Maybe it was all an act, though. Lying never came easily to her, but she had learned by now that Jason was rather more skilled at it. 'I don't want to listen to this paranoid crap,' he said. 'I'm not going to leave, and you need to stop this nonsense right now.'

'Or what?'

He didn't reply, and she picked up her phone and opened the camera.

'What are you doing?'

She held her phone up and he knocked it out of her hand.

'If you've nothing to hide, why not let me do it?'

'I don't have to prove anything to you! Relationships should have trust–'

'Don't give me that! You won't let me do it because you're not really who you say you are. Just tell me the truth!'

'You know already! You know my name isn't really Jason. You know I'm not telling you certain things to protect you. If you don't trust me, that's your problem. I don't have anything to prove to you, and if you ever loved me, my word would be enough for you.'

'Whose blood is on those clothes you've hidden in your bag?'

Now his face went pale. 'You've been looking through my stuff?'

'Yes I have. Why do you have clothes with blood on them?'

'You know why! I used to deal with people who owed money, or were causing problems. I used to go and… and scare them a bit. You *know* that. I never tried to pretend otherwise.'

'Did you beat any of them to death?'

'No! No, of course not. What use would that be anyway? They can't pay their debts back if they're dead. I just used to… rough them up a bit. For God's sake, I've told you all this before.'

She shook her head. 'I'm not buying this.'

'Why haven't you called the police then? If you're so sure about what I've done?'

She swallowed hard, and didn't answer.

'Because you've been hiding me,' he said. 'You've covered up for me for years. If I go down, you go down too.'

Stephanie nodded. 'I know,' she said. 'That's why I'm not going to the police. But you need to leave. You need to leave tonight.'

He stared at her a moment longer, then, to her horror, he laughed. 'Yeah, I'm not going to do that,' he said, 'and I'd like to see you try and make me.'

In a fit of rage, she got up and tried to pull him from the bed. 'Get out!' she screamed at him. 'Get out, get out!'

She kept trying to move him without success, until he lashed out, using the arm she was grabbing hold of to give her a firm shove that sent her sprawling to the ground. He stood over her, pointing his finger in her face. '*You* are nothing but a stupid little girl,' he yelled at her, 'who let a stranger stay in her house, because she'd only had sex once before in her miserable twenty-three years of life and wanted a man who was willing to shag her.'

Stephanie's eyes filled with tears, but she refused to let them fall. She wouldn't give him the satisfaction of seeing her cry. 'You let me stay here,' he continued, 'because you were thinking with what's between your legs. And I didn't disappoint, did I? You got what you wanted, I got what I wanted. Let's face it, you weren't likely to get any action from anyone else, were you? Now accept you've brought this on yourself, and let me carry on living here as long as I need to, or things are going to go very badly for you.'

'Did you... didn't you ever care for me?'

'A little,' he said. 'That's why I kept your dad's address. I could have destroyed that – you should be grateful I didn't. But you need to get real, Steph. Guys that look like me don't love girls that look like you. I'll admit that for a quick shag, you're better than nothing, but come on. You've been living in a fantasy world.'

'What are you actually doing all the time?' she asked shakily. 'Where do you go?'

Now he smiled. 'To spend time with a real woman,' he said. 'The one I imagine I'm screwing to get me through a session with you.'

At this revelation Stephanie did cry, though she hated herself for it. Jason left her on the floor, and not long after she heard the front door close, but she stayed on the carpet, crying in huge, painful sobs.

Jay

5

He didn't have a plan, but somehow the van steered itself in the direction of Alstercombe. It would be very late by the time he got there – Felicity would be in bed, so he stood no chance of seeing her – but he just wanted to be near her.

He parked his van on her street, a good way away from her and Scott's dormer bungalow, the building silent, all its windows dark. Being close to Felicity soothed him briefly, but then the questions started. What was he going to do about Stephanie? He could still just about control her for the moment, but soon she was going to crack. If she got desperate enough that she decided to go to the police, it would ruin everything. He'd be caught. All the work he'd done to find Felicity would be for nothing – his life would be over. He drummed his fingers against his knee, trying to stay calm, but everything was turning into a nightmare. Finding Felicity had been amazing, but finding her was just one small step. Figuring out what the hell to do now, *that* was where it got really difficult. And he had to decide what to do soon, before Stephanie snapped.

Should he approach Vicky? He'd been reluctant, since he still wasn't entirely sure of her motivations, but what choice did he have? He knew where she lived – he'd followed her home one day after she dropped her little boy off at Scott and Felicity's house. He had to find out what had happened to scare Felicity. And if he could get Vicky to help him somehow, that would be even better. After all, she had been pretty keen for him to take Felicity and Leo away, so maybe she still would be.

With a sigh, he started the engine and pulled out into the road. What he was planning could be suicidal, but if Vicky had gone to the police, or told Felicity and Scott about him, she must

19

not have given them much, or he would have been found.

It was gone midnight when he arrived at Vicky's neat little house. It was at the end of a row of terraces on a new estate, and a light was still on in the downstairs window, though the blind was down and he couldn't see inside. He rang her doorbell, and when the door opened he found himself face-to-face with a woman in black and pink leopard-print pyjamas, red-blonde hair loose around her shoulders, a confused expression on her face. Then she realised who he was, which happened about the same moment he accepted that this woman really was Vicky, because she'd looked a lot smarter when he'd met her before.

'No,' she said, and began to close the door.

He put his foot in the way. 'I just want to talk.'

'I've got nothing to say to you.'

'I think you do. As you can see, I know where you live. I know where you work, and I've figured out why you're so bothered about Scott, too. You have a son with him, don't you?'

He flashed her a smile, pleased with himself as he added, 'Your boy goes to that nursery where you first met me. I know what he looks like. I've seen him plenty of times, with Scott and Felicity.'

Her eyes widened in shock. Good. Those words had obviously hit home. 'Are you threatening my son?' she asked, her voice unsteady.

'Not if you let me in to talk to you for five minutes. Just five minutes, that's all I'm asking.'

'You need to get away from here. I am not talking to you. I'm not letting you in my house.'

He gave the door an almighty shove, throwing her backwards and allowing him to force the door fully open and step inside. 'I'm in now,' he said, 'so you can start talking.'

...

'You did *what?*' he asked, incredulous. It had taken several minutes, more threats from him, more protests from her, but finally she'd caved in and told him what she'd done.

'You heard me,' she said.

'What did you think was going to happen? Putting a stupid flower on Felicity's car won't solve any of your problems! Or did you think it would make me get caught somehow?'

She didn't reply.

He looked at her closely. 'That's it, isn't it? You wanted me caught, but you didn't want your name dragged into it.'

'I would never have come to you if I'd known... that you've killed...'

'But you did. You *did* come to me. You still want Felicity gone, right? You want her out of the way so you can get your hands on Scott.'

She watched him, her expression unreadable. What *did* she really want? Well, whatever it was, it had been enough to make her approach him, and though she'd got cold feet, her original motivation probably hadn't vanished. 'If you help me, no one need ever hear your name,' he said. 'But if I get caught, and I believe it's down to you...' He shook his head. 'Everyone is going to know. Maybe you'll get that kid taken off you, for helping somebody like me.'

Her eyes flashed with anger, though she spoke calmly. 'I can't help you. Even if I wanted to, what could I actually do? I told you where she lives, she's moved now, but–'

'Yeah, I know where she's moved to.'

'Then I've already helped. You want to do something to her, you can go ahead and do it. It's nothing to do with me. I won't stand in your way, but I'm not going to help, either.'

'You know, me and you aren't so different,' he said.

'Yeah, we are.'

'We've both had partners screw us over. When did Scott leave you? After the baby was born, or before?'

'Before,' she said, after a short pause.

'He left you while you were pregnant?'

She shrugged.

'I would never do that to a woman,' Jay said. 'Whatever I

might have done in the past, I've done it out of love. To protect people I care about, to keep them safe. Family is everything. I just want to be with mine, but it's not straightforward. I need a bit of help. I feel like perhaps you understand what that's like.'

Vicky didn't reply straight away. But was that a flash of emotion in her eyes? She hadn't immediately told him he was wrong. He smiled faintly, as a flicker of hope sprang to life inside him.

Vicky

4 YEARS AGO

6

Vicky hovered in the doorway of Scott's workshop, and watched him for a moment. He was applying dark wood stain to an antique desk. The small radio on the shelf in the corner was playing rock music that she didn't recognise, and he was completely absorbed in his work, so much so that he jumped when she stepped further inside.

'Vicky!' he said. 'You gave me a fright.'

'I need to talk to you.'

'Can it wait just for a bit? I'm kind of in the middle–'

'I'm pregnant,' she said. There was no point in beating about the bush.

He stood and stared at her, looking almost comical with the brush still in one hand, a drip slowly running down the bristles, before it fell and made a splodge of brown on his left shoe. Not that he noticed. The colour had drained from his cheeks, and the half-finished desk was now forgotten as he searched her face for answers. 'You – you what?' he said. 'Is this a joke?'

'Of course it's not a fucking joke!' she exploded. 'Why would I joke about something like this?'

'I'm sorry,' he said, shaking his head. He put the brush down, and turned off the radio. 'Are you... so you're sure?'

She reached into her handbag and took out a couple of pregnancy tests, showing him the blue lines. He frowned as he looked at them, then he met her eyes. 'It's from that night we...'

'Well, we haven't done it any other time, have we?'

He sank down onto an old dining chair in the corner. She sat on a second chair beside him.

'Vicky, I can barely remember that night. I was so drunk...'

'What are you trying to say?'

'How could this have happened? When I can only vaguely remember...'

'What do you mean, how could it happen? Do you need me to draw a diagram?'

He rubbed his forehead, and she glared at him in disgust. Could he not even try to disguise the fact he was horrified, for her sake?

'Are you... okay?' he asked. 'How long have you known?'

'Not long.'

'Do you need anything? What do we, like, *do*?'

'How should I know? I thought when I had a baby it would be with Tim, not' – she waved her hand at him dismissively – 'you.'

'So you're going to... Do you want to keep it?'

'You know what,' she shouted at him, 'I should have known better than to think you'd have the slightest interest.' She got up and started towards the door, but he followed her. 'I didn't mean anything, Vix. I just wondered what you felt about it.'

'I'm not thrilled about it.' She gave him a meaningful look before saying her next words. 'But now I don't have Tim, perhaps it might be good for me.'

'I've told you I'm sorry for what happened to Tim.'

'Words don't help me. What would have helped is you not making him go climbing with you.'

He looked like he wanted to argue, but he didn't. 'Vix, I can't take all this in. I'll help you with whatever you need, I'm just... I don't want to end up saying something stupid, I need a bit of time to think.'

'And don't you think I feel exactly the same? But I don't have time to think. I can't escape this situation. Your baby is growing inside me right now. As we *speak*!'

He looked miserable.

'I need to know if we're going to make a go of it,' she pushed him.

Now he just looked confused. 'A go of what?'

'Us.'

'Us? Vicky, there is no "us"! It was one night–'

'–that's going to change the rest of my life. I don't think you understand quite what this means.'

'No. I don't. I barely know anything about kids, or babies.'

'I'll tell you then. It means you need to grow a pair and take some responsibility. I don't want to be a single mum, and if Tim could see us right now, he wouldn't want you to make me go through this alone. He'd be furious with you for even thinking it.'

'You're seriously telling me that you want us to be a couple?'

He waited for her to answer, and when she didn't he said, 'I can't have a relationship with you. I'll help you with the baby, I'll do whatever you need me to, but I can't be your partner! I don't… I don't love you. You don't love me. You don't even like me! You blame me for Tim's death. I thought you hated me.'

'So you don't even want to give our child a *chance* at growing up with both its parents together, under one roof.'

'Do we have to talk about this now? You only just found out, perhaps when you've had a bit more time–'

'I want to talk about it now.'

He sighed heavily. 'Okay, well, I don't think that growing up with two people who don't love each other is going to do a whole lot to help the baby. I don't think it will do a whole lot to help us. We'd argue, we'd fall out, we'd resent each other. I'm not doing that to myself. I'm not doing it to you. I'm certainly not going to do it to a… to *our* baby.'

'You're abandoning me.'

'No!' he said. 'No, I'm not abandoning you. I'm just not going to make promises I won't be able to keep. But I'll be there for you, I promise. You're not going to be alone.'

'Yes I am,' she said. She walked out while he stared after her helplessly. She was angry; furious, in fact, but not only with him. *What did you expect? Of course he doesn't want you.* Hot tears filled her eyes. A few weeks ago she'd been in a relationship, living with

Tim, her life all mapped out. Now she was single, expecting a baby, and facing a future not even vaguely resembling the one she had planned. True, she didn't love Scott, but almost anybody was better than being alone.

Vicky

PRESENT DAY

7

Jay was still watching her. 'Is that what happened then?' he pressed her. 'Did Scott ditch you when you told him you were pregnant?'

She didn't answer. She wasn't going to start dredging up all the details of her past with Scott. Especially not to this man, whose idea of family and love was about as twisted as you could get.

'He really hurt you, didn't he?' Jay said, his voice soft. 'You didn't deserve that.'

He'd moved closer to her, alarmingly close, and his fingers brushed her arm. 'Are you... coming on to me?' she asked, as she pulled her arm away. Her mind kept going back to what she'd heard about him from Scott, and now here she was alone with him in her house. She swallowed hard. *Don't let him see your fear.*

'What has Felicity said about me?' he asked. He'd obviously guessed her thoughts. 'I can imagine some of it, actually.'

'I think you need to leave.'

'The truth is, Felicity liked a bit of rough sex. Once or twice, it got too real for her. I didn't mean it to end up like that, but she shouldn't have played with fire if she was scared of getting burned. Now she's found Scott, she's ashamed of the sort of shit she used to get up to with me, so she's turning it round and saying I forced her. It's her word against mine, but I'm telling you, Vicky: Felicity might look innocent now, but she used to like doing some properly filthy stuff. I'm not surprised she's trying to pretend it never happened.'

Vicky didn't believe a word of it, but she nodded. Jay was still standing very close to her, close enough she could smell him – some sort of aftershave or deodorant, she wasn't sure which, but the scent of him made her skin prickle with fear. She remembered how quickly he'd grown angry when she met him in the pub and told him Felicity was pregnant.

She waited for Jay to move away from her, but he didn't. He stayed claustrophobically close, until she became so afraid he was going to touch her that she tried desperately to think of something, anything, to distract him and make him stop whatever game he was playing.

The night in the pub. When she'd told him Felicity was pregnant. Of course! He probably *still* thought she was pregnant!

'Did you know Felicity lost her baby?' she blurted out. 'She's not pregnant any more.'

She was sickened when Jay's face broke into a smile, yet equally as relieved when he took a step back from her. 'Really?' he said. 'That's good.' He thought for a moment. 'Are they trying again?'

'How should I know? They don't talk to me about stuff like that.'

'You know, you and me really should work together on this. Scott and Felicity aren't meant to be together, we both agree.'

'You killed somebody,' she said in a small voice.

'No, not just "somebody". I killed a man who was trying to ruin my relationship with Felicity. He'd ruined one of my previous relationships; he was hell bent on stopping me from being happy. He was not a good man, Vicky. He was twisted. Evil. He drove me to it – I don't think anyone could have taken the kind of shit he was giving me without lashing out.'

An image of the lacy underwear that Scott and Martin had planted in hers and Tim's bedroom filled her mind. *They* had been determined to break up her relationship. She'd never been so angry in her life, but could somebody ever make her so angry she could kill them? She thought of Felicity – her innocent blue eyes, her awful wishy-washy mumsy clothes, the way everyone treated her like the sun shone out of her bum, when she was really just pathetic. She hated her. She hated her more than anyone she'd ever met. There had been times she'd wished Felicity was dead. She wouldn't kill her, though. Apart from anything else, the woman wasn't worth risking doing time over. If she'd fully understood who Jay was from the start, she wouldn't have considered approaching him worth the risk either, but she'd already gone a fair way down that path, too far to turn back now.

'What is it you actually need, Jay?' she said. 'What are you trying to do?'

'I need a good opportunity to get hold of Felicity and Leo, when I'm not likely to be seen, and it won't be discovered straight away. Then I need a place I can take them while I talk to her. It should only take me a day or two to talk her round. I want her to *want* to be with me. Then everything will be okay. At the moment she's always with Scott, or she's at work. She's barely ever on her own – even when he's working at that chip shop she goes down there with Leo. There's never an opportunity for me to do anything. It's always too big a risk.'

'Okay,' she said, 'I get it. Look, meet me at the White Hart again. In a couple of months. I'll see if I can figure something out.'

'Can't you just phone me, if anything comes up?'

'No.'

'Why–'

'I don't want records that we've been calling each other.'

'My phone's not in my name, if that's what you're worried about. Or I can get a prepaid one, that's a thing, isn't it?'

'I'll meet you at the White Hart,' she said firmly. She grabbed some notepaper and a pen from the kitchen. 'This date, this time. Don't come to my house again.'

He looked at her suspiciously. 'How do I know this isn't some kind of set-up?'

Honestly, she wasn't even sure herself if her offer to meet

him again and help him was genuine. She just wanted him to leave. She'd worry about the rest later. 'You don't,' she told him. 'But I'm the best chance you have.'

He took the paper from her. 'I'll be there.'

Stephanie

8

Long after her sobs had died down and she'd begun shivering with cold, Stephanie forced herself to get up from the floor. She wasn't going to let Jason do this to her. She dried her tears, and found her laptop.

First she typed in "what happens if you help someone hide from the police", which didn't give very useful results, so she took a few deep breaths and tried "assisting an offender", and finally "assisting an offender sentencing guidelines uk". The words on the screen swam before her eyes. How had she ended up here, having to look up this sort of information? She hadn't known Jason had broken the law when she invited him into her house. He'd spoon-fed her information about himself, waiting until she couldn't get through a day without him before he'd started telling her about his past. Even then, he'd confused her with stories about who he was hiding from, saying she could be in danger, making out that he was trying to do the right thing.

She saw the words "three to ten years", and she dropped the laptop down on the bed and ran into the bathroom to be sick.

...

Eventually, she made her way back across the hall. She was shaking all over. If she turned Jason in now, would that help her chances? She didn't know. She'd done so much to help him. She hadn't thought it all through. She'd blocked it out. She'd needed him so much, and she'd believed him that he'd never really done anything that bad, but now she was no longer sure.

He's killed somebody. The words swirled around in her mind. *You know it in your heart.*

She shook her head. She might suspect it in her heart, but she didn't *know* it. Even so, a war was going on inside her brain. Should she come clean to the police, or should she try again to get Jason to leave? It was almost two o'clock in the morning. Jason was still out, and Stephanie had no chance of sleeping now. Grabbing his backpack from the wardrobe, she made her decision. It was always better to tell the truth. Adults had always said that when she was a kid. They always said you'd be in less trouble if you owned up.

Once she'd put her coat on, she slipped the backpack's straps over her shoulders, a shiver of disgust passing through her body as she thought of the bloodied clothes inside. She was too shaky and panicky to drive. She'd walk to the police station. It was about twenty-five minutes away, in the centre of Wrexton. Plenty of time for the cold air to clear her head and give her a chance to think about what she was going to say.

She opened the front door, but before she'd taken ten steps from the house, Jason's van came around the corner. She froze. Had he seen her? Should she try to run back inside the house, or continue towards the police station?

Jason was driving fast, and when he saw her he slammed on the brakes, as if he knew what she was trying to do. *But how could he? I'll just say I was going for a walk.* Keeping her eyes fixed dead ahead, she heard the driver's door slam. He'd left his van in the middle of the road in his haste, and he grabbed her by one of the straps over her shoulder. 'Where are you going with this?' he hissed at her.

The backpack! She couldn't answer. There was no reasonable explanation as to why she had it. She stared blankly at his face, so different now from the man she'd fallen in love with, and not just because of his dyed hair and glasses, but because he'd used to be kind and thoughtful, and now he was full of nothing but hate and anger.

'Get inside the house,' he said. He released his grip on her and she ran inside, locking the door behind her and putting the security chain across, while he went over to his van to park it properly. She ran upstairs for her phone to call the police, just as she heard him struggling and failing to open the front door. She glanced hurriedly around the bedroom. Shit! Where was her phone? She was still searching as the back door screeched open, and Jason's feet pounded up the stairs. No phone – it must be downstairs – but before she could do anything, Jason had burst in through the bedroom door.

'I hope you weren't going where I think you were going with that bag,' he said.

Jay

9

'Please don't hurt me!' Stephanie said. She held her hands up as if expecting a physical attack. Jay paused. Why did women always assume he was going to hurt them? Vicky had been afraid of him. Now Stephanie. What the hell did she think he was going to do? He had no interest in hurting her. He was more scared than angry.

'If this is about what I said earlier, Steph, then I'm sorry,' he told her softly. 'I didn't mean a word of it, you know I didn't.'

She lowered her hands, and he took a look at her face, which was red and blotchy, her eyes puffy from crying. Could he smell sick? What the hell had been going on since he left? Her laptop was open on the bed. The screen was dark, but he pressed a key and it woke up. He quickly scanned the words. 'Why on earth are you looking at this?' he asked. 'Steph, you're not going to go to prison.'

'Yes I am!' she cried. 'You said yourself how stupid I am, and I am, aren't I? I can't do this any more, I can't hide you here–'

Jay's skin prickled with fear. 'If I ever do get caught, and that's a big if, I'll make sure you don't get in trouble–'

'They will work it out, Jason! Please, you have to go. I'll give you a head start, but I have to call the police, I can't just wait for them to find me...'

He stepped closer to her and held her face in his hands. 'Stop. Stop it. You're making yourself ill.'

He let go of her and she sank down onto the bed.

'Please try to forget what I said to you earlier,' he said. 'I *do* care about you. It's not all been a lie, and I don't think you're stupid.'

'It's not about that.'

'You're angry with me, and you have every right to be. But I'll be leaving soon.'

'You... you will?'

'I don't want to hurt you any more.' He kissed her on the forehead. 'You've done so much to help me, I don't want you to be unhappy.'

An idea occurred to him. One that would make him a little less reliant on Vicky. He smiled, pleased with himself. 'There's just one last thing I need you to do to help me.'

Stephanie's eyes searched his face. She still looked terrified. 'What is it you need me to do?' she asked, her voice barely above a whisper.

'I need to use the house. Just for a day or two. Maybe a week. I don't know exactly when yet.'

'You need to do what?'

'So you'll have to go on a little holiday. Will you be able to do that?'

Stephanie stared at him. 'I'm not leaving you alone in my house!' she said. 'How do I know you won't change all the locks and throw me out?'

'You don't. But you want me gone, don't you?'

'I'm not letting you use the house.'

'Stephanie, I just want to stay here a few more months, have the house to myself for a little while, and then I'll leave. As long as you don't do anything to spoil my plans, none of this will ever come back to you. You'll never get in trouble, you can have your life back.'

'It's too late for that!'

'What do you mean?'

'I might get my life back, but I'll never have my *conscience* back! I can't keep turning a blind eye! I don't know why I let this go on so long. Well, I do. I did it because I loved you, but that's not an excuse. I've broken the law–'

'You don't even know what I actually did. I've never told you. You don't know my name. All you're guilty of is being gullible and naïve.'

Her eyes glittered darkly. 'And you say you don't want to hurt me any more.'

'I'm reassuring you. That's all anyone would think. You're not a criminal – no one in their right mind would see you like that.'

She shook her head. 'I can't live like this.'

'I'll move out of the bedroom if that helps. I'll sleep in your granddad's old room, and I'll stay out of your way.'

She looked utterly defeated. He sat down beside her, and put his hand over hers, but she snatched it away. 'Stephanie, listen, when we argued earlier, I was hurt because you said you don't love me any more. I lashed out. I know our relationship isn't quite what you once thought it was, but I truly am fond of you. And although I don't... love you, it meant a lot to me that you loved me. I didn't even realise how much. I didn't like it when you said you don't love me and I guess I was trying to... to bring you down to my level.'

Stephanie was clasping her hands in her lap, her face pale, but at these words she turned to him. 'If your self-esteem is so low that you have to say hateful things to make yourself feel better, then you need help,' she told him.

'That's probably true.'

'That blood on the clothes,' she said slowly, 'is it a *woman's* blood? Tell me the truth, Jason. Did you attack a woman?'

'No!' he said, as an image of Mark cowering on the ground in the woods, face bloodied and terrified, flashed through his mind. 'It was a man. What sort of person do you think I am?'

She backed away from him on the bed. 'I'm not going to get taken in by you again. You've always been this way; you say these spiteful little things, then you say you're sorry. You say worse things, and then you say you're sorry. Then it isn't just words any more, is it? It stopped being just words with me, last year. Last year when you... when you forced me–'

'I don't want to talk about what happened last year!' he snapped. 'That was your fault as much as mine.'

Stephanie put her hands over her face. 'Why won't you leave?' she pleaded. 'Why won't you just leave?'

'Stop it,' he said. 'Stop it now.'

She didn't stop. She was crying, caught up in some wave of horror, obsessed with the idea that he'd hurt other women. How could she think that about him? She didn't understand. No one ever understood. They didn't know what it was like inside his head, how much everything hurt. How lashing out was sometimes all he could do to make it stop, even for just a second. He grabbed her. 'Stop it,' he yelled into her face. 'Just calm down, and go to bed.'

He released her and she fell back onto the bed, curling up into a ball. 'Do as I say, and everything will be okay,' he told her. 'Don't concern yourself with anything else. Everything else is my business.'

Felicity

Two months later

10

I woke with a start. My heart was hammering, and I was desperately sucking in air. I opened my eyes and tried to make out familiar shapes in the near-darkness – the outline of our wardrobe, the chest of drawers with framed photos of me and Scott and the children on top of it, the metal stand shaped like a tree that I hung my necklaces and earrings on.

Scott, thank goodness, was fast asleep beside me and none the wiser. I must not have made any sounds as I dreamt. Gently I slipped out from under the covers and made my way up the staircase to the attic room, putting my feet down ever so gently on the steps to try not to make a sound. The door to the boys' bedroom was slightly ajar and I pushed it open, peeking in. Leo was curled up in his bed on the left-hand side of the room under the sloping ceiling. Although they were dim now, the ceiling was covered all over with glow-in-the-dark stars that he liked to look at before he fell asleep. My eyes travelled over the mass of brightly coloured train track that sat permanently in the middle of the room, and I looked at Den asleep peacefully in his bed. I hugged my arms around myself. Being part of a family gave me such a sense of well-being, though the feeling was always tainted. I felt like a cuckoo, enjoying its nest, but really having no business being in it. It was Jay who had made me feel this way, making me doubt myself at every turn, but no matter how much I told myself not to let his poison get to me, some days it felt like it had seeped right into my bones.

Nevertheless, as the days lengthened and we found ourselves

in a surprisingly warm and sunny May, I felt ready to have the housewarming barbecue to thank all of Scott's family and friends for the support they had shown us. I threw myself into preparations with such zeal that when Scott found me preparing marinades at ten p.m. the night before, he put his arm around me and said, 'If you put this much effort into a barbecue, what will you be like if we get married?'

I stopped what I was doing and looked at him. Had he said that by mistake? Was it a hint? Was he waiting to see my reaction? I laughed, not unkindly, but perhaps a little nervously. 'What are you talking about?'

I tried to get back to what I was doing, but he stepped between me and the fridge. 'We've bought a house together,' he said, 'we're already halfway there.'

I stared at him, my mind blank. 'Scott, this is so out of the blue—'

'Is it really? Fliss, I thought about surprising you – a ring, going on one knee, the whole thing – but I don't want you to feel pressured into saying yes. I... I'd like to marry you, though. I'd like it a lot.'

Before I could stop myself I said, 'Why?'

'Because I love you, you doughnut!'

I closed my eyes for a second, and then I looked at him properly; the way he was smiling at me, though I could tell he was nervous, and I thought of how much he made me laugh, how I felt safe when we were together, how much I enjoyed being with him – even if I found it difficult to show it sometimes. The word popped out of my mouth before I was truly conscious of it. 'Yes,' I said.

'Yes, what?'

'Yes, I'll marry you.' I gave him a little push out of the way to the fridge. 'You doughnut,' I added.

...

The next day, when all our friends arrived, it was as if Scott and I were inside our own happy little bubble. Nobody knew about our engagement yet, and little flutters of excitement filled my stomach when I thought about our secret. After we'd eaten, Scott whispered, 'Can we tell everybody?' and in the heat of the moment I agreed. The afternoon passed in a hazy blur of hugs, congratulations and well-wishing that left me overwhelmed, and my mood began to turn. What had I been thinking? Did I *really* want to be bound to Scott this way? I'd thought so earlier, but now the idea was scary, and doubts crowded in.

I got through the rest of the night, but I woke very early and walked down to the beach, sitting on my own while Scott and Leo were still sleeping. It was a still day, the air mild, and the sea and sky were both the palest, milky blue so that I could barely tell where the water ended and the sky began. I took out my phone and looked at one of my favourite pictures of Scott with Leo, a complicated mixture of feelings fighting away inside me. In the end, once it got past eight a.m., I called Leanne. She sounded a bit groggy but listened as I tried to explain how I felt, and then she said, 'I'll come and see you.'

'You don't have to do that—'

'I'll come today, if you want?'

I hesitated, but I really did want to see her, and sooner rather than later. 'I'd like that,' I said.

'That's settled then. Me and Kayleigh could do with getting out of Coalton for a day. It'll be good to have a change of scenery.'

It wasn't until lunchtime that she arrived at the door with Kayleigh, and she gave me a tight hug.

'Sorry it's a bit of a drive,' I said.

She shrugged. 'Can't blame you for wanting to put some serious miles between you and Coalton.'

Once she and Kayleigh had been introduced to Scott, she said, 'So, I hear congratulations are in order.' She didn't wait for us to reply before saying, 'I bet he did something really romantic, did he?'

'We were just here at the house. I was marinating chicken.'

She laughed. 'Aww,' she said, 'well, I guess that's as good a time as any.'

. . .

We spent a pleasant afternoon together, walking along the beach, and while Scott and Kayleigh went on ahead with Leo, Leanne and I hung back and talked.

'Scott seems very genuine,' she said. 'Nice, kind, honest, funny. All the things…' She stopped herself, but then, having started the sentence, decided she should carry on. 'All the things that Jay isn't.'

I looked round at her briefly. 'I'm being stupid to worry, aren't I?'

'No, you're not being stupid. You've been through a hell of a lot. You probably haven't even processed everything that happened to you, and now you're engaged. And even though you haven't heard from Jay, this whole thing is bound to shake you up. Are you scared somehow he'll find out?'

'Yes,' I said, 'and no. Sometimes I feel like I'm going mad. I don't feel… at home anywhere. Sometimes I look at Scott and even though I love him it's like looking at a stranger.'

'But you said yes when he asked you,' she said.

'Yeah, without even thinking properly.'

'And you felt happy, when he asked?'

I thought about it. 'Yes, I suppose I did. Surprised, but… yeah. Happy.'

'And it was only after that you started doubting it?'

I looked ahead to where Scott was with the two children. Leo had picked up a stick and was dragging it along in the sand behind him, and Scott was talking to Kayleigh. I smiled despite myself.

'If you want my opinion,' Leanne said, 'this is the same as what you were worried about when you came to see me before. You love him, but you're scared because you don't want to make a mistake and end up trapped.'

'So you think we should get married?'

'I didn't say that. Look, Fliss, you don't have to marry him right now. You don't have to marry him *ever*, if you don't want to. You should do what you feel comfortable with, and if he loves you as much as it seems like he does, he'll understand.'

We were silent for a while, and I found my mind turning back to a wedding I'd been to while I was still with Jay. 'Do you remember Grace's wedding?'

'Yes.'

'Jay... Jay raped me at her wedding. In our hotel room upstairs. While the music was just starting.'

Leanne stopped in her tracks and stared at me.

'He did it because he discovered I was still taking my contraceptive pills. He thought he'd got rid of them all, but I still had some. He wanted me to have a baby.'

'He did it at the wedding?'

'Yes.'

'While we were... while *I* was downstairs dancing and stuffing my face with cake?'

'I guess so, if that's what you were doing down there.'

She looked at me a while longer and then she hugged me fiercely. 'I'm so sorry,' she said, 'I'm so sorry, Fliss.'

'It wasn't your fault.'

She loosened her grip on me to look at me squarely. 'I let it happen, though. I handled all the stuff with Jay so badly. When I should have been supporting you, I just ignored you. I wanted to say how sorry I was when you came to see me last year, but I couldn't find the words–'

'It's okay–'

'It's not okay!' she said. She was crying, and it shocked me because I couldn't remember the last time I'd seen her cry. Certainly not since we'd left school. 'That bastard was hurting you, really hurting you,' she said through her tears, 'and all I was thinking about was how I was pissed off that you were choosing him over me. I was *jealous*. And I was angry with you, because I couldn't understand why you were making the choices you were making. But I should have been there for you instead of judging you. I should have listened instead of jumping in and trying to take charge. I made it so you couldn't talk to me. I don't think I'll ever forgive myself.'

I looked at her, my friend who I'd known since I wasn't much more than Leo's age, whose hair I'd seen dyed nearly every colour under the sun, who had talked to me before anyone else when she'd found out she was pregnant with Kayleigh, and had confided in me how scared she was and that she wasn't sure what to do. As I looked at her, suddenly all I wanted was to forget the rift that had formed between us over Jay, to close it up and never talk about it again. I could see she wanted me to say something, so I said, 'What sort of cake was it?'

'What?'

'At Grace's wedding. What sort of cake did she have? I never had any.'

'Fliss, why on earth–'

'I don't want to talk about the bad stuff any more.'

She was silent, and then she nodded. 'It was… ah… let me think.' She screwed her face up. 'Lemon. That was it. Lovely and light. Summery.'

'Mm,' I said. 'If I was to marry Scott, I'd have one of those cheese cakes. You know, where they stack the cheeses up like a wedding cake. And some little cupcakes for the kids. Dennis loves cheese, though. The stronger the better. But Leo's more of a cake and icing fan.'

'It sounds like you've already started thinking about it.'

I smiled, and she put her arm around my waist. 'Well, just remember that the marriage is *your* choice as well as his. It's what Scott wants, clearly, but don't do something you don't want to do. Or something you're not *ready* to do. You don't have to marry Scott to show him you love him.'

Felicity

11

'I'm so pleased I got to meet one of your friends,' Scott said once Leanne and Kayleigh had left, and we were going to bed. 'I felt like you'd met all my family and friends, and I didn't know anybody from your life.'

'There aren't many people from my life,' I said, thinking of my parents.

He was silent briefly. 'What were you and her talking about earlier? Anything important?'

'Just… things.'

I sat down on the edge of the bed and he sat next to me. 'Leanne talked to me for a bit as well,' he said, 'I think she was trying to suss me out. See if I'm good enough for you. Did you ask her to visit because you aren't sure about marrying me?'

I didn't answer, and he put his hand over mine. 'Felicity, listen, we don't have to get married if it's not what you want.'

I searched his face. 'Did she say something to you?'

'No, but she didn't have to. I can tell that something's changed since I asked you. I know we've already told everybody, but we can say we've changed our mind. I'm sure everybody will understand.'

'It's not because of you,' I said, feeling it was important he knew. 'You've done nothing wrong.'

'So is it because of him?'

I couldn't work out how to reply, and Scott gave my hand a squeeze. 'Fliss, I didn't ask you to marry me to trap you, if that's what you're scared of.'

'I know that.'

'But I understand why you're nervous. After what happened with Jay, I get it if you don't want to be in a situation that you

44

feel you can't walk away from.'

'I don't *want* to walk away from you.'

'You might not want to, but if it's important for you to feel that you can, if that's what makes you feel safe, then that's okay.'

'What about what you feel? You must want to get married or you wouldn't have asked me.'

'I asked you because I want to share my life with you and Leo, and I want to say in front of all the people we care about that I love you. *That's* why I asked you. I didn't ask you because I want you to feel like you're mine, or to make it so that you can't leave without it being messy and complicated, or so that I can start telling you what to do, or anything like that.'

I shook my head, as a wave of sadness washed over me.

'What is it?' he said.

'You shouldn't have to tell me that. I should know that. I should know you. And I do know you, but I still…'

'We won't do it then. It's too soon. We know how we feel about each other – that's all that matters, not a piece of paper.'

I smiled, though my eyes had filled with tears. I hated that Scott had to keep reassuring me, and reminding me he wasn't like Jay. It wasn't fair. 'That's pretty much what Leanne said,' I told him. 'She said I don't have to marry you to show you I love you.'

'Then she's right.'

I took a deep breath. I'd already decided what I wanted before I started the conversation, and the things he'd said convinced me I was making the right choice. 'Scott, I wasn't sure. But I am sure now.'

'You… you are?'

'Yes. Scott, I want to get married.'

'Are you really, really sure?'

'Yes.'

He threw his arms around me and kissed me. His delight was infectious and I giggled as we fell backwards onto the bed.

...

The next morning over breakfast, we started thinking about the people we hadn't told yet.

'What will you do about Vicky?' I asked him while I sat eating a bowl of cereal. Leo was by my side with his own breakfast, fishing out cornflakes with his fingers and ignoring my encouragement to use a spoon.

'I'll have to tell her today,' he said. 'She needs to hear it from me, not from anybody else.'

I nodded. 'She's going to flip,' I said.

Scott sat down with a mug of coffee. 'Yeah, I know.' He watched what Leo was doing with his breakfast, and Leo switched to using his spoon nicely.

'I don't know how you do it,' I said quietly to Scott. 'He'll do anything to make you happy.'

'Not always. Did I tell you he buried my phone in the garden last week? He wouldn't tell me where he'd put it, I had to go digging about in the flowerbed for fifteen minutes. And he lay down on the floor and screamed when I said we had to leave the soft play the other day.'

I stifled a laugh. 'Seriously, though, what on earth will you say to Vicky?'

'I'll just have to say it like it is. There's no way of sugar-coating it, and she must realise that me and you getting married was always on the cards.' He drank some of his coffee, then he looked at me. 'There's something else, actually. I wasn't going to mention it, I already kind of told him no, but at the barbecue yesterday Martin mentioned that he wants to go to Chamonix this summer. He thought I might want to come along. He wants to try to climb Mont Blanc.'

I raised an eyebrow. 'Isn't that... would you be able to do that?'

He laughed. 'Thanks.'

'I just mean–'

He gave me a quick kiss across the table. 'I know what you meant. I reckon we could do it. We'd just need to make sure we got ourselves acclimatised well, maybe start on some smaller peaks around Chamonix. Besides, there's a few different routes up Mont Blanc so we could always just see how we get on nearer the time.'

I thought about it, and then I realised why he was asking me, and why he'd said no to Martin at first. 'So you'd want to go away for a while, then? A week? Two?'

'That's why it's not really an option.'

I met his eyes. 'You should do it,' I told him firmly. 'Honestly, it'll be okay. I can manage a week or so on my own with Leo.'

'Well, I don't need an answer right now. We can take a few weeks to think about it. There's no rush.'

We fell into silence, but as he finished his coffee he said, 'I told Vicky I'd be a bit early to pick Den up this morning. It'll give me more of a chance to talk to her. So I'd better go. Will you be okay dropping Leo off at nursery before work?'

I nodded and watched as he left, and then I smiled at Leo, who grinned back. 'We love Daddy, don't we?' I said.

He held his spoon up in the air and said, 'Daddy!' which I took as a yes.

Vicky

12

Grabbing a vase from the mantelpiece, Vicky hurled it across the room, where it smashed into pieces against the wall. Then she sank down to her knees and cried brokenly into her hands for a minute or two, before getting her breath back. How could Scott do this to her?

It was bad enough he'd abandoned her, that he'd never said sorry for Tim's death – not properly, since he maintained it wasn't his fault – and now he was making their son live with a woman with a violent, dangerous ex-boyfriend, an ex Felicity was so scared of that she would scream in the middle of the night and terrify Dennis and Leo. Why did Scott put up with it? The idea of how much Scott must love Felicity to be able to overlook all these things filled her with a fresh wave of anger. All she could be grateful for was that the meeting she'd arranged with Jay was now only a week away. She'd tell him about the engagement, and see what he made of it. No doubt he wouldn't be too pleased.

. . .

The week passed far too slowly for Vicky's liking, but finally, the following Monday, she sat down at a table with Jay in a secluded corner of the White Hart pub. She swirled her red wine around in its glass, scared now he was in front of her to say the words.

'What is it?' Jay asked. 'I can see there's something.'

She delayed a moment longer. 'There's been a development.'

Jay narrowed his eyes. 'She's not pregnant again, is she?'

'Not that I know of.'

'Then what?'

She couldn't put him off any longer. She *wanted* him to know, but she had to admit she was scared of his reaction. 'They're engaged,' she said finally.

He was silent for a long time. Had he understood her? 'Jay?' she said. 'Did you hear what I–'

'How dare she?' he exploded, 'How fucking dare she?'

Vicky glanced around nervously. 'Don't overreact–'

'Overreact? She's not marrying that prick. Or if she is, it'll be over my dead body.'

'Jay, you have to calm d–'

'What's wrong with you?' he said, 'Why fucking tell me if you don't want me to react? I'm not going to be fucking calm!'

A few people were looking at them now. She gave a vague smile and nod at the couple nearest to them to show she was okay, and they turned their gazes away.

'I'm going to Alstercombe,' Jay said. 'I'll go right now and drag her and Leo out of their house. This has gone on long enough.'

He started to stand. 'Jay, no!' she said. 'You'll blow the whole thing if you go and do that. You'll get caught!'

He was off now, making his way towards the door, and a thick sense of dread settled in the pit of Vicky's stomach. It was like the first time she'd approached him – when she'd seen him hanging around Den's nursery. She'd been angry and wanted to lash out, but Jay's idea of lashing out was off the scale. If he went to get Felicity right now, he'd have Scott to contend with, and in his current mood, for all she knew, he could end up killing him. Plus Dennis was in the house.

She rushed out to her own car. Why had she been such an idiot again? *You're always an idiot.* 'Shut up,' she muttered under her breath to the little voice in her head. It was done now. All she could do was try to get to the house before him and stop him doing anything crazy.

But when she arrived at Scott and Felicity's, she was surprised and relieved to find that Jay was not there. She'd lost sight of him on the drive to Alstercombe, and she'd been afraid he'd got ahead of her, but instead he must have been held up. She sat in her car stewing for a while. What could she do? Maybe the best thing was to go inside the house. She wasn't exactly sure what good she could do from there, but neither did she want to start reasoning with Jay in the street where anyone might look out of their window and see.

When they opened the door, Scott and Felicity weren't happy to see her, that much was painfully clear. They invited her inside awkwardly, and although they were polite and appeared happy when she congratulated them on their engagement, saying she had come to clear the air, she could almost imagine them whispering behind their hands to each other, wondering why she was here, what she was up to. The two children were in bed, so she launched herself into conversation, pretending not to notice the way Scott and Felicity kept trying to close every topic quickly, keen, no doubt, to get her to leave. Anger bubbled away inside her. She was here to protect them from Jay's wrath! *They* should be grateful to her, not that they knew, of course. To them she was just an inconvenience. *And it was you who caused Jay's wrath. You told him about their engagement.* Her stomach twisted uncomfortably. There were times she got so angry that the thought of Jay murdering Felicity and Scott in their beds was almost appealing, but that wasn't what she wanted. She wasn't cruel or violent: she wasn't like Jay. But why couldn't Felicity just go away? Not be hurt, just leave. She should go back to wherever she came from and leave Vicky's family alone.

'Tell Vicky what you told me last week,' Felicity said to Scott.

Scott turned to Felicity, his fingers touching hers where they rested on the sofa. They were so easy with each other, so relaxed. It made her sick. Felicity didn't even *look* good – she was just slouching there on the sofa, in faded grey leggings and an oversized floral t-shirt, her short brown hair scruffy. Did Scott really find her attractive?

'What do you mean?' Scott asked Felicity.

'About you going away this summer. To Chamonix, with Martin.'

'Oh… yeah. Well, it's not definite yet.'

Vicky listened as he outlined his plans.

'So you'd want me to have Dennis while you were there?'

'I guess, yeah. But it's all up in the air at the moment. I don't have dates or anything.'

Vicky was about to start complaining – she was going to tell him it would be awkward with her work, even though it wouldn't be really – but she held her tongue. She hadn't come here to argue. She'd come here to stop Jay, so she didn't want to leave too soon. How would she stop him, though? Hopefully just the fact he'd see her car and know she was inside the house would be enough to make him pause. Perhaps he had already reconsidered; after all, he should have been here by now.

'So you'll be here on your own with Leo?' she asked Felicity nicely.

'Yeah.'

Vicky was just opening her mouth to speak, when there was an almighty crash. The front window in the living room shattered, and a stone landed near her feet.

Vicky

13

In the aftermath of the smashing glass, the room seemed to ring and reverberate with the sound. Scott and Felicity hadn't seen where the stone landed, they were still looking around. They probably hadn't realised yet that anything definitely had come through the window. Scott's attention soon turned to Felicity, who was now frozen with shock. 'Are you hurt?' he asked her. Vicky's skin prickled with irritation. The glass had gone nowhere near Felicity.

Vicky bent down to take a closer look at the stone. On closer inspection, it was in fact a garden ornament. A frog – a grotesque-looking thing, which Vicky vaguely remembered having spotted in Scott and Felicity's front garden. There was a note taped to the frog which she tore off and stuffed into her jeans pocket. Scott was on his feet now, striding across the room to the window. 'It's here,' she told him. 'It's this ornament.' She held it up and he said, 'Don't touch it. Put it back down where it was.' He was still looking out of the window, trying to see who had thrown it.

She did as he asked, placing the ornament on the carpet by her feet, and Scott considered it for a moment, his brow furrowed. Then he looked up at Vicky. 'Please tell me this wasn't you.'

She leapt to her feet, immediately seeing red. 'I'm inside your fucking house! How the hell–'

'And why are you inside our house? Coming here to wish us well, let's face it, it's not really your style, is it? And I know full well that you hate Felicity, after that rose–'

'That rose, that rose, that fucking rose!' Vicky yelled. 'Stop going on about it! I've apologised!'

'Yes, I know. But if you were twisted enough to do that, God knows what else you'd do. Did you get a kick out of it? Telling someone to come and throw this thing while you were in the house so that you could watch Felicity's reaction? Is that it?'

Vicky glanced across to Felicity, and Scott followed her gaze, then he rushed over to her. Vicky rolled her eyes. Felicity had fainted, and now Scott was all over her. It was pathetic.

Vicky began to shake with anger. How could they just assume it was her? But if she convinced them it wasn't, would they start to suspect Jay? A plan had started to hatch in the back of her mind, and if she wanted it to work, Scott and Felicity definitely needed to be unaware that Jay was on the scene.

'Fine,' she said. She held her hands up. 'You got me. I did want to see the look on Felicity's stupid face, because you know what, you need to open your eyes, Scott. I don't want her around our child. She is a wreck. She's damaged. I'm not sure she should even be trusted with her own son, let alone with *mine*.'

Scott turned to her. Felicity was awake in his arms now, but she was dazed, and Scott's eyes flashed with anger. 'Get out of our house.'

'No. Not until you hear me out.'

Scott rested Felicity back against the sofa and leapt to his feet, pointing his finger at Vicky. 'Get out, or I'll throw you out.'

'Oh yeah? Go on then. I'm sure Felicity would be really impressed to watch you behaving like that.'

Scott took out his phone. 'I'm calling the police. You've harassed us enough, and if you won't stop because I ask you to, maybe you will when they *tell* you to.'

'Go on then. That's really fair, isn't it? You did plenty to harass me and Tim, but nothing ever happened to you, did it? The police didn't give you a hard time about that underwear. And yet what do I get when I leave a rose on your stupid fiancée's car? The police at my door. People looking at me like I'm something on the bottom of their shoe.'

'I am sorry,' Scott said through gritted teeth, 'for that business with the underwear. I'm sorry for trying to interfere with you and Tim. I'm sorry you got stabbed, I'm sorry about the agoraphobia, I'm sorry Tim died, I'm sorry you have this *fixation* on me. But perhaps you need to take a look at yourself rather than blaming me for every single thing that has gone wrong in your life!'

A sly tingle of pleasure ran through her. His punishment was only just beginning. When he went on his trip with Martin, she would make sure Jay paid Felicity a little visit, and then he would *really* be sorry. 'If you don't leave her,' she said, savouring the words, 'something terrible is going to end up happening. You mark my words.'

'Are you threatening us?'

'You're making a mistake.' Vicky pointed her finger at Felicity. '*She* is not worth all this.'

'All of what? *You* are causing all these problems! And if anyone's a wreck, Vicky, it's not her, it's you. And right now, I'd trust her with Dennis far more than I would trust *you*.'

She was stung. 'You don't mean that.'

'I do.' He took a deep breath. 'Vicky, I know you're hurting, I know you don't want me to be with Fliss, but this is how it is. For God's sake, please, this is your last chance. If you do one more thing like this…' He trailed off, and she stepped closer to him.

'Go on then. What?'

'It doesn't matter. Just go away. Please. Just leave us alone.'

'I want to know what you were going to say.'

He sighed. 'All right. Fine. If you threaten, or scare, my family like this again, not only will I go to the police, but I will make sure that Dennis lives here full time.'

She gaped at him, the silence heavy in the room. She felt like she'd been punched in the stomach. 'Just try it!' she screamed at him. 'You wouldn't be able to. No one would agree that he was better here with your nutcase fiancée than with his own mother, and you're not as much of a father to him as you think you are!'

'Vicky, you need to calm down. Leo and Dennis are asleep upstairs. Go home, and cool off. We'll talk about this another time.'

Vicky picked up her handbag and took a fistful of cash from her purse. 'If this is about the window, here,' she said, thrusting it at Scott, 'I'll pay for your sodding window.'

He didn't take the money, and suddenly Felicity was at Scott's side. 'I thought my ex was going to kill me,' she said quietly. 'Do you think that's a joke?'

Vicky couldn't contain herself. She gave Felicity a shove, but to her surprise, Felicity shoved her straight back. Vicky flew at her, enraged, and Scott caught her. 'Stop. Now,' he said.

Vicky fixed her eyes on Felicity. 'You're pathetic,' she said. 'You're such a wet blanket, I'm not surprised you let your ex walk all over you. If a man started knocking me around, I'd cut his balls off.'

Felicity didn't reply straight away, but she kept eye contact. The woman obviously did have some sort of backbone after all. Vicky paused, feeling a twinge of guilt at the things she'd just said, but then she quickly shoved those feelings aside.

'You...' Felicity said slowly, 'You have *no* idea what you're talking about.'

Vicky shook her head. 'Whatever.' She pushed Scott away from her. 'I'm going. And if you even *think* about trying to take Dennis away from me, you're going to get one hell of a nasty surprise.'

She waited until she was inside her car and out of sight of the house before she took out the note that had been attached to the ornament.

You fucking bitch, I'll kill you before I let you marry someone else

In the past, that note would have sickened her. But after Scott's threats to take Dennis away from her, her mouth twisted into a smile.

...

Once she was a couple of streets away, Vicky was surprised to spot Jay's van parked at the side of the road. She pulled over behind the van, and found him sat inside, his head in his hands, so lost in his thoughts that he didn't notice her approaching. When she knocked on the window, he jumped out of his skin, and only opened it when he was sure she was alone. 'I'm fucked, aren't I?' he said.

'If you thought that, why the hell are you hanging around here? Shouldn't you be trying to get away?'

He shook his head despondently. Christ, he could be as pathetic as Felicity. As far as she was concerned, they both needed a good slap. If it wasn't for the fact that the things Jay did were genuinely scary, she'd liken him to Dennis; having a temper tantrum one minute and wanting a cuddle the next.

'Scott is going away this summer. Climbing, in the Alps,' she said quickly.

Jay's eyes widened. 'On his own?'

'With a friend, but if you mean, is he going with Felicity, then no. Her and Leo will be home alone.'

'So that's when you think I should…'

'Yes!' she said, exasperated. Why wouldn't he just get a grip? 'Write your phone number down. I'll get a second phone, and *I* will call *you*, okay?'

'What about the window?'

'I said I got one of my friends to do it. They believe me. I took your little note.' She thrust it through the window. 'Here, have it back.'

He took it and screwed it into a ball. 'Was she scared?'

'She fainted.'

Jay nodded grimly. 'I should be able to tell her how stupid she is to her cheating little face, not sneak around like I'm the one who's done something to be ashamed of.'

Vicky tried not to raise her eyebrows. Jay was completely delusional. Still, she didn't care. 'You'll get plenty of time to talk to her face-to-face soon.'

He smiled as he scribbled his phone number down for her,

and her heart chilled. Her resolve didn't weaken, though. Scott had gone too far this time, threatening to take Dennis away. He'd pushed her into this. It was his own fault.

Felicity

14

I turned Vicky's words over and over in my mind for the next few days. Not so much how she told me I let Jay walk all over me – I wasn't going to let her hurt me with spiteful, ignorant words like that – but what she said when Scott had threatened to go for full custody of Dennis. Two things had struck me as odd.

The first was when she said Scott wasn't as much of a father to Dennis as he thought he was. And the second was when she said that if he tried to take Dennis away, Scott would get one hell of a nasty surprise. Of course, the first statement could be a criticism of his parenting, the second an idle threat. Scott hadn't mentioned Vicky's words since that night, and though he was furious and barely slept a wink after the argument, he soon put the whole thing behind him, though he maintained the next time she did anything he would go straight to the police.

I couldn't forget it so easily, nor the idea that was going round and round in my head. Should I speak to Scott, and tackle my concerns head on? In the end, I couldn't face doing it to him, not without more evidence, so one evening when Scott was helping out at Driver's Plaice and Leo was fast asleep upstairs, I phoned Martin and asked him to come round to see me.

He arrived quickly, and followed me through to the kitchen.

'I didn't expect to get your call,' he said, concerned. 'Is everything all right?'

I smiled reassuringly at him, as he took off his jacket. 'Yes... and no,' I told him. 'Do you want some tea? I just boiled the kettle.'

He nodded and I made us each a mug. 'Let's talk in the lounge.'

'So,' he said once we'd sat down, 'what's this all about? I don't know whether to be worried or intrigued.'

I took a sip of tea. I was nervous now. Did I really want to start asking about this? 'It's kind of delicate.'

'Okay…'

'It's about Scott and Vicky.'

'Oh man,' Martin said, 'what's happened now? Scott told me about that big argument you all had, when she got someone to break your window.'

'Nothing new has happened. It just made me start to question something.' I took a deep breath. I couldn't keep beating about the bush. 'There's no easy way of saying this, so I'm just going to come out with it.'

'Go ahead.'

'Okay. Here it is. Do you think there's a chance Scott isn't Dennis's biological father?'

Martin raised his eyebrows. 'Wow. Okay. I wasn't expecting that.'

'Am I really the only person who has ever wondered? I mean, just look at the dates. It was so soon after Tim died that Vicky and Scott slept together, I can't help but question…' I trailed off. Was it an appalling thing to ask? Was Martin disgusted with me for thinking Vicky would lie about such a thing?

'You're not the first person to wonder about it,' he said. 'When he told me she was pregnant, it was the first thing I asked him.'

'And?'

'Well, I thought he was just going to say that she wouldn't deceive him about something like that. You know what he's like, he doesn't want to think badly of anyone until they prove otherwise. He's like… an eternal optimist about stuff like that.'

'So what did he actually say?'

'He came up with a pretty convincing reason why he was sure Vicky was telling the truth.'

I leaned forwards, as though being closer to Martin would make the answer come sooner.

'It's obvious when you really think about it. You know how

Vicky talks about Tim, and about the life she had with him. She wasn't all that great a partner to him when he was alive, but she idolises him now. She goes on about how he was the love of her life, and Scott took him away from her. If Dennis was Tim's, she wouldn't hide it, she'd shout it from the rooftops. Because then she could say that Scott hadn't only taken Tim from her, but that he'd also left Dennis without his dad.'

I let Martin's words sink in. They made a lot of sense.

'On top of that,' he went on, 'Tim was going to end things with her. If their relationship was as rocky as he was making it out to be, I can't imagine they were exactly ripping each other's clothes off by the end. I think it's quite likely they weren't sleeping together much, if at all, by that point, no matter what Vicky says now about how happy they were together.'

I nodded. 'I've let my imagination run away with me,' I said. 'You know, I'm so glad I was wrong. I've been worried sick about how Scott would react if I ended up having to talk to him about this. I didn't want to hurt him.'

Martin was quiet for a time. He normally had a lightness to him, an air of not taking anything too seriously. But now he looked decidedly like something was dragging him down. 'What is it?' I asked. 'Are you not so sure?'

'There were some things I found odd. Things to do with the pregnancy, and the birth.'

I looked at Martin closely, nerves fluttering in my stomach. 'What things?'

Felicity

15

Martin finished the rest of his tea, the small flowery mug I'd given him looking slightly ridiculous in his hands, which were large and always looked a bit rough and dry, presumably from the amount of time he spent outside in his work as a landscape gardener. I waited impatiently for him to answer, beginning to feel nauseous. I'd been so glad when it had appeared my fears were unfounded, I didn't want Martin to cast doubt over Dennis's parentage again. But I'd brought him here to get to the truth, so I had to face it, whatever it was.

'It's nothing particularly big, or obvious,' he said eventually. 'It was little things. She was a bit secretive. Like she wanted Scott at arm's length until Dennis was born.'

'Did he ever go to any appointments with her? Her midwife appointments, or her scans?'

'No. But then, they weren't in a relationship. They weren't a couple, so I can understand her not wanting him there.'

I frowned as I thought about it. 'Was Dennis born on time?'

'No. He was early. A few weeks, I think.'

My pulse quickened. 'But Scott wasn't at the birth, presumably.'

'No. He didn't even see her in the hospital – she wouldn't let him. He only saw Dennis once Vicky had gone home with him.'

'Do you think she didn't want Scott to see Dennis when he was first born?'

'I have no idea.'

'When Leo was first born, he looked so much like Jay it used to take my breath away,' I said. 'Babies often look just like their dads right at the start, it's like… it gives them an evolutionary advantage, or something.'

'Is that really true?'

'Well, whether it is or not, that could be what happened, couldn't it?'

'Maybe. It's hard to say. I saw Dennis when he was small, and to be honest, I'll admit he didn't look much like Scott, aside from the dark hair. But actually, he didn't look like Tim either.'

'I should stop thinking about this,' I said, trying to calm down. 'I'm winding myself up. She's said some pretty vile things to me and now I've started believing all sorts. But this speculation could really hurt Scott. It's not worth it.'

'Yeah, I think this could be an ignorance-is-bliss situation,' Martin said. 'Scott loves being a dad. I think it's possible that he may have suspected at some point, perhaps he still does now, but he's choosing not to question it because he loves Dennis and as far as he's concerned he's his dad no matter what.'

'You're right,' I said. 'Except…'

'What is it?'

I sighed. 'It's beginning to look like we might get into a custody battle with Vicky. She's getting more and more threatening towards us, and it may end up impossible to carry on the way we are. It's not good for Dennis either when there's so much bad feeling. Scott threatened her about going for full custody, and that's when she said something that made me start wondering about all this.'

'Ah.'

'I don't know if the parentage thing would even affect that, though, would it? Scott's been there for Dennis all his life. And if Dennis ended up being Tim's biologically, then I mean… Tim's not here. So surely Scott wouldn't really be at risk of losing Dennis, would he?'

At that moment a sound made us both look up. Scott had got home and was standing in the doorway, but we'd been so intent on our conversation that until now we hadn't heard him.

…

'Scott!' I said. 'Did you hear what we…'

He nodded and came to sit beside me, so I tried to explain. 'I didn't mean to go behind your back. I just wanted to talk to Martin first. I thought it would be unkind to ask you about something so upsetting if I was just being stupid. And I probably am just being stupid–'

'It's extremely unlikely Dennis could be Tim's,' Scott said quietly.

I looked across at Martin, who gave a small shrug. 'I'm sure you're right,' I said. 'Even Vicky wouldn't lie about something like–'

'That's not what I mean.' He sighed, and then looked at Martin. 'It all happened that year you went travelling,' he said.

I frowned in confusion and waited for Martin's reaction, but he looked as mystified as I did. 'That was years ago,' Martin said, 'before Tim and Vicky were together. What does that have to do with–'

'Tim had cancer,' Scott explained. 'Testicular cancer. They treated it, it's one of the more treatable types of cancer, apparently. I looked it all up at the time. In fact, I think quite often men are still fertile after, with one testicle, but in Tim's case...' Scott shook his head. 'He was going to do sperm banking before the operation, but then it turned out he couldn't. I don't know all the details, but I think basically his... he already had...' Scott paused and my heart ached for him.

'You don't have to say any more,' I told him softly.

'I've said this much. I might as well say the rest. Basically it wasn't viable for him to do the sperm banking. His sperm wasn't good enough quality. So in fact, it would have been difficult for him to have kids anyway. He just wouldn't have found out until he was with someone and they started trying. Having cancer meant he found out about it much earlier.'

'How could I not know about this?' Martin said, unable to contain himself any longer. 'He had *cancer!* I was one of his closest friends, why didn't he–'

'You weren't here, and by the time you were I guess he wanted to put the whole thing behind him, or try to, anyway. He didn't want everyone knowing his business, not if they didn't have to.'

'Why didn't you tell me when you came to me and said Vicky was pregnant, though?' Martin pressed him. 'I even asked you if you were sure the baby was yours.'

'I couldn't bring myself to tell you then. It wasn't long after Tim's death, and I couldn't bear the thought of saying all this personal stuff about him, not when he wasn't there to... I don't know. I just felt that it would be abusing his trust.'

'My God, Scott,' I said, 'I'm so sorry I started this whole thing. I feel awful for making you say all of this.'

'It's all right. It's not your fault. You were worried because we had that argument with Vicky about Dennis, and I would be worried too if I didn't know about Tim.'

I gave Scott's hand a squeeze. 'I'm sorry about Tim as well,' I said, 'I wish I could have met him.'

'Me too,' Scott said.

For a while we sat in silence, until Martin said, 'So, there can't really be much doubt that Den is yours. That's good, right? Considering things between you and Vicky are beginning to break down.'

Scott still looked troubled. 'There was an odd thing, though.' He took out his phone and after a few moments he showed us an image. It was a baby scan photo. 'Aww,' I said, 'so that's Dennis?'

He nodded. 'It's from Vicky's twenty-week scan. She emailed it to me.'

'What's weird about it?' Martin asked.

Scott pointed to the image. 'I've never seen the original,' he said, 'but she had this scan done at the same hospital where Natasha and Zack had their scan of the twins. I imagine scans from any hospital are much the same, anyway.'

I looked up at him curiously. 'What are you getting at?' I'd never had a twenty-week scan. I'd never even seen a midwife while pregnant with Leo, until I escaped from the house where Jay held me prisoner.

'It's supposed to have information at the top. I can't remember what all of it is now, but one of the things is the date of the scan. Look at the way she's taken this picture. All the information is missing, on both images.' He swiped to the next picture, and sure enough, the top of the second scan was missing again.

'So you think the date she had a twenty-week scan doesn't add up with the date you and her slept together.'

'Well, that's the question, isn't it? Why didn't she want me to see it? Nobody would normally take a photo like that, it looks kind of weird. Also, I mean, I don't know a huge amount about newborns, but Dennis didn't seem small or anything. He was only three weeks early from the due date she told me, so I knew he wasn't going to be really tiny or anything, but I remember thinking he seemed a pretty healthy size.'

'So you think Dennis might not be yours, *or* Tim's?' Martin asked.

'Honestly, I try to never think about it. I don't want to think about it. I don't know either way, and I don't care either way. He's my son; I'm the one who's been there for him. As far as I'm concerned, that's all there is to it.'

I put my arms around Scott and gave him a squeeze. 'You're right,' I told him. 'That's all that matters: who has actually been there for him.'

'I just hope we don't ever have to fight Vicky about this. I hope she gets her head straight and lets us get on with our lives, and that she switches her focus to getting on with hers. She's not a bad mum, and I don't want to stop her spending time with Dennis. She's just—'

'A bad person,' Martin said.

'No. Look, I know you really don't like her, Martin. But she finds things difficult. I don't want to be part of the problem, but if I end up having to go to the police over something she does to me and Fliss, it's going to start getting messy. I hope she can see that it's not worth messing up Dennis's life out of jealousy and resentment. He doesn't deserve that, and I'm sure she'll realise that herself, before it's too late and she does something she can't so easily come back from.'

Scott

16

Scott woke up in the small hours, panicky and disoriented. What had he been dreaming about? He couldn't remember, but he'd been on edge ever since Vicky had escalated things by getting someone to break the window. He'd pretended to Felicity that he was fine, and though Vicky had been perfectly civil towards him since she'd done it, that had only served to make him more nervous. Had she really arranged it just so that she could be in the house and see how scared Felicity was? It was so strange, but then, what other reason could there be? She'd even said herself that's why she had done it. But it didn't seem normal. Was she just playing games with them, or was something truly wrong with her?

On top of that, Martin and Felicity had made him start questioning his true relationship to Dennis, and now he was gripped by a sense of foreboding, but couldn't put his finger on exactly where the danger was coming from. He rolled over to put his arm around Felicity, but she wasn't in bed beside him. His heart rate spiked. Where was she? Had something happened? He shook his head to clear it. It was anxiety left over from the dream, that was all. Felicity had probably just gone to the bathroom, or maybe she was checking on Leo.

He made his way out of the bedroom and down the hall. Soft light was coming from the living room, and the door was open a crack. Felicity was inside, curled up on the sofa with a book, a mug of hot chocolate on the side table next to her. She sat up when he came in and put her book down. 'Sorry,' he said, 'I didn't mean to disturb you.'

She gave a big stretch and rubbed her eyes. 'I wasn't concentrating on it anyway. My head's all over the place tonight, I don't know what's wrong with me.'

He sat down beside her. 'I've been feeling uneasy too. This stuff with Vicky – I don't know. I feel like there's something badly wrong, but I can't put my finger on it.'

'If there's one thing I've learned, it's that people can do some pretty dark stuff when they're jealous,' she said. 'Jay...' She faltered and didn't finish her sentence.

'Is that what's keeping you awake?' he asked. 'Thinking about Jay?'

'No. Well, yes, but not like you mean. I'm not thinking about what he did. I'm thinking about me. When Vicky was here–'

'Don't listen to anything *Vicky* says.'

'At the time I didn't. I've tried not to since, but tonight I started asking myself if she had a point. Her words keep going round and round, what she said about me being a wet blanket, and that I let Jay walk all over me.'

'She has no idea what she's talking about. You told her that at the time. You shouldn't give it a second thought.'

Felicity turned to him. 'I have to, though, Scott. I'm trying to work out whether I could have seen it coming. If there was anything different I could have done.'

'Look, it's easy for her to judge. She has no idea what it was like. Nobody *wants* to be in a situation like you were in with Jay. Nobody asks for it. Nobody deserves it.'

'The first time he...' She paused and took a deep breath. 'The first time he did anything... violent, it was like it came out of nowhere. He was always moody. Clingy. And he got in fights, well, picked fights – when we went out he'd go looking for trouble, but he'd never made me feel scared before. I'd been out for the evening, for a friend's hen night, and he hadn't wanted me to go. He said some pretty despicable things to me before I left. I was angry with him for trying to stop me going out, but at the same time it wasn't all that unexpected for him to behave like that. I thought that by the time I got home he'd be fine. I never imagined...' She took another long pause. 'When I came back home, I was very drunk. It was all... some of it's a blur, but I remember him grabbing my hair. He…' She swallowed hard. 'He held me near the gas burner on the hob. He didn't burn me, but he let me think that he would, and he held me there until I apologised for going out and hurting his feelings.'

Scott stared at her. Had he heard her right? Jay had threatened to *burn* her just because she'd gone out with her friends? He felt sick. 'Fliss–'

She held up her hand and he stopped talking. She so rarely wanted to speak about it, he didn't want to interrupt her now.

'I just couldn't believe it was happening. It was like… it was surreal. My mind couldn't make sense of it. I was terrified, I just did what he wanted, said all the things he wanted me to say, to make it stop. When I woke up the next day I wanted it to not be real. But it *was* real, and I didn't know what to do. That's what Vicky doesn't understand…' She sighed. 'I couldn't just leave. It's far more complicated than that. I had nowhere to go, certainly nowhere that Jay wouldn't come looking for me. And he wouldn't have let me walk out the door. He was always watching, and checking up on me. I had to be so careful. But now I'm going over and over it, and I can't figure out if I made a mistake. I can't figure out how it all happened. And I… I still loved him, even after he did that. I still loved him for a while after, even though…' She trailed off and looked round at him again. 'How did it happen, Scott?'

'It's like you just said. You loved him, and by the time you realised how dangerous he was, you were in too deep to get out easily, and too scared to make any wrong moves.'

She picked up her mug of hot chocolate and took a few shaky sips. 'I don't want to feel like this. I don't want to keep questioning myself. It's not like I can change the past.'

'I know it's not quite the same, but I've had plenty of nights sitting up questioning what happened to Tim. Going through the day of the accident and asking myself the same things over and over – did I make a mistake? Could I have foreseen what was going to happen? Could I have reacted differently? Sometimes I talk myself into thinking I did something wrong, but I didn't. I didn't make any mistakes, I didn't forget anything or take unnecessary risks. Neither did Tim. Nobody can stop a rock falling. It's just...' How could he explain it? In a lot of ways, what had happened to Tim had changed the course of his whole life. 'It still messes with your head, though, you know? The fact he was gone but also... I suppose this sounds selfish, but the fact he died when he was barely thirty, it made me realise *I* could die. It seems impossible, otherwise. People don't die when they're that young, that's what you think, until somebody proves otherwise.'

She smiled slightly. 'I wish I could go back to thinking like that. I can just about remember what it was like when terrible things were just something on the news, not in real life.' She thought for a moment. 'How old was Tim when he found out he had cancer?'

'Twenty-two, I think. Maybe twenty-three. Early twenties.'

'There have been a lot of times I never thought I'd make it this long,' she said. 'A lot of times when I've looked at Jay's face, and I thought he would kill me.'

'I can't imagine what that feels like.'

'Hopefully you'll never find out. Hopefully nobody else ever will.'

'This trip I've got planned,' he said after a long pause, 'to Chamonix, it's kind of – maybe this sounds silly, but it's kind of a tribute to Tim. He always talked about going there, and we should have done – it's not even that far, but life kept getting in the way and somehow it never happened. He died before he got a chance.'

'I've already said you have to go,' she said. 'That just makes it even more important. Don't leave it because it feels like this summer isn't ideal. You can't wait for "ideal". You just have to do stuff when you get the chance.' She finished her hot chocolate and put the mug down. 'You know we should start planning the wedding, too. I've already made one decision. I made it just now.'

'What's that?'

'I'm going to dye my hair blonde again. Back to its natural colour, and I'll grow it longer too. I didn't change the way it looked because I wanted my hair different, I did it because I was trying to hide. But I don't want to hide when I marry you; I want to look like me.'

Scott put his arm around her, filled with different emotions – happiness, sadness about the things she'd been through with Jay, admiration for her. He didn't say anything, but it seemed Felicity understood how he felt, because she snuggled against him and closed her eyes.

Felicity

17

Though I tried to bury my feelings of unease, and Scott tried to do the same, neither of us could manage it, especially as Scott's trip to Chamonix drew closer. I grew so frustrated with myself: after all, surely there was no real risk from Jay now. The more time that passed since I escaped, the more likely it became that he would have moved on. Looking for me would put him in danger; he wouldn't risk it. But it was as though deep down I believed the opposite. I constantly imagined there were eyes on me, and one warm day in early summer when I took a picnic down to the beach with Leo, my fears were brought home to me in a terrifying way.

Leo was in his element. We'd finished eating and he was filling up his bucket with sand and tipping it out again while I sat nearby, occasionally looking around at the path and the road behind us – nowadays I couldn't go more than a couple of minutes without doing a quick visual sweep of my surroundings. If I tried to ignore the compulsion to check all around me, anxiety would build until I had to give in to it, sure that something dreadful would happen if my attention was elsewhere. Today my eyes settled on the small café not far from the shore – really it was more of a shack, which only opened in the summer. There were a few people sat on picnic benches outside, some small children running around.

Then I did a double take. There was a man, on his own, with a coffee in front of him on the table. I couldn't see him very clearly, I was too far away, but something about him made me stare. It wasn't like the times when I "saw" Jay in the street – those waking hallucinations that convinced me some random man looked *exactly* like Jay, and then I'd snap out of it and he'd morph back into an innocent stranger. This man didn't look exactly like Jay. He was wearing a baseball cap, and he had glasses. But he was looking right at me and Leo. I stared closer, and when he realised he'd been spotted, he turned away quickly – too quickly. I stood up. My heart was pounding. The man was facing away from me now, drinking his drink, looking at his phone. I rubbed my eyes. Was I going mad? It couldn't be him. It didn't *really* look much like him, not superficially. His clothes, his glasses, the hat, everything was all wrong. And besides, would he be so brazen as to come and watch me playing on the beach with Leo?

I looked down at Leo, who was still playing happily, and when I turned towards the café again, the man was gone. All my composure suddenly left me. I ducked down beside Leo, holding him close. Where had the man gone? Was he coming down to the beach?

'Mummy?' Leo said. He started to climb into my lap, but it was as though he thought better of it and he tried instead to get away. 'Stay here,' I said, clutching hold of him. 'Stay down here…'

Leo pulled away from me. 'You're being scary. I don't like it.'

He started to run across the beach and I leapt up and grabbed him. 'Stay here!' I said, my voice rising. 'He might be coming for us! He might be coming for us!'

...

'It must not have been him,' I said quietly. It was evening. I was home with Scott, having called him to come and rescue me from the beach. 'If I'd been completely sure, I would have just called the police straight away, not waited until I got back here. I must have known in my heart it wasn't really him and that's why I phoned you instead. It was just me panicking. I was being stupid.'

'You weren't,' Scott said. 'DI Miller said you did the right thing to let them know. After all, you knew Jay very well. If you thought the man looked like him–'

'But he *didn't*, not really. And I see things. You know I do.'

I thought back to my conversation with DI Miller. She'd been perfectly friendly and understanding, she always was, but did she secretly think I was losing the plot? I couldn't blame her if she did.

…

That night, my nightmares woke the whole house. Scott calmed the boys down and got them back to sleep, but the next morning Vicky came back mere moments after picking Dennis up to look after him for the weekend. I was in the living room with Leo, and Scott went to answer the door.

'Do you know what Den was saying to me in the car just then?' Vicky said, her voice carrying easily through to me in the living room, even though the door was shut. 'He was talking about Felicity again. About her nightmares, and her panic attacks, or whatever…'

'Please, not now,' Scott said.

'Not now? What could possibly be more important?'

I got up and went to the window. Den was sitting in the back of Vicky's car outside the house. He spotted me through the window and waved, and I waved back, but then I quickly sat down again. I didn't want to hear the conversation so I turned on the TV, but I still managed to catch some of the words during a quiet part of the programme. 'I can't believe you're putting that woman above the well-being of your own son!' Vicky was shouting. 'Either she gets her head together, or you can only see Den when she's not around!'

'Are you serious?' Scott said. 'Are you seriously saying that to me, when *you* were the one who got someone to come and smash our window–'

I couldn't stand any more of it. I opened the door and immediately their eyes fell on me.

'You might be able to wrap Scott around your little finger with all your crying and hysterics,' Vicky spat at me, 'but I am *not*

74

letting you terrify my son—'

'You have no idea!' I yelled at her abruptly. 'You have no idea what you've done!'

She stood there looking like I'd slapped her, and I went back into the living room.

'Why is everyone shouting?' Leo asked, looking up from a book he was flicking through on the carpet.

'Don't worry about it,' I said. I kissed the top of his head. Scott and Vicky's raised voices carried through to me, though I couldn't make out the words, and then they went quiet. The front door closed. They must have decided to talk outside where I couldn't overhear them. Either that or Vicky had decided to leave.

'You know there's nothing to be scared of, don't you?' I said to Leo. 'Just so long as you stay near Mummy and Daddy, or somebody you know very well, like Natasha. Do you understand?'

'Yes, Mummy.'

I held him close. 'And don't ever talk to or go anywhere with somebody you don't know, okay? Even if they say they know you. Like, if a man said he was your daddy, or something. *Especially* if they say something like that.'

'Why would someone say they're Daddy if they're not?'

'Because sometimes people do strange things.'

'Like how you are scared of white vans, and men in the street?'

'I'm not scared of white vans, or men who go past in the street.'

'Yes, you are.'

I sighed. Scott hadn't returned.

'The important thing is that we have each other,' I told Leo. 'You'll always have me, and I'll always look after you.'

'And Daddy,' he said.

'Yes, and Daddy.'

'Why does Vicky not like Daddy?'

'That's hard to explain.'

Leo frowned intensely.

'It's nothing to worry about. Sometimes... sometimes these things just happen. But we're safe here, I promise.'

I closed my eyes and the image of the man I'd seen yesterday filled my mind. *It wasn't him. There's just no way. Even the police didn't take it seriously.*

Jay

18

Jay drove home in a panic. He'd become complacent, sitting in a café in broad daylight watching Felicity and Leo on the beach. She'd looked right at him. *Right at him.* Had she recognised him? She'd started acting funny immediately afterwards. That was when he'd made a quick exit.

God, why did he have to be such an idiot? There was no reason for him to even go to Alstercombe at the moment – Vicky had called and given him the date in July when Scott would be going away, so the best thing he could do would be to lay low. But it was as if Felicity and Leo kept calling to him subconsciously, so that he'd find himself in his van on his way to Alstercombe before he'd had a chance to think about it rationally.

You're obsessed. It's not healthy. Well, if he was, it was all Felicity's doing. The pregnancy, the engagement, the house move – all of it pushed Jay's buttons.

It's so soon now. Just hold it together. He pulled over and spent a few minutes flicking through pictures of her and Leo on his phone until he became more composed. Felicity wouldn't have recognised him. He looked too different now, and she had been too far away. It would be fine. But perhaps he really should lie low for a couple of weeks. It wasn't that big a sacrifice, when it was so soon that he'd have her with him again. He'd be able to touch her, kiss her, hold her. *And fuck her.* He put his phone away. That wasn't a good thing to think about right now. He needed to calm down, not work himself up.

He started the engine. Going home and looking at Stephanie would be the equivalent of a cold shower. He smirked, but then the smile faded as he thought about how things had ended up with Steph. She had been so subdued, practically lifeless, after he'd caught her trying to take his backpack to the police station. She looked pale and ill, and she'd lost weight. It was as if she'd made a conscious decision to withdraw from the world around her – emotionally detaching herself from him. Recently she'd begun to try to lose herself in other pursuits, namely reading her silly fantasy books more than ever, and playing equally ridiculous-sounding games online.

Today, as he stepped inside the house, he was surprised to hear her burst out laughing inside her bedroom upstairs. He froze. Was somebody else in the house with her? There were no other voices, just hers. He pushed the front door closed as quietly as he could and tiptoed towards the staircase, making his way up painstakingly slowly to avoid making a sound. Eventually he made it to the landing, and he peeped round the bedroom door, which was slightly ajar. Stephanie was sitting cross-legged on the bed, talking animatedly on her phone.

He frowned. Who could she be talking to? He couldn't imagine her dad had suddenly called her, and in the past she'd barely spoken to anybody. But she was chatting away to this person like she'd known them for years. Laughing like that – it was what you'd do if you were talking to a close friend, or somebody you loved. Jay shook his head. Where could she possibly have met anybody?

Nevertheless, he waited until she was asleep that night, picked up her phone and took it into his own room. She'd never had a password on it in the past, but he was shocked to find that now it did. He frowned down at the screen, his anger building. What the fuck was this all about? He had enough on his plate without dealing with some bloody Stephanie drama too. He was tempted to throw her phone across the room – let's see her try to talk to her new friend with her phone smashed to pieces. She'd think twice about keeping secrets from him then. He didn't love Steph, but the idea of her betraying him made his insides tie themselves in knots. How *dare* she? Should he pull her out of her bed, force her to explain herself? No. That would be a mistake. He had to be careful how far he pushed her; there was too much at stake. He put her phone back in her room and went to bed. He'd talk to her in the morning, when he'd slept on it.

...

When he came downstairs to make himself breakfast, Stephanie was already sitting at the kitchen table and he watched her carefully. She smiled when she checked her phone.

'What's making you so happy?' he asked her.

She jumped, and looked round at him over her shoulder. 'It's nothing.'

'You won't mind me looking then.'

He made a grab for her phone and she moved it out of his reach.

'Steph,' he said firmly, 'show it to me.'

She held it further from him, but he managed to reach across and snatch it before it locked, and he read the message that had made her smile. 'Can't stop thinking about you,' he read aloud. She wouldn't meet his eyes so he held her chin in his hand to make her look at him. 'Who is this from?' There had been a name with the message: Xavier. Jay already hated him. He sounded like a twat. What was Stephanie doing? If she'd decided to find herself a boyfriend, it could jeopardise everything for him. Not to mention it was ridiculous. If she thought some guy was really interested in her, she was fooling herself. It would all end in tears.

'You can read the name as well as I can,' she said.

He let go of her chin, giving her a shove at the same time. 'Don't get clever with me. I mean who is he to you? Why is he thinking about you?'

Stephanie took her phone back and started to stand so he pushed her back down. 'Are you cheating on me?'

'Are you being serious? Jason, we're over! I'm... I'm just waiting for you to leave!'

'Where did you meet him?'

'I don't have to explain myself to you.'

He grabbed her shoulders and shook her. 'Where did you meet him?' he shouted.

Stephanie met his eyes. Spots of colour had risen in her cheeks. 'I've known him for years. He's just somebody I've played games with online. I've never really *talked* to him before, not until recently.'

'So he's never seen you?'

'Not in person, no.'

'What about a photo?'

'Well... no, what's that got to do with anything?'

Jay started to smile. If this guy saw what Stephanie looked like, he'd probably lose interest pretty quick.

Stephanie

19

'How dare you?' Stephanie said. She'd pretended not to know what Jason was getting at when he'd asked if Xavier knew what she looked like. Why give him the satisfaction of seeing she was hurt? But suddenly she was overwhelmed with anger, and she couldn't hold her tongue any longer. 'How dare you judge me like this, and treat me like this, when I've done so much for you? When I loved you...' She stopped. Tears were threatening, but she swallowed them back down. 'Why don't you have the decency to get out of my life? I helped you. Can't you do this one thing to help me? Don't you have any compassion?'

Jason rolled his eyes. 'Have you finished?'

She paused. 'Yes.'

'Good. Because I don't want to talk about this crap. And this *Xavier* is only talking to you because he wants to get in your pants. But once he catches sight of you, all he'll want is for you to keep your clothes firmly on your body.'

Stephanie was silent for a moment. *Don't react. He's not worth your anger. It'll just encourage him.* It was no use. She let out her rage in a screech, and lunged at Jason. 'I hate you!' she yelled. 'Why won't you just go? Just get out of my house! Get out of my house!'

'No. I'm not ready yet.'

'Well, I am! You need to leave. Now!'

Jason just watched her silently. If anything, he looked mildly amused. She took a deep breath. 'When will you go?' she asked as calmly as she could. 'When will you be ready?'

'Soon.'

'How soon?'

'July. Just a few weeks away. Then I will go, I promise. But remember, I want to use the house for a few days first.'

Stephanie fixed her eyes on him and he held her gaze. 'Steph, you can trust me. Don't fight me on this. If you fight me, I won't be able to do what I need to do, and I'll have to stay here longer.'

She couldn't bring herself to answer, but when she got to work, she wrote a hasty message to Xavier: *I know this is sudden. I need to be out of my house for a few days in July and I don't know where to go. Can I come and see you? Xx*

...

As July approached, the house filled with tension. Stephanie watched Jason closely. He could barely sit still. He kept checking his phone, restless and unsettled. Xavier had told her he was happy for her to come and stay. Despite Jason's insistence that seeing what she looked like would put him off, she had had several video calls with Xavier, and he was as keen as ever. Butterflies of excitement filled her stomach when she thought about going to visit him, but they were quickly smothered by fear. Dread. What was Jason going to do in her house? What if whatever it was went wrong, and he was caught? What if he was planning on doing something truly awful, like hurting somebody? How could she come back to her house knowing that she had helped him to do it? She felt sick near-constantly as the days slipped by, until she could only manage to eat a few mouthfuls at mealtimes. Her nights were sleepless, her days filled with anxiety. Jason was surely planning to do something bad in her house, which would make her into an accomplice, and she couldn't let him. She wouldn't let him.

She set about searching the house for clues about who Jason really was and what he was planning. She looked again in the backpack, she went through his wardrobe, drawers, his coat and trouser pockets, but found nothing. Could he have got rid of everything from his life before he came to Wrexton? Everything apart from those bloodied clothes, anyway. It would probably be sensible for him to have done that, but somehow she couldn't bring herself to believe he had. When she'd met him, he hadn't had much with him, just the backpack, and the clothes he stood up in. He'd had a wallet, though – he'd bought drinks for them both, that first morning when they met. She hadn't seen inside, and he'd paid with cash, but it must have cards in it – even if there was no driver's license or any sort of ID, surely he had a bank card at least. Would he have kept it? It would be difficult to just discard everything you owned, wouldn't it? Or maybe it wouldn't. Jason told her often enough that she was over-sentimental; she'd kept all sorts of things of her granddad's. It was different for Jason. She'd often seen him glaring at various ornaments and treasured things in her house like he wished he could throw the whole lot away. Probably he didn't form much attachment to his own possessions either.

Eventually, she had to admit defeat. Just a week before the date he'd told her he needed the house, Stephanie sat quietly in the kitchen as Jason made himself spinach and poached eggs for breakfast, lost in thought until he looked at her and said, 'What?'

'Nothing.'

'You daydreaming about bloody Xavier, or something?'

'No.'

He shrugged and lifted the eggs out of the pan with a slotted spoon to place them on a plate. One of them skidded across the china before coming to a halt near the edge. 'You shouldn't look back so negatively on the time we had together,' he said, as he moved the egg back to the middle of the plate. 'We had some good times. It's not my fault you're suddenly getting so hung up about my past. You were happy enough not to give it too much thought in the beginning.'

'I *believed* you in the beginning!'

'Yes. Well, I think it's really yourself you're angry at, not me.'

Stephanie tried to ignore him as she poured herself a bowl of chocolate-flavoured cereal. Jason raised an eyebrow at her meal choice, but didn't say anything. Before long he'd finished eating, and after meticulously washing up his plate, pan, cutlery and utensils, he made his way down the hall to the door, taking his keys from his jeans pocket.

Then an idea hit her with such force that her breath caught in her throat. The van! If there was anything he didn't want her to see, he was probably hiding it in there. She never went in it, and he'd probably prefer to keep things in a space he felt was truly "his", even if the van was technically hers. She forced herself to finish her breakfast. She was going to need all her strength. The van. That's where she needed to look. She'd wait until that night when he was asleep, and then she'd take his keys and find out what he was hiding from her.

Felicity

20

'So you're absolutely sure you're happy with me going?' Scott asked me, for probably the hundredth time.

'*Yes,*' I said, determined to convince him.

'You're scared, I can see it in your face.'

Reluctantly, I nodded. 'Okay. I am scared, I'm not going to deny it, but we have to work around it.'

'Well, I do have a possible solution. You can stay with my sister, if you'd feel more comfortable.'

'With Natasha?'

'Yeah.'

I thought about it. I had to admit staying with Natasha, Zack and the twins held a lot of appeal. 'Are you sure they're okay with it? Do they have enough room for me and Leo?'

'It'll be a bit of a squeeze, but she says they can manage. She knows how much this trip means to me–'

I cut him off. 'That's why you have to go. I *want* you to go.'

He smiled. 'I know. But listen, you and Leo come first. And Den, of course, but he's going to be at Vicky's. I want you to feel safe, and be safe too.'

'I will be. And I will stay at Natasha's, I think. Leo will love it, and I'd prefer not to be in an empty house.' I glanced down at the engagement ring sparkling on my finger – Scott and I had chosen it together, and I was still getting used to wearing it. 'Maybe Natasha and I could sort out some wedding stuff together. I need to go dress shopping soon if we're getting married later this year.'

'That's settled then.' He paused briefly, and then said, 'Vicky will be pleased.'

'Vicky?'

'Yeah. She's pretty keen for me to go. I think she really wants to make things right.'

'I guess she's looking forward to a week with Dennis.'

'Yeah, but I don't have to go anywhere for her to do that. She's gone on holiday with him before when I've just been here at home. It's not like I'd ever stop her spending time with him.'

I frowned. 'Why else would she want you to go? She never usually wants you to be happy.'

'Well, if she has decided to start now, I'm not complaining.'

I laughed and he gave me a hug. 'I won't be away for long,' he said, 'not really. And it's still a week away yet.'

'Just promise me you'll be careful. When you're out there, I mean. Don't take any risks…'

'It's always a risk, Fliss.'

'Just be as careful as you can.'

He grinned. 'I will be. Honestly. I'm not going to take any silly risks, I'll stay within my comfort zone as much as I can, I promise.'

I snuggled into him. 'Good. I won't be happy unless you tell me you're having a thoroughly thrill-free time, okay?' I teased him. 'Zero excitement.'

'I'll do my best,' he said, and kissed my hair.

'You know, I hope we really have turned a corner with Vicky. It'll be so much better for everybody if we can get along, her included.'

'We'll just have to wait and see. I'm cautiously optimistic, though. She does seem different. People can't carry on fighting forever. I think she always hoped I'd break up with you to save myself the grief, but perhaps now that she's realised I'm not going to do that, she can't see the point in trying to make problems for us any more. Maybe she just got tired of it all.'

Stephanie

21

Try as she might, Stephanie could never find a good opportunity to get the keys to the van. Jason always kept them with him, as if he suspected her. In the past he would hang them on a hook in the small cupboard in the hallway, but even though she kept checking, hoping that one day he'd let his guard down and follow his usual habit, he never did. He had to be keeping them in his pocket, and taking them into his room when he went to bed at night.

The problem was, the deadline for her departure from the house was fast approaching. Every night she steeled herself to go into his room and take the keys, but she was always too afraid, until the night before she was supposed to be leaving, when desperation forced her to act.

She waited for a good amount of time after Jason went to bed – enough time for him to have fallen soundly asleep – before tiptoeing out of her room and making her way slowly across the landing to his door. She took several deep breaths. There were no sounds from inside. She turned the handle slowly, and slipped into his room, glancing around quickly. The keys weren't immediately obvious, and her heart sank. Would she have to scrabble around in the dark? The chance of her waking him if she had to go looking through drawers or inside cupboards was so high she almost turned around to leave. *No. You have to do this. You have to.*

She stepped further inside. The jeans he'd worn that day were neatly folded on top of a chair in the corner and she made her way across to them, her breath catching in her throat as a floorboard creaked underfoot. Carefully, she lifted the jeans enough to put her hand inside one of the pockets. Nothing. She reached for the other pocket, her heart hammering so hard she thought she would pass out. Her fingers closed around something metal. Keys! She quickly snatched them from the pocket, wincing when they made a soft jingling noise, and darted back out of his room again, closing the door softly behind her.

Every hair on her body stood on end as she began her search through the van. It must have been about ten minutes, and she still hadn't found anything, when a small envelope caught her eye, tucked inside an innocuous-looking takeaway menu inside the glove box. She'd ignored it the first time she gave the van a once-over, but the presence of the menu prodded at her mind – Jason didn't eat takeaways. The envelope wasn't sealed shut, and inside was a photo and a folded page from a newspaper. She set the newspaper aside while she stared at the photo. It showed three teenagers: one she recognised as Jason, a second boy with messy dark hair, and a blonde girl with blue eyes and a happy smile. Jason had his arm around the girl's shoulders, and all three were wearing school uniform. Stephanie turned the photo over in case anything was written on the back, but it was blank. She turned her attention to the newspaper article, engrossed now in what she was doing, so that when the front door of her house opened she wasn't quick enough to react.

In a panic, she tried to fold up the newspaper clipping again, having only looked at it long enough to see the words "missing girl", and a name, Samantha Haragan, but Jason had already reached the van. He opened the door and grabbed the photo and the article, his face contorted with anger. 'What the hell do you think you're doing?' he asked her.

He dragged her back inside the house, and shoved her roughly against the wall. His face was so close to her that she could feel his breath. 'This is nothing to do with you! Stay out of my business, or so help me…' He stopped, and she pushed him away. 'What?' she spat at him. 'What will you do? Are you going to kill me, Jason? Is that your plan? Because I'm right here, so come on, what are you waiting for?'

'Don't tempt me.'

Her stomach flip-flopped. Why had she yelled at him? She needed to tread carefully, not give him reason to get angry with her. 'Who is she?' she asked softly. 'That girl in the photo?'

'It's none of your business.'

'Is she why you're hiding from the police? Did something happen to her?'

He slammed his hand against the wall, right next to her head, and she cried out in shock. 'Stop talking!' he shouted. 'For God's sake. Don't push me like this.'

He stepped away from her, and she quickly moved out of his reach. 'Jason, you can tell me. Perhaps if I understood–'

To her surprise, he took his phone from his pocket, and after pressing the screen a few times he held it out to her. She took it, and was confronted with a blurry photo of a woman and a young boy, taken from some distance away. She swiped through a few more, all of them of the woman and the boy, or sometimes the woman on her own. All taken from some distance. A cold feeling spread through her. So this was why he'd been disappearing so frequently. Perhaps it was the reason he wanted to use her house. She didn't like to think what for.

She shook her head. 'What is this?'

He looked back at her as though he thought the whole thing was obvious, like these photos explained everything, and justified all the threats he'd made, all the things he'd done. 'They're my family,' he told her. Stephanie nodded. Her eyes prickled with tears, and she gave his phone back to him. 'And you want them back?' she said.

Jay

22

Jay glared at her, frustrated. Of course he wanted them back! Was Stephanie stupid?

'The woman is my girlfriend, Felicity,' he explained. 'And she has my son.'

Stephanie nodded. 'Okay.'

'Why are you looking at me like that?'

'I'm not looking at you like anything.'

'Yes, you are. You're looking at me like I'm crazy. They're my family, Stephanie. My *family*!'

'Come and sit down,' she invited him, her voice soft. 'Tell me about them.'

He followed her into the living room, and he spilt out his story. Not all of it – there were some details she definitely didn't need to hear – but the fact that Felicity was his girlfriend, that things had gone wrong between them, that he wanted her back but she was moving on.

'I don't believe she's really moved on, though,' he said. 'She loves me. I know she does, because she's doing all this to punish me.'

'Jason, listen–'

'No! You're going to tell me I'm doing the wrong thing, but nobody else knows what goes on inside a relationship. You don't know anything about me and her, or what we were like together. And she had my baby! I've never even met my own son.'

'What went wrong between you?'

He glanced up at her, and then down at his hands in his lap. He couldn't explain. If he told her any of the things he'd done to Felicity then Stephanie would think he was a monster. People never understood that Felicity drove him to it herself by constantly pushing him, testing him, betraying him. Then, after he'd hurt her, she'd drive him even crazier when she looked so scared, when she sat there or lay there with her cuts and bruises, making him sick with guilt about what he'd done, never realising it had been all her own fault. Jay caught himself. This train of thought never went anywhere good. 'She cheated on me,' he said. 'But I forgive her. All I want is to care for her and my son.'

'Have you spoken to her?'

'What do you think?'

Stephanie nodded slowly. 'She doesn't want you to go near her, does she? That's why… you've been stalking her, Jason, haven't you? That's what you go and do all the time.'

'It's not stalking. She's my girlfriend and the boy is my son.'

'If she was your girlfriend, she'd be with you now. She's your ex, surely…'

'No.'

Stephanie was looking at him with a mixture of fear and pity. 'Jason,' she said slowly, 'did you do something to her–'

He couldn't take any more of this. 'What right have you to question how my family feels about me, or how I feel about them?' he exploded. 'How dare you suggest I *did* anything to them! The only thing I ever did was love them too much.'

'I know… perhaps it feels that way,' Stephanie said, 'but if you really loved them, perhaps you should let them live their own lives.'

'And let my son grow up without his real dad? I would have thought of all people you–'

'If you want to see your son, you can do it through official channels.'

The look on his face betrayed him.

'You can't, can you?' she said, her voice taking on an awful *knowing* tone, like she understood everything about him now. 'You know that you'd never be allowed access. You'd go to prison.'

'What sort of world is it where she can take my son and get engaged to someone else? She can let my son think some other

91

man is his dad, and no one bats an eyelid. I might have done wrong, but my heart is in the right place. Where's her heart? Does she even remember me at all, or is she happy to just let me rot?'

'Jason, listen–'

'My name's not Jason! My name is Jay Kilburn. Look me up if you want, I don't care any more. Soon, I'll have my family back, and if you stand in my way…'

Her eyes widened, but her voice was defiant. 'What? If I stand in your way, what? What will you do?'

'You don't want to find out.'

Jay waited for Stephanie to reply, but she didn't. Her earlier boldness was gone; her face had a greyish tinge to it now. He stood up and made his way out of the room, his leg brushing hers as he walked in front of her, and she shrank away from his touch.

Jay

23

Leaving Stephanie in the living room, he made his way up the stairs, making sure his feet landed heavily on each step so that she would hear. Then, moving as silently as he could, he made his way back down again, creeping towards the living room door, which he'd left open a crack. He manoeuvred himself to a spot where he could look through. Stephanie was still on the sofa, her face illuminated by the glow from her phone screen. His palms began to sweat. What had he done? He wanted her to understand about Felicity, to see that he was doing the right thing, but clearly his explanations were lost on her. She was presumably looking him up, since she now knew his real name.

Sure enough, she gasped softly, and looked up from her phone. Her hair slipped forward from behind her ear, obscuring her face from his view. What would she do? On some level she had to understand, surely? She understood about family, about how important it was, how you should fight for it. She pressed urgently on the phone screen. He froze. Surely she wouldn't dare… He couldn't take the chance. His mind filled with blind panic. He burst into the room, grabbed the heavy ceramic table lamp from the table beside her, and smashed it into her head.

Silence filled the room, broken only by the thud of her phone dropping to the floor. It had the numbers 999 on the screen, but she had not pressed Call. He'd stopped her in time. Taking hold of her shoulders, he gave her a shake. 'Steph?' he said. 'Stephanie?'

Her body was heavy. He dropped her back against the sofa, and when he said her name again his voice came out as a frightened squeak. Was she breathing? She didn't look like she was breathing. He pressed his fingers to her neck and then her wrist, but he couldn't feel a pulse. Tears filled his eyes. He turned her head to the side, and recoiled with a cry at the blood in her hair. He scrambled across the room away from her, stumbling and nearly falling when he collided with the coffee table. 'Why did you do it?' he moaned. 'Why did you try to call them? I thought you loved me. I thought you *loved* me!' His voice had become a shout. As he caught sight of the blood again, his nausea intensified so he ran into the kitchen, scrubbing at his hands with washing-up liquid even though no blood had gone on him. He had to leave the house. He still needed to get Felicity and Leo, more urgently now than ever, but he could no longer bring them to Stephanie's house. People might come looking for her. Her work colleagues would miss her. Xavier might wonder what was going on. After grabbing some clothes and his backpack containing his stash of money, he dashed out to the van and tore away down the street, a few tears drying on his cheeks.

Once he'd put a bit of distance between himself and Wrexton, he pulled over and started to cry in big, painful sobs. To calm himself he looked at the photo of Sammie that Stephanie had found, swiping angrily at his tears when they blurred her image. 'I didn't mean to hurt Stephanie,' he told Sammie. 'You understand, don't you? I know you understand.' He brought the picture to his lips and kissed her face several times. 'I know you understand me. You're the only one who ever has. I'm doing it all for my family. It's the right thing, isn't it? I couldn't care for you and our baby, and I'll never stop regretting it, but I can make it right. I can look after Felicity and Leo instead. I'll look after them until I die, and then I can be with you again.'

His tears subsided. He always felt better after talking to Sammie. It was like praying. She would always forgive him. She was sweet and innocent and perfect, and she knew he had a good heart, despite the world's constant attempts to turn him bad.

Jay

24

It was hard to focus on the drive to Alstercombe. Worries filled Jay's mind. Should he still use the van? Once the police found Stephanie – and they would, sooner or later – perhaps they would start looking for the person she'd been living with. They'd realise Stephanie owned a van, and that it was missing. His palms began to sweat, slipping on the steering wheel. He was getting ahead of himself. The police wouldn't figure it all out instantly, and besides, somebody would have to realise Stephanie was missing first, and care enough to do something about it. That probably wouldn't be instant, either.

God, why had he been so stupid? He'd just left her body there, along with the lamp he'd hit her with. Why hadn't he tried to hide what he'd done, at least? An image flashed through his mind. Him and Mark, rolling Sammie's body into the grave they'd dug in Tatchley woods. She'd been inside a sleeping bag – Mark had put her in it, he'd been too scared to touch her body – and she'd fallen with a heavy thud that still turned his stomach as he remembered it.

And now you've killed Steph.

No. It had been an accident. And he had to forget about it. Felicity and Leo were all that mattered now. As long as he found a way to snatch them quickly, he'd bully Vicky into giving him the address of her cousin's half-finished cottage. If it really was in the middle of nowhere, nobody would figure out where he was for a long time. Vicky would be a weak link, of course. She might crumble and talk, so he'd need to make sure he scared her enough to keep her quiet.

He arrived in Scott and Felicity's street, and frowned as he stopped near their house. Her car wasn't there. It was the dead

95

of night – where could she have gone? Was she staying with somebody? His mind began to race. Where the fuck had she gone? After everything he'd done for her, where was she?

Stop it. Calm down. He took a deep breath. There was nothing he could do right now. There was probably some simple explanation. Perhaps her car was in the garage, getting fixed. Once he'd got a bit of rest he could figure it out in the morning.

His plan to sleep in the van was futile. Images of Stephanie kept running through his brain. *I'm losing my mind.* He rubbed at his eyes. What the fuck was wrong with him? He had to stay rational. He had to stay focused. But now he'd got Steph out of his head, the absence of Felicity's car began to worry him again, until he couldn't take it any more and he called Vicky.

'Jay, what the hell? Do you know what time it is?'

'Why isn't Felicity's car outside her house?'

Silence.

'Vicky, why isn't her car there?'

She still didn't reply, and he shouted, 'Answer me!'

'You need to call the whole thing off,' she said finally. 'I was hoping perhaps you'd get cold feet.'

'Well, I haven't. I'm here right now. I want to take my family. That's what *you* wanted too.'

'They're not at the house. You can't take them. You need to turn around and go back to wherever it is that you're hiding.'

'I can't. I've burned my bridges there. I can't go back again, not ever.'

'That's not my problem.'

'It is your fucking problem! Tell me where Felicity is or I'll come to your house.'

Silence again.

'Vicky! Tell me where the fuck my family are, or I swear to God I'll come to your house and break every bone in your body. Don't think I won't.'

'There is no point in me telling you. You can't do anything now.'

Was that fear in her voice? Good. 'There's no point in *not* telling me either, then, is there? Unless you *want* me to come round.'

She didn't reply straight away. Jay's frustration was boiling over. Did she want him to go and beat the shit out of her? Why wouldn't she just fucking talk to him? He was about to start yelling down the phone at her, outlining exactly what was going to be in store for her when he paid her a visit, but she spoke just in time. 'They're at Natasha… Scott's sister's house. She lives with her husband and their twins.'

'You mean…' He was too horrified to even be angry. 'Felicity and Leo are surrounded by *more* people now than they are when Scott is at home?'

'Yes.'

'Why are they there?' he said, his voice rising again. 'Why has she gone there? Did you warn them—'

'Of course I didn't.'

'Then why is she there? You must have said something to spook them—'

'You're the one who threw that bloody garden ornament through their window. You scared Felicity half to death. It's a miracle the trip didn't get cancelled. And you've got me to thank for that. I've been encouraging Scott to go.'

'Yeah? Well, you're the one who put a rose on her car. You started all this.'

'No I did not!' she said, her voice shrill. 'None of this is what I want! None of this has *ever* been what I want!'

'So you don't want Felicity and Leo to disappear?'

'Not like this. We are both going to get caught, and I'm not prepared to go down for this. Just forget it. For God's sake, turn around and leave.'

'I'm not doing that. I'll get her. And Leo. I'll take them both, I'll find a way.' He hung up before she had time to argue, and threw the phone down. 'Fuck, fuck, fuck!' he yelled, and then he stopped and sat very still and silent. Vicky hadn't given him the address of Scott's sister's house, but she hadn't needed to. He'd seen Scott visit a house from time to time, where there were a couple of very similar-looking children; a boy and a girl. Twins. He remembered where the house was.

It's now or never.

Jay

25

It was the beginning of rush hour, and the sound of cars pulled Jay from his stupor. Somehow he'd passed the hours until morning, neither sleeping nor fully awake, slumped behind the wheel of the van, parked near Scott's sister's house. The road was getting busy now – lots of traffic, lots of cars, and white vans like his. The hustle and bustle all around would help him. Nobody would notice a face that didn't fit on a busy road like this. Felicity's car was parked outside Natasha's house. That had been the first thing he'd checked. Now, he would wait. She'd have to come out sooner or later.

Sure enough, around nine-thirty, Felicity left the house with Natasha, Leo and the twins just behind them. He squinted at them all through his windscreen, frowning at the sight of Natasha. Felicity certainly had a knack of surrounding herself with women who turned his stomach. Leanne had always been bad enough, with her daft-coloured hair and crazy outfits, but Natasha was possibly even less pleasant to look at. She was basically Scott, but with a ponytail. Her clothes certainly had nothing feminine about them; knee-length denim shorts paired with a bland navy t-shirt. By her side Felicity was beautifully feminine in a pretty lemon-yellow summer dress, and his eyes lingered on her hair. She'd dyed it blonde again! It was still short, though perhaps not quite so cropped as it had been. Was she growing it longer too? It was a sign. She wanted to look the way she had when she'd been with him. He smiled for the first time in a while.

Once the small group had piled into Natasha's car, his optimism deserted him again. How the hell was he going to get Felicity and Leo on their own? They had some bags with them, like they were going swimming, or for a day out or something. His head throbbed. He didn't deserve this. He didn't deserve for it to be this hard.

There was no point in him being there while they were out, so he went to buy supplies for staying in the cottage with Felicity, returning to the house around lunchtime. Natasha's car was there, so the two women and the children must be back inside again. Jay sipped slowly from a fresh bottle of water. He'd bought himself lunch as well, but he had no appetite.

Before long, another car turned up and a man got out. Natasha's husband, possibly? Whoever he was, he was tall, and carried himself with a confident stride. He was big – not overweight, but powerful-looking, with light hair cropped very short and muscled arms. He opened the front door with a key. So it *was* Natasha's husband. This was getting beyond a joke. He couldn't fight that man. Felicity might as well be in a fucking fortress.

But then, just minutes later, Felicity ran out of the house, followed by Natasha and the man. Jay sat up and watched carefully. Felicity was clearly distraught, and Natasha too. Jay raised an eyebrow. Now this was interesting. If something bad had happened, this could be a good time to strike.

NEVER LET HER GO

Felicity

26

The living room door burst open, and Zack came to stand in front of Natasha and me, his eyes searching our startled faces. 'I've been trying to call the two of you all morning. Has Martin spoken to you?'

'Martin?' Natasha said slowly. 'No, we've been at the swimming pool, I haven't checked my phone. Fliss, have you...'

She trailed off as she began to suspect what had happened, and we looked at each other. Shaking my my head, I started to say, 'No–'

'It's Scott,' Zack said, confirming all of my fears. 'There's been an accident.'

I couldn't bring myself to stay in the room and hear any more. I ran out into the hall, yanked the front door open and darted into the street. The afternoon sun beat down on me, making me dizzy. Tears rolled down my cheeks, and my whole body began to shake, so that when Zack and Natasha both came outside to talk to me I could barely take in what they were saying.

'We don't know exactly what happened yet,' Zack tried to reassure me. 'You know Scott, he's tough–'

'Martin just told Zack that there was an accident,' Natasha continued, her voice shaky. 'For all he knows Scott might be absolutely fine. Mountain Rescue are–'

I stopped listening. My stomach clenched and I felt faint. Crouching down, I covered my face with my hands until the dizziness passed.

'When...' I said, getting shakily to my feet, 'how long...'

They seemed to understand what I was trying to ask. 'Martin just said Mountain Rescue are out there now, looking for Scott. I don't know when we're likely to hear anything. We just have to try to be patient.'

'Does Martin think he'll be okay? Did he...'

The two of them exchanged a look.

'What? What did he say?'

'He... Oh, Fliss.' Tears were streaming down Natasha's cheeks. I made my way towards her and we put our arms around each other.

'He said he thinks we should prepare for the worst,' Zack said.

...

For a time – hours maybe, or perhaps just minutes – it was like I'd dropped off the face of the earth. Nothing felt real. Scott's parents turned up, and Zack kept making tea, while everyone waited and cried, and waited and cried. Leo and the twins were running about, not able to understand what was going on, until in the late afternoon Zack took them all out to the park to give us some space while we waited for news.

My eye rested on the wedding magazine next to me on the sofa. I'd been flicking through it just that morning, before we went swimming. This week I should have been going dress shopping. And not only that, I was beginning to suspect that when Scott arrived home I'd have some exciting news to tell him: my period was three days late. I hadn't bought a test yet; I'd been planning to do it this afternoon. I should have been finding out if we were going to add one more to our little family, not sat here scared about whether Scott was even alive! Pain swept through my body as I recalled Martin's words. *Prepare for the worst.*

I turned to Natasha, who was beside me on the sofa. 'I think I'm pregnant,' I said quietly. 'I need... I want to know. For sure.'

She stared at me for a moment, and then said, 'Come upstairs.'

I followed her into the bathroom and she handed me a pregnancy test. 'Zack and I have started trying for another baby,' she said. 'I've always got tests in the house at the moment.'

I nodded, taking it from her, and she left me on my own.

Felicity

27

I waited a long time before going back downstairs. Natasha looked up as I joined her in the living room, and at the unspoken question in her eyes I nodded. The test had been positive. But I'd barely managed to sit down and ask if there was any news when Natasha got a call from Zack, who was still out with the children. Her eyes widened as she listened and she put her hand up to her mouth, shaking her head.

'What is it?' I asked urgently, 'is it Scott? Have they found him?'

She shook her head. 'Oh, Fliss, I'm so sorry... he's called the police, and he's still there searching...'

I frowned at her. What was she talking about? Then it hit me. Leo. 'No,' I said, 'oh God. No—'

'Leo ran off after the ball. Rory wasn't too far behind, and he said he saw a man near Leo...'

I leapt up from the sofa. 'Which park are they at?' I asked urgently. 'Where are they?'

'I'll come too,' she said. She looked across at Scott's parents. 'Call us if you hear anything about Scott,' she said. 'And we'll call you when we know more about Leo.'

They nodded, and we left. Natasha kept apologising, and saying that perhaps there was some other explanation – perhaps Leo was just hiding, or he'd got lost and would turn up again. Then she got overwhelmed about Scott, and her voice was choked with tears.

'We'll find Leo,' she said, once she'd got control of herself again. 'We will. It'll just be some misunderstanding. He'll be okay. He'll be okay, Fliss.'

I nodded dumbly. But nothing anybody said could possibly

reassure me. It was clear what had happened. Zack had had his hands full with the three children, Leo had gone out of his sight, and Jay snatched him. I had no doubt it was Jay. Though I'd had no contact from him since I escaped from the house in Tatchley, I knew it in my heart, and I knew that by the time I got to the park, Jay and Leo would be long gone.

. . .

The evening was consumed by waiting. Waiting for the police to find a trail to Leo, waiting for Martin to call with news of Scott. A witness was found who said she'd seen a man carrying a boy about Leo's age. He didn't really match Jay's description. But he matched very closely the appearance of the man I'd spotted by the beach café. I cursed myself. Why hadn't I trusted my instinct that day? I should have insisted to the police that I'd seen him, not doubted myself for a second. Jay had been watching me for weeks, months, for all I knew maybe even *years*!

Hours passed. Scott and Leo remained missing. I alternated wildly between an almost trance-like state, and then flurries of desperate activity. I didn't know what to do with myself. I started scratching at my wrist again, but this time while I was awake, scratching and scratching and scratching. At eleven p.m., an email from an address I didn't recognise snapped me out of my stupor:

Felicity, it's Jay. Leo is in a safe place. If you want to see him again meet me in 20 minutes, at the corner where Redcroft Road meets Grange Street. Leo is not with me. If you tell the police about our meeting it won't lead them to him. If they arrest me, I won't say where he is. By the time they figure it out, he could have been on his own for days. I know you don't want that. I love you Felicity, and I just want to talk. 20 minutes. Be there.

Cold dread seeped through my body. Jay was using Leo to make me go to him! An awful tearing sensation ripped through my mind. I wanted to scream, but I didn't. I had to be calm, sensible, logical. I needed to arouse no suspicion. After taking a couple of minutes to clear my head, I changed out of my summer dress into jeans and a t-shirt, and slipped a cardigan over my arms. I wasn't sure exactly where everybody was, as I'd spent the last hour or so in Natasha and Zack's spare room where I'd been sleeping the past couple of nights. Scott's parents had probably returned to their own house, the twins had gone to bed, and Natasha and Zack might be either in their bedroom or downstairs in the living room or kitchen. I peeked out from behind the curtain in my bedroom. There was a police car on the street right outside, and I was pretty sure there was another around the side of the house, watching out for any signs of Jay coming to get me. Or, I suspected, any signs of me trying to leave to go to him.

Opening the bedroom door as silently as I could, I glanced down the landing. No lights were on in the other two bedrooms, nor in the bathroom. I couldn't imagine Natasha would be able to sleep. She must be downstairs, and Zack was probably with her. My footsteps silent on the thick carpet, I crept down the stairs into the hall and grabbed my trainers, slipping them on to my feet in the dark. There was a strip of light under the closed living room door, and faint sounds of the TV. I tiptoed down the hall, into the kitchen, towards the small utility room and the back door out into the garden. The under-cupboard lights in the kitchen had been left on, thankfully, so I could see where I was going without turning on any lights. I had a brief moment of panic as the back door was locked and my mind went blank about where they kept the key. I searched around on the worktop, relieved when my fingers closed around a set of keys. I tried a couple, and the second key worked. After opening the door silently, I stepped into the garden.

Vicky

A few hours earlier

28

The sound of the doorbell made Vicky jump. She'd just settled down in front of the TV, a glass of white wine in hand, and she wasn't in the mood to be disturbed. She hesitated, tempted to ignore whoever was outside, but then they rang the bell again. She froze. Surely it wasn't...

She got unsteadily to her feet just as there were several loud knocks on the door. 'I'm coming,' she called out. But it was like one of those dreams where she'd will her feet to move but they wouldn't. *It's him. It's Jay. He's come here.* Could she ignore him? No. If she tried, he'd stay out there banging on her door, drawing the attention of her neighbours. Maybe he'd even try to break in. She would just have to try to calm him down and get him to leave.

When she made it to the door, the sight that greeted her was worse that she could possibly have imagined. Jay stood there, holding a sleeping Leo in his arms. She was so shocked that she froze, and he pushed past her into the house. She snapped back to her senses. 'What the hell are you doing?' she said, her eyes flicking from Leo to Jay's face. 'You need to go. Now.'

Jay was looking past her, trying to see further into the house. 'Is anyone else here?' Leo stirred in his arms. 'Can I put him down somewhere?' He began to make his way down the hall.

'What are you doing?' she said, standing in his way. 'You can't be here! Why have you brought Leo here? Are you... what are you...' She stopped and swallowed painfully. Her mind was racing. Had anyone seen him come to her house? Did anyone realise he had Leo? They must do – if he'd snatched the little boy, it would only be moments before his disappearance was noticed. Felicity never let Leo out of her sight except for when he went to nursery. Her panic rose. If Felicity knew, or suspected, that Leo was gone, then the police would know. 'You can't be here!' she said again. 'Get out! Get out!'

She pushed him towards the door, but he wouldn't budge. Leo's eyes flickered open, but then closed again. If they made much more noise he would wake up properly.

'You need to help me,' he said. 'At least let me put Leo down.'

'I'm not helping you! What were you thinking? Where's Felicity? I thought you would take them both! In fact, I told you not to do it at all!'

'I'm still going to take her. It will all be fine. Just calm down.'

She stopped talking, eyeing him warily. The look on his face when he'd first burst into her house had been wild, crazed. He was calmer now, though he held Leo awkwardly in his arms, desperate to put him down. 'Felicity will come to me,' he said, 'but you need to keep Leo here. Just for the moment.' He tried to step past her again.

'Are you fucking crazy?' she hissed at him, blocking his path. 'I can't keep him here! You've abducted him, the police will be combing Alstercombe looking for him–'

He barged past her, stopping her mid-sentence. 'He's going to wake up. I can't talk to you with him asleep on me.' This time she didn't stop him. She stood by helplessly and let him lay Leo on the sofa in the living room, her stomach twisting itself into knots as he placed the stolen child down in her house.

'He's not staying here,' she said as he came back into the hall, closing the living room door behind him. 'You need to take him back. You can't just steal children, Jay!'

'Well, it's done now,' he snapped, 'so we just have to work with it. Look, Vicky, you want this to be over, don't you? Keep him in your house, just for a day or two. I need to talk to Felicity alone. If Leo is with us it's not going to work.'

'What's not going to work? What the hell are you thinking is going to happen now? Her *and* Leo, that was the deal. The original deal, anyway. I *told* you not to do it at all. This is… this is all wrong! Once Felicity went to Natasha's house, it was impossible. This… this is…' Her panic overwhelmed her, and her voice became a cry. 'Just get Leo away from here! Away from me!'

'I want Felicity to *want* to be with me. This is the only way.'

Was he serious? The man was deranged.

'Don't look at me like that! She loves me, she's just forgotten that she does. Once she spends some time with me, she'll want us to be together, and we'll come and get Leo. Together.'

'Leo is *not* staying here. You need to pick him back up and get out of here, right now.'

'No one will know–'

'My son will know!' she exploded. 'He *knows* Leo! If he wakes up and finds him here, he'll tell Scott and Felicity about it as soon as he sees them.'

As if on cue, Dennis started crying upstairs. She couldn't take any more of this. 'Take Leo and get out!' she demanded. 'Or so help me I'll call the police and tell them you're here! I'll tell them you turned up and threatened me. Who are they going to believe, after all? A criminal who's already on the run, or me? They won't believe I already knew you. Why would they? You can't prove it–'

He took his phone from his pocket. 'Yes, I can. I've been recording everything you said since I came through your front door.'

Vicky froze in her tracks. What had she said? She couldn't really remember. It would be obvious she knew him, though. Had she said anything else about how she'd helped him? She glared at him, her body shaking. Upstairs, Dennis's cries subsided. He had gone back to sleep. Jay stopped the recording and faced her. 'I don't know what you'll do about your son telling people Leo was here,' he said, 'but that's your problem. You are going to help me, because helping me is the only way you're going to get away with what you've done.'

Vicky shook her head. This couldn't be real. This was a

nightmare. In a minute she'd wake up.

'I don't want to hurt you, Vicky. I just want you to help me one last time.'

'I never should have helped you the first time.'

'I need to know the address of this cottage of your cousin's, so I can take Felicity there.'

'You can't be serious.'

'I am serious. You'll do it. Now.'

Vicky was going to argue, but then he took a step towards her. He was reaching for something inside his jacket. There was a glint of metal. 'Don't hurt me!' she said as he drew out a knife. Her body turned to jelly, her mind returning to the night she'd been attacked when she was just a teenager; the night she'd ended up lying on the pavement, bleeding, crying out weakly for help.

Her eyes fixed on the blade in Jay's hand, and when he took a step towards her she turned and bolted for the kitchen, but he grabbed her arm and before she knew it the knife was against her throat. 'Do as I say.' His mouth was at her ear. 'Everything is going to be fine.'

Tears spilt down her cheeks. The metal was cold, and felt like it was already cutting into her. She imagined thick drops of blood spilling down her top, but she couldn't look down. She didn't want to move her head a single millimetre and risk the knife digging any further in to her. A drop of something warm splashed against her ankle and she thought it was her own blood until she became aware of the warmth and wetness of her leggings. She'd wet herself. Jay had noticed too.

'For God's sake,' he said. 'Just give me the fucking address, keep your mouth shut and this will be over before you know it.'

'I… I'll get it. I'll get it now. It's on my phone. My phone is in the kitchen.'

Jay took the knife away and followed her to her phone, on the worktop near the kettle. She desperately searched her emails to find the one from her cousin, while Jay stood by her side, still holding the knife in his hand.

'Here,' she said finally. She showed him the screen. 'It's remote. It's an old bothy, in Scotland, that they're turning into a holiday cottage. It doesn't even have mains water; it has its own supply. I don't know if it has any electricity yet. It's not really habitable. It... it's all locked up, half-finished. I...' She shook uncontrollably for a moment, then took a breath. 'Please don't go there. Don't involve me any further. Perhaps it's just not possible for you to get Felicity back. You could stop this now, take Leo back, show that you're a reasonable man. A *good* man...'

He was noting down the address on his phone, the knife now back in his jacket. He was barely listening to her.

'Jay, please—'

'I am a good man,' he said. 'I'm proving that by bringing my family back together. Even if it is just a piece at a time.' He gave her a look. 'Don't even think about telling anybody where I've gone. If you mess this up for me, I will make you pay. If I get caught, don't think you're safe. Even if I go to *prison*, I'll find a way of getting somebody to come after you.'

She didn't reply.

'Do you hear me?'

'Yes.'

'Are you sure?'

He was reaching for the knife again. 'Yes!' she cried.

'Good.' He put his phone away and walked back down the hall, and out of the front door, while Vicky dropped to her knees in the kitchen, shaking and crying. Her phone vibrated and she tried to focus on the screen through her tears. She had a message from Martin.

I'm afraid I have some bad news. A few hours ago there was an accident, Mountain Rescue are out looking for Scott. I'll call you as soon as I know anything more.

She covered her face with her hands. She wanted to scream, but the thought of the two sleeping children in the house was enough to stop her. She began to cry in huge sobs that she tried her best to stifle with her hands. Scott was hurt? Lost? *Dead?* What was happening? What the hell was happening?

Jay

29

Jay hastily left Vicky's house and drove away, relieved that he no longer had Leo with him. As amazing as it had been to look into his son's face, and hold him in his arms, the three-year-old boy had been a nightmare to deal with. Jay's heart had felt like it was going to pound right out of his chest when he'd grabbed Leo and made his way back to his van. The little boy had cried while he drove, until Jay pulled over and demanded, 'What? What do you want?'

A crease had formed between Leo's eyebrows. 'Where's Mummy?'

'You'll see her soon.'

'I don't know you.'

'No.'

'I want to go home.'

'Well, you can't.'

'Why not?'

'Because you need to stay with me a while.'

'I don't like you.'

Jay had wanted to grab Leo and give him a shake, but he didn't. He tried to see it from Leo's point of view. 'I'm Mummy's friend,' he said. 'She must have forgotten to tell you that you'd be seeing me later.'

Two wide round eyes fixed on him. 'We'll see Mummy later?'

'Yes, later.'

'I'm hungry.'

Jay rolled his eyes. What the fuck did small children eat? He had no idea. 'Do you like sandwiches?'

Leo nodded. 'Cheese.'

'Okay.' Jay took a deep breath. 'Okay. All right. You stay here and I'll be back.'

Fortunately, he'd stopped near a petrol station and he dashed inside to buy a sandwich for Leo, who sat quietly tearing it into strips and ate about half of it. The crumbs and mess set Jay's jaw on edge, but he let Leo do what he wanted, and concentrated on driving, and thinking. Once he'd finished eating, Leo said, 'Will Daddy be back soon?'

A jolt of pain went through Jay, and he ignored the question.

'I want Daddy,' Leo said. 'Where's Daddy?'

Jay took a deep breath and let it out slowly. *Don't let it get to you.* There would be plenty of time later to re-educate Leo on his parentage. But the boy kept saying it over and over. 'I want Daddy. I want Mummy. I want Daddy. Where's Daddy?'

'If you mean Scott,' Jay said loudly, 'then he isn't your daddy. Scott is just some man who has sex with your mummy.'

Leo was deep in thought. 'What's sex?'

'Oh, for God's sake.'

'Are you sad?'

Jay stopped at some traffic lights. 'Why would you ask that?'

'Red means stop,' Leo said.

'Why do you think I'm sad?'

'You're all shouty.'

'I'm sad because you think Scott is your daddy. But he isn't. *I'm* your daddy.'

At this, Leo screwed his face up with concentration. 'Mummy said... Mummy said it's bad if someone says they are Daddy when they're not.'

'She said what?'

Leo was clearly confused about what to say next, but Jay didn't need him to answer. It was clear what had happened. Felicity had warned him against going near somebody who said they were his daddy. Felicity had warned Leo against *him*.

Gripped by a spasm of anger, he didn't realise the lights had turned green until the car behind beeped its horn. He made a noise of frustration, stuck his middle finger up at the car behind, and got moving again. He was exhausted, the adrenalin of taking

Leo beginning to be eaten away by wearying fear and anxiety. God, why couldn't he just have Felicity now? Why couldn't it just be over with? He drove around a bit longer, getting everything straight in his head, and to his immense relief the driving eventually lulled Leo to sleep.

By the time he left Vicky's, his mind had turned into one big checklist. Get Leo. Done. Get Vicky to take him. Done. Get the address. Done. Trusting Vicky was a risk. He was only fifty-fifty about whether she would stay silent or talk. But what choice did he have? There was nowhere else to leave Leo, and the boy had to be left somewhere – otherwise, aside from Leo reducing their opportunities to be alone together, there would be no incentive for Felicity to spend time getting to know him again. If Leo was with them, all she'd try to do would be escape with him. But now she didn't know where Leo was, it would be in her interest to listen to him.

As for the bothy, that was a risk too, because if Vicky ignored his dire warnings – which were really just empty threats – and talked to the police, they'd have an exact location for him. He shook his head helplessly. There was nothing he could do about that. He'd have to chance it. He wasn't sure exactly what a bothy was, but it must be some kind of cottage, since that was what Vicky had called it originally. In any case, he'd bought all sorts of supplies – he was prepared for no electricity, no water. Everything was in place now. All that remained was to summon Felicity.

Jay

30

'Tell me where he is,' Felicity demanded, the second she got into his van. He ignored her, speeding away from the spot where he'd waited for her, and out of Alstercombe, drowning out her questions about Leo as he concentrated on driving. She wouldn't be so easily put off, though. 'Where is he?' she screamed at the top of her voice, after several minutes of him not replying. 'Where is he, Jay? Where is Leo? Tell me where my son is!'

'Stop asking me. I need to concentrate. We'll talk in a few minutes.'

'We'll talk *now!*' She grabbed his arm and he tried to shake her away but she wouldn't budge. 'Now!' she said again. 'Tell me what you've done with him!'

The stress of the last couple of days was more than he could bear. He couldn't take it any more. 'Shut up!' he yelled at her. 'Shut up, shut up, *shut up!*' He tore her hand from his arm, almost swerving into the oncoming traffic, and she cried out in fear. 'You almost made me crash the fucking van,' he shouted at her. 'Just shut the fuck up and let me drive.'

'Are you taking me to Leo?'

'No.'

She was silent for a moment, frozen. 'Jay, tell me where my son is,' she said very slowly and clearly.

'No. Not right now. No–'

Her desperation to find Leo had clearly made her lose all sense of reason as she lunged at him again, almost making him lose control of the van. He took his hand from the steering wheel and swung it at her face. The blow wasn't enough to deter her, and she was still clutching at his arm. God, why was she doing this? Why wouldn't she stop?

'Tell me where Leo is! Tell me right now!' she yelled at him.

'Stop it,' he pleaded. 'Not now. Just calm down, and let go of me.'

'I will not *calm* down!' Her hand tightened on his arm.

In a spasm of fury, he tore her hand away and hit her in the face as hard as he could. 'Stop,' he said, 'stop it. Just stop.' He was almost in tears. Why wouldn't she just calm the fuck down?

He glanced round at her. She was cowering in her seat now, her nose bleeding. *Blood!* He shuddered and looked away. 'I don't want to hurt you,' he said. 'Just let me drive. Please.'

She huddled against the window, silent now, thank God.

A little while later he pulled over in a quiet lay-by. Felicity sat forward, pinching the top of her nose, not meeting his eye.

'You okay?'

'I want Leo,' she said quietly.

'Give me your phone first,' he said, 'and then we can talk.' She handed it over, and he turned it off and slipped it into his jeans pocket. It might come in handy at some point, though he'd need to get rid of it soon. He wasn't sure how phones were traced, and he couldn't take any chances.

'I'm sorry I didn't answer your questions about Leo,' he said. 'I needed to get away from Alstercombe. Away from the police. They didn't spot you leaving, did they?'

Instead of answering, she continued to sit forward holding her nose, her shoulders tight, like she was trying to curl in on herself.

'Felicity,' he said softly, 'don't be afraid of me. You were going to make me crash the van, that's the only reason I lashed out like that. You're not thinking straight. You're worried about Leo, I understand. But you have to calm down, or you're going to end up hurting us both.'

She lifted her head. Her eyes had a strange glint to them as they fixed on him, and then she looked away. Her face was ashen. Now her initial rush of adrenalin had passed, she was terrified of him. Too terrified to even speak, it seemed.

He opened the glovebox and took out a pack of paracetamol.

'Take some of these for the pain,' he told her. He handed her his near-empty bottle of water. 'And drink the rest of this.'

She did as he asked. He gave her a moment to compose herself, though she didn't look much better. 'Fliss, I need you to tell me how you got out of Natasha's house. Could you have been seen?'

She shook her head with small, jerky motions.

'So how did you do it?'

'Just… just tell me where Leo is. Please.'

'Answer me first.'

'I climbed the fence into Natasha's neighbour's garden,' she said finally. 'And then I climbed into the next garden along from that. I managed to slip out onto the street without being seen.'

He nodded. 'Good.'

'Tell me then,' she said urgently. 'Where's Leo? What have you done with him?'

'What have I *done* with him?'

'You said you left him on his own.'

Her comment made him angry. Was that really what she thought of him? That he'd put their son in danger? Instead of answering straight away, he took a bit of time to look at her close up. She looked older. Her blonde hair was a little lank and greasy where it parted in the middle of her scalp, like she'd been running her hands through it over and over, and her eyes were puffy. It was a warm evening, and she was wearing cropped jeans, along with a grass-green top with a pattern of little white flowers all over it, an oatmeal-coloured cardigan covering her arms.

'Tell me where he is, Jay!' she insisted, her voice shrill. 'If anything happens to him—'

'I'm glad you came,' he cut her off. 'I'm so happy to see you.'

She didn't reply. She was white and shaky; her skin had an unpleasant sheen to it, like she was feverish, and she'd started scratching at her wrist. He reached out to her and she flinched. Her eyes were huge, fixed on him the way Vicky had stared at the knife when he'd taken it from his jacket.

'He's not on his own,' Jay snapped. 'I can't believe you think I'd put our child in danger.'

Her voice trembled. 'Who's he with, then?'

'I'm not telling you that.'

'I'm his mother! Who have you left him with? Who have you left my son with, Jay–'

'Stop with the "my". He's not just yours, he's *ours*. And he's safe. I promise you.' He reached towards her again. His fingers brushed her cheek and she stiffened. 'I want Leo,' she said, her voice a near whisper now. 'Please, Jay. Tell me where he is.'

'I will, soon. Please try to understand. I'm only not telling you because I want us to have a chance to talk and get to know each other again before Leo is back on the scene. It's not because you won't approve of where he is. If you knew where he was and who was looking after him, you'd be okay about it, I promise.' This probably wasn't true, though surely she'd rather Vicky than a total stranger. He lifted her chin. 'I promise, Flissie. I wouldn't do anything to harm Leo. I love you and him, you know that. You *do* know that, don't you? When I think of what I've had to go through to get to this point, to get to see you again–'

'What *you've* had to go through?' she whispered.

'Yes. I've had to stay hidden all this time. I've had to find you again.' He gestured at his face. 'I mean, look at me. I look ridiculous. But you'd know all about making yourself look stupid, wouldn't you. You made your hair look like shit. And you changed your surname.'

She didn't reply.

'You know, everything is going to work out okay,' he told her. 'Once we've had a chance to talk–'

'How did... how did you find me?' she asked. She was rubbing at her wrist again.

'I hung around near Leanne's for a while. You visited her, and when you were leaving you left your handbag in your unlocked car for a minute or two. I took a photo of your driver's licence.'

Felicity looked appalled. Her eyes glistened, but then she pulled herself together, her voice hard. 'I saw you. You watched me on the beach with Leo one day, you were in the café. I told myself I was seeing things.'

'Yes, I was there. I've been watching you for a while. This thing with Scott, I forgive you. I know it's not real. You're using him to get back at me.'

She didn't respond, so he pressed her. 'I know you still love me, Fliss.'

She was silent, and he looked around at the road. He'd put some distance between them and Alstercombe, but they were still a bit close for his liking. He started the engine. 'We'll talk,' he said, 'I'll explain everything. I'm not trying to hurt you, Felicity, you know that?'

'I want my son,' she said. 'I need to know Leo is safe.'

He didn't answer, though the temptation to shout at her was almost overwhelming. She had said "my" again. *My* son. As if Leo was nothing to do with him. Instead of shouting, he drove and hoped she would start being more rational, but when he glanced back at her a few moments later, she was huddled in her seat. Her skin, if anything, was even paler, and her hands were trembling where they rested in her lap. He turned his attention to the road again. It was fucking ridiculous, the way she was behaving. She'd better stop her rabbit-in-the-headlights act soon, or he was going to seriously lose his patience with her.

Jay

31

'What are you going to do to me?'

Her voice startled him. It came out of nowhere, after she had spent so long in silence. 'What?' he asked, appalled by her question. What did she think he was going to do to her, for God's sake? He'd told her how much he loved her. Yet she still expected the worst.

'I'm not going to *do* anything to you. I just want to show you I've changed. I want us to spend some time together.'

'And then you'll let me have Leo?'

Christ. Leo, Leo, Leo. Yes, the boy was important, but he was just one part of the whole picture. Why didn't she understand? 'Yes,' he said, unconvincingly. 'Once we've got to know each other again.'

She watched him, eyes glittering.

'We need to be a couple again before we can be a family. You need to put in some effort with me. You need to earn Leo back–'

'You bastard!' she screamed, her face wild now, desperate. She flew at him again and her nails scratched his face. 'I don't need to *earn* my own son!' He tried to fight her off with one arm while keeping control of the van with his other hand. Not this again. Had she gone crazy?

'Stop!' he said, 'stop it, stop, *stop!*' He gave her an almighty shove and she fell back against her seat. The stupid bitch. He should have shoved her even harder. Or given her another smack. Anything to make sure she properly shut up and gave him some space for a few minutes. How could she be so selfish and ungrateful? Didn't she realise what he was trying to do for her? For all of them? Tears were pouring down her cheeks and she brought her knees up and hugged them to her chest. 'I want my son,' she told him. 'I want Leo. I want Leo.'

...

Jay's knuckles were white on the steering wheel. He had hoped that their exchange in the car would be more pleasant than this. One of her nails had caught his face quite badly and he was bleeding, and there would be no talking to her while she was in this state. Fortunately he had made some preparations for this. When they neared a service station, he stopped and said, 'I'll get you a coffee. It'll help.'

'I don't want anything from you.'

'Or one of those fancy fruit things blended with ice. It's a warm evening, it'll make you feel better. I bet you haven't eaten or had a drink for ages. Or I could get you an iced coffee – you used to love those.'

'Do whatever you want.'

Jay gave up and got out of the van. He'd get her a drink anyway. He locked the van and started walking across the car park. Then he paused. Felicity's phone was still in his pocket. It might be worth having a look at it now. He turned it on and found she had a missed call from "Natasha". Scott's sister. He glanced over at the van, but Felicity wasn't watching him, she was staring out of her window, so he listened to the voicemail message. Natasha's voice was stressed and emotional.

Fliss! Where are you? We thought you were asleep! Are you safe? Please reply. You're scaring us. And listen, we've had some news, it's about Scott...

That bastard again! Why the fuck did anyone care about him? Jay almost flung the phone into the bin by the door, but then he came to his senses. This information could be important. He made his way to the drinks counter, Natasha's piercing voice drilling into his ear.

Once the message had finished, he bought a bottle of water for himself and an iced coffee for Felicity, and then he took the drinks over to the stand with sugar sachets, wooden drinks stirrers, and serviettes. He quickly took the top from her takeaway coffee cup, and from his jeans pocket a small clear plastic packet with some white powder inside. The café was moderately busy – enough people around that he wasn't conspicuous by being one of the only customers, but few enough that no one was standing right by him. He opened the packet and quickly tipped in the powder, then threw the packet away and stirred the drink thoroughly. As long as he could get her to drink it, soon he'd be free of her questions and her anger, and he could talk to her again when she was thinking more clearly. As for the news he'd just heard about this prick Scott – well, she didn't know anything yet. He would speak to her about him in his own time. When he was good and ready.

He was just picking up the coffee when Felicity's phone rang. He didn't answer and it beeped again. Another answerphone message, from Natasha. The woman's voice was urgent, frantic.

Fliss, where are you? Leo is back! The police found him in the street, he's safe and well. They think Jay took him to trick you into going to him, but really he never took Leo anywhere, he left him in Alstercombe! Fliss, please, please don't go to Jay. Come home, or tell us where you are. The police are searching for you. You need to come back, please, Fliss! Jay doesn't have Leo!

The phone started ringing again so he turned it off and quickly left the café. Once outside he dropped the phone on the ground, smashed it under his foot and threw the pieces in the bin. Then he took out his own phone and called Vicky.

'What are you doing?' Her voice filled his ear, full of distress. 'Don't call me–'

'You dumped Leo.'

Silence.

'Well?'

'What the fuck did you think I was going to do? I couldn't keep him here, Jay, are you fucking crazy? I left him in the road, no one saw me–'

122

'You left my son in the street?'

'You gave me no fucking choice! Now leave me alone!' She hung up. Jay turned his phone off and glanced thoughtfully over at the van. Leo had been found. Vicky had lost her nerve, and made sure Leo was out of her house. Hopefully that meant she wasn't likely to tell the police about his plans, because if she had any intention of talking to them, surely she wouldn't have dumped Leo in the street to cover up her involvement.

A thought struck him. Would Leo's safe return be on the news? Felicity could turn the radio on in the van! He shoved his phone back in his pocket, and dashed over to Felicity.

Jay

32

Thankfully, Felicity hadn't done anything so rash as turn on the van's radio. It probably hadn't occurred to her. In fact, she hadn't moved at all; she was still gazing listlessly out of the window. But he'd barely managed to put the drinks down when she suddenly sprang up and leapt out of the van. Swearing, he got out himself, but she wasn't trying to run. 'Tell me where Leo is, or I will start screaming,' she said.

Jay glanced around. Though the car park wasn't packed full, there were a lot of people who would hear if she started making noise – several people nearby were taking a break or eating inside their cars, and there were a few small groups making their way to and from the service station.

'I mean it, Jay.'

He stood in front of her. Her eyes were fixed on him. But he wasn't convinced she would really start screaming. 'Go on, then,' he said.

She wasn't expecting that. She faltered. 'Just tell me, Jay,' she said desperately. 'Tell me where he is. Tell me where he is!' her voice was rising. 'Tell me where he is, tell me where he is!' She took a deep breath, as though she truly was about to start screaming. He couldn't risk it. He clapped his hand across her mouth. 'I told you, getting other people involved won't help,' he said into her ear. 'I won't tell the police where he is, so drawing attention to yourself will achieve nothing. But if you cooperate, I *will* tell you. Just not right now.'

She was making noises in her throat, and he took his hand away. She took another big breath, readying herself to scream. Jesus, what was wrong with her? He grabbed her arms and shook her. 'Stop it! Fucking stop it,' he hissed at her.

'I'm not going to stop asking where he is until you give me an answer.'

'Yes you are. You're going to get back in the van, you're going to sit down, and you're going to shut up.'

'No.'

'Then I won't ever tell you where Leo is. I'll make sure you never set eyes on him again. Do you want that?'

Her eyes flashed with anger, but she didn't reply.

'Do you?'

Still nothing.

'I said, do you *want* to never see Leo again? Answer me.'

'No,' she said finally.

'Then do as I say. Everything will be fine if you do as I say. But if you start screaming, I will have to leave you here, and if I leave you here, you won't get Leo.'

It was a lie, but she didn't know that – she still believed Leo was in danger. Reluctantly, she made her way towards the van. She took the iced coffee from him without a word, and he started driving again, watching her out of the corner of his eye to see if she drank any of it. Just as he was beginning to lose hope, she took a sip, then another. He sighed inwardly with relief. Soon he wouldn't have to worry about her. He'd get some peace and quiet, and she'd get the rest she obviously needed.

When Felicity had drunk about half of her coffee, she became drowsy, but not yet suspicious. 'I need a wee,' she told him.

'I don't want to stop.'

'Jay, I need to go! I'll go in the bushes if I have to, just pull over. I…' Her voice was slurred and she rubbed her eyes. 'I'm not going to make a run for it, not when I don't know where you've put Leo.'

Her eyelids were drooping as she finished speaking. He stopped in a lay-by and helped her out of the van towards the grass verge, and she swayed a little. 'I feel weird,' she said.

'You're exhausted. It's not surprising with everything you–'

'You've drugged me!' she said abruptly, staring at him.

'You've *drugged* me, Jay, haven't you?'

'You need some sleep.'

'No, I… you…' She swayed again. 'What did you give me?'

'Nothing that will do you any harm. Come on, I'll help you and then you can sleep inside the van.'

He supported her while she squatted down in the grass behind the van, and by the time she was climbing back inside, her eyes were barely open. She slumped down in her seat, and Jay pulled the seatbelt around her. He got in next to her and sat back with his eyes closed for a moment, rubbing his temples. He was exhausted himself, tired right down to his bones. Why did it have to be this hard?

By the time he'd driven to the bothy, broken in through a window, brought all the stuff inside, and set up the airbed to lay Felicity on – all by the light of a wind-up camping lantern – he was so weary he was shaking, his body weak from exertion and the stress of it all. He threw himself down onto the airbed beside Felicity and pulled the duvet over his body. He reached out for her in the darkness – it really was pitch black, too, with no streetlights outside the curtainless windows. His fingers brushed against her cheek, and her breathing was gentle and even. The sound of it relaxed him, and he snuggled closer to her, closing his eyes.

Felicity

33

I opened my eyes slowly. I was groggy and nauseous, and for some reason, my nose hurt like hell. Where on earth was I? How had I got here? The previous day was a blank hole in my memory.

I stared stupidly around at the bizarre space. It seemed to be some sort of building site, with bare pinky-brown plaster on the walls and electrical cables sticking out, but no sockets or fixtures. The air was cold. Early morning sunlight spilt in through a small window, and I sat up, rubbing my eyes. I was on an airbed in the middle of a dusty floor. Although it was just an airbed, it had proper bedding on it – a duvet and pillows, and by my side a camping lantern. I frowned. What was going on? Where was this place?

Then, the memories hit me with such awful force that I curled up into a ball as if I was wrapping my body around all the hurt and trying to squeeze it away. Leo was gone. Scott was gone. I was with Jay. I started to cry and it was a while before I could stop, then I wiped my eyes with the duvet cover and sat up again. I couldn't fall apart, I had to find Leo. And I had to keep believing that Scott was alive and would be found. After all, nobody had told me otherwise.

But you're here with Jay. Jay!

I put my hand up to my chest, where a pain had started. Already my body was growing tense, my mind starting to freeze up with terror. Where was he? What had he *done* to me? He'd drugged me, and I couldn't remember anything that had happened since. Had he spent the night in here with me? Had he raped me? I began to shake, and I swallowed hard. I pulled the duvet aside and looked down at myself. My cardigan was gone, but I was still dressed in the same green top and jeans I'd put on the night before. That brought me a small amount of reassurance.

I moved my feet tentatively over the side of the airbed, and stood up slowly, my legs weak. Wherever this place was, it certainly wasn't lived in. This couldn't be where Jay had been hiding all this time. I walked over to the window, and was so astonished by the view that I took a step backwards. We were somewhere very remote. I should have guessed that before I even looked – after all, Jay was hardly likely to take me somewhere vulnerable to prying eyes – but the big, dark blue expanse of water a hundred metres or so from the window, the swathe of trees, the isolation of it, took me aback. There wasn't going to be any phone signal here, that was clear, not that I had my phone any more. The small track outside the window looked barely used, and though it was the kind of place you might get the odd hiker or cyclist, to all intents and purposes I was completely alone here with Jay. My knees buckled, and I grabbed at the wall to stay standing.

Why had I done this? Why the fuck had I done this? *You're going to die here.* I gulped in air. The room felt like it was spinning. *I came here because of Leo. Because Leo is in danger.* I closed my eyes and took a few deep, calm breaths. As I turned away from the window, a note on top of a pile of clothes in the corner of the room caught my eye, so I went to take a closer look.

I bought this stuff for you Fliss so help yourself to what you need

Under the note were toiletries as well as clothes, a couple of books and magazines, a box of chocolates. I stared at the little collection in bewilderment. Did Jay think this was a holiday? That I would be in the mood for reading and eating chocolates?

'I thought I heard you moving about,' he said, his voice startling me. He was standing in the doorway, and my composure left me. I backed away from him, my skin prickling with fear. 'I was just making some breakfast,' he said.

'What is this place?' I asked.

'It's our home for a few days.' He pointed at a door across the hall. 'I've put a fresh towel in the bathroom for you. It's the pink one. There's no hot water, but the plumbing seems to work. The water's kind of brown, though. I brought bottled water for us to drink.'

I needed to use the bathroom so I followed his directions, grateful to be able to close the door behind me and not see his face any more.

...

I jumped when Jay knocked on the door.

'Fliss, you've been in there ages. Are you okay?'

I couldn't find my voice to answer. I hadn't wanted to come out of the bathroom and face him. Instead, once I'd used the toilet and washed my face, I sat down on the edge of the bath and stayed there, frozen, unable to stomach the idea of talking to him. How could I have been so stupid? Had I really believed he'd just give me Leo? The door handle turned. There was no lock, so before I knew it Jay was in the room with me.

'Flissie,' he said gently, 'what's wrong? You can talk to me.'

He sat down beside me, and put his hand over mine. I glanced round at him. It was so strange to see him with dark hair, and though he'd taken off the glasses that had previously formed part of his cover, the pale yellow t-shirt with a picture of a camper van on the front looked completely alien on him. I fixed my eyes on my lap.

'I've made you some breakfast,' he told me. 'Come and eat. You'll feel better.'

'I'm worried about Leo. I can't do anything until I know Leo is okay.'

'We'll talk about him later.'

'But, Jay–'

'Later.'

There was little point in arguing. Making him angry would get me nowhere. I followed him out of the bathroom, and took the opportunity to get a closer look at my surroundings. The building was small; it only had one bedroom, and the living room and kitchen was one large room. One of the windows on the far side was covered with a couple of sheets of cardboard. Had Jay needed to smash the window to get inside? How had he found this place? Who did it belong it to? The room was mostly bare, apart from a half-finished kitchen area with cupboards and a kitchen sink, but gaps where appliances should be. Jay had laid out boxes and tins of food on the work-surface. There was a bag of fruit and vegetables, and he'd set up a camping stove on the floor. He must have planned out carefully how we were going to live in this shell of a house.

'Can I have a glass of water?' I asked, eyeing the several large containers of mineral water lined up against the wall.

He poured some into a plastic cup and held it out to me. 'How's your nose?' he asked.

I was reluctant to answer. There was an edge to his voice, as if he was daring me to complain that he'd hurt me. 'It's... all right,' I lied. It was pretty painful, though feeling it tentatively with my fingers had reassured me. I didn't think it was broken. Jay grabbed a pack of painkillers from the kitchen and handed them to me without comment. 'I've thought of pretty much everything,' he continued. 'It's not going to be luxurious, but it's quite romantic, don't you think? Have you looked out of the window?'

I nodded. 'Where are we?'

'Never mind about that. I've made some porridge. Here.' He held out a bowl and I took it from him.

'I forgot to get any folding chairs, though,' he said. 'We'll have to sit on the floor.'

I did as he suggested and sat cross-legged a good distance away from him.

After taking the painkillers, I forced the bowl of porridge down, though I didn't feel hungry. I had to keep my strength up. I needed to do everything I could to stay strong. 'I want to know how Leo is,' I said to Jay as soon as I finished my breakfast.

'I told you we'd talk about him later.'

'No,' I said. 'Now.'

Jay ignored me as he polished off the last of his breakfast. Then he met my gaze squarely. 'We need to talk first,' he said. 'I want to explain about everything that happened.'

'Let me speak to Leo first, Jay, please,' I said. I was taking a risk by pushing him, but I was desperate. 'You said he's being looked after by somebody. You can phone them, and I can speak to him.'

Jay was silent.

'Jay!' I insisted.

'There's no phone signal here,' he said. 'Surely you realise that.'

I had realised, but I didn't want to budge. I wanted him to make it happen somehow. 'Then I'm not going to talk to you. I'm not going to say another word until I know Leo is safe.'

'Don't be childish. We're going to be here too long for you to not say a word to me.'

I was silent for a moment, and then I lost my temper. 'Let me tell you something,' I said. 'You think you're a dad to Leo? That we're a loving, happy family? If I hadn't got out of that house in Tatchley when I did, I would have *died* giving birth to Leo. You would have lost us both, because you were keeping us prisoner. That's what would have happened to your *family*.'

'I would have taken you to hospital.'

'No, you wouldn't!' I cried. 'Not in enough time! Maybe right at the last moment, but by then it would have been too late. I had all sorts of complications. Leo was early, I had to have an emergency Caesarean, and Leo was in hospital for a while afterwards.'

Jay shook his head. He looked genuinely upset. 'Fliss, I wouldn't have... I didn't mean...'

As abruptly as my anger had started, it left me. I gulped down the rest of my cup of water, my mouth suddenly dry, and stared down at my lap. What was I thinking, winding Jay up like this?

He couldn't handle his emotions; he might be upset and sorry now, but how long until that turned to anger?

Jay

34

'Let's go for a walk,' he said. 'I think we both need some fresh air.'

'Yes, okay,' Felicity said, her voice subdued. After breakfast, she'd got changed into the clothes he'd bought for her: grey jeans and a pink t-shirt. The clothes weren't a perfect fit, but they were good enough, and once she'd brushed her hair she looked a bit more like herself. But she was rubbing at her wrist again. 'Why do you do that?' he asked her.

'Do what?'

'Your wrist.'

She tried to hide her wrist in her lap, covering it with her other hand, so he grabbed her arm, and drew in his breath sharply as his eyes fell on the scratches and scars. 'What is this?' he asked her, recoiling. 'Are you cutting yourself?'

She snatched her arm back and shook her head. 'I do it in my sleep,' she said.

'What are you talking about?'

She clearly didn't want to give him a straight answer. Why wouldn't she just tell him, rather than turning it into a fucking riddle? 'Fliss, tell me why you have those scratches.'

'I don't think we should talk about it.'

'Well, I do. Tell me. What are they?'

'Jay, please drop it.'

He grabbed her hands and she stiffened, her eyes bulging with fear. He wanted to give her a shake. Why was she so afraid? He wasn't a monster. She should find it romantic, the lengths he was going to to get her back. How many women could say they had a man as committed to them as he was to Felicity?

'Tell me the truth!' he said.

She shook her head.

'Tell me!'

'All right!' she said. 'It… it's where the handcuff used to be. I have nightmares I'm still there. In Tatchley.'

Jay felt like he'd been punched in the stomach. 'I didn't mean to do that,' he said in a low voice. 'You made it so I had to do that to you. It was your fault, Felicity.'

She was trying to pull her hands away from his grip, and he let her go. 'It was your fault,' he said again. 'You know that, don't you? Tell me you understand it was your own fault.'

There was a long pause. 'Nothing you did could be worse than you taking my son from me. If you separate me from Leo, you're killing me.'

'Then tell me you understand it's all your own fault.'

This time, when she looked at him, her eyes were defiant. She said the phrase he'd asked her to; she said she was to blame, but the expression on her face made her words meaningless. She was taunting him. She was playing along to get Leo. Well, she wasn't playing nearly hard enough to convince him to give her what she wanted.

'Let's go for a walk,' he said.

...

Instead of making their way down the track and towards the water, which would be the obvious thing to do, he took a different route up behind the house, where there would be less chance of running into people. Even though it was summer the air was chilly, and Felicity crossed her arms over her chest. But before long the sun came out from behind the clouds and warmed them both, the air fresh and pleasant. Far preferable to the dusty atmosphere inside the half-finished building.

The path climbed towards some trees, and Jay sat down on a fallen tree trunk at the edge of the woods. He had been thinking about the argument they'd had about her wrist, and he hated the way it had ended up. Felicity obediently sat beside him.

'I want to make it up to you, you know,' he told her. 'I do know I was wrong. I shouldn't have said it was all your fault back in the house just then.'

She didn't reply.

'I'm so ashamed,' he continued. 'I wasn't in my right mind. You... you did upset me, but I know I shouldn't have acted how I did.'

She still didn't speak. He looked at her more closely. Her gaze was on the engagement ring around her finger. Anger pulsed through him, but he tried to push it aside, continue with his explanation. 'All the stuff with Mark. It made me crazy.'

He put his hand on her knee. 'It will all be okay,' he said. 'You can trust me. I'm not the person I used to be. That person makes me sick. I want to get better, and I know if you're with me I can get over it, all the... the anger.'

She was still looking at the ring. It was unbearable. 'Take that fucking thing off!' he said, undermining all the words he'd just said, and making her jump out of her skin.

'What thing?'

'That ring! That fucking ring – you were staring at it the whole time I spoke to you.'

She brought her hand up helplessly. 'I didn't mean to. I didn't realise I was–'

'Take it off and give it to me.'

She did as he asked, and he held the ring between his thumb and index finger, turning it as though he was admiring it. 'Pretty small, isn't it?' he said.

'What is?'

'The stone. The diamond. It's tiny.'

'We don't have much money. And I don't really care about stuff like that. It's not important.'

With a derisive laugh, Jay drew his arm back and threw the ring as far as he could into the trees.

Jay

35

Jay studied Felicity's face as they walked through the woods. She was hard to read. She'd been in turns angry, subdued, sad, and afraid. Most of all she'd been afraid. What was going on inside her head? Were his words getting through to her at all?

They were going uphill through the trees, and it was cool again in the shade. Jay wasn't keen to walk too far, though equally the idea of spending the whole time cooped up inside wasn't appealing. The fresh air would do them both good. Felicity was walking at a good pace, as though she was appreciating the chance to be outside and stretch her legs. *Or perhaps she's just trying to get it over with. She doesn't want to be with you. She's probably trying to take her mind off of worrying about Scott.* Jay almost stopped in his tracks as the man's name popped into his head. He'd been trying his hardest not to think about Scott, or at least, not to wonder how often the prick was in Felicity's thoughts, especially after she spent all that time staring at her bloody engagement ring. He was looking forward to telling her Scott was dead. But not yet. He was planning to, if a moment arose when it would be useful, but saying it right now would stop her from focusing on him, and he needed to get through to her.

Felicity had got ahead of him and he sped up to catch up with her, until they ended up in a clearing, where logs were stacked up in piles, and there was a rough track running through the trees. Jay stopped abruptly and looked around. He hadn't been expecting this. People had been working in this area. Felicity stopped too. 'I can't see anyone,' she said, 'if that's what you're worried about.'

She was watching him as if she was daring him to say how concerned he was about being caught. He was about to snap at her in irritation, but then the expression he thought he'd seen was gone. Now she was watching him warily. 'Don't look at me like that,' he told her.

She looked away.

'I'm not a psycho!' he said, his voice rising. 'It's like you think I'm going to flip out and attack you for no reason.'

She didn't reply, and he walked over to her. 'Fliss,' he said gently, 'Flissie. I don't want you to be afraid of me. Didn't we just talk about this? How I regret who I was? How I want to be better? I can't... I can't move on if you keep reminding me of who I used to be.'

'I'm not trying to remind you. I'm sorry, Jay. I'm just so worried about Leo. Is there really no way you can prove to me he's okay?'

He gripped both her arms. 'He's my son!' he said, giving her a shake. 'He's my flesh and blood, how can you possibly believe I would harm him?'

'Because you don't know what you're doing!' she shot back. 'You don't think! And you don't know what a three-year-old child needs!'

Jay let go of her. 'No. You're right. I don't know anything about children, because you stopped me from having the chance to learn.'

'Leo is just a little boy,' she said. 'If he's somewhere he doesn't know he'll get frightened. He needs routine, familiarity, people who know what he likes and what he needs.'

A sound from deep in the trees made them both jump. A vehicle. It was still a fair way away – they couldn't see it – but it must be coming along the track towards the clearing.

'We need to go back to the house,' Jay said.

Felicity nodded reluctantly. The clouds through the leaves above them had thickened, and turned a forbidding dark grey. Even if they hadn't heard the truck, it still looked like a good time to go.

...

They didn't quite manage to make it back before the rain began. A few fat drops to start with, but then the heavens opened, soaking them through to the skin. Back inside the bothy they made their way to the bedroom, where he quickly stripped off his wet clothes.

'Take yours off, too,' he said. 'I bought more than one outfit for you.'

She stood, shivering, water dripping from her hair and running down her face. He sighed in exasperation. 'I won't look, then, if that's what you're worried about.'

Turning his back, he finished getting changed, listening to her moving around the room behind him, collecting some clothes from the pile, and getting undressed. He did glance round at her: she was side-on to him, pulling her t-shirt over her head. Her chest was bigger than he remembered, due to having Leo, presumably. Was she going to take her bra off? He'd get her to sooner or later. Preferably sooner. He looked away. Just that short glimpse of her body had been enough to get him hard. If he didn't snap out of it he was going to end up doing something he'd regret. He had to go about things the right way. He had to remind her how great they'd been in bed together at the start of their relationship, not how messed up things had become.

When you used to rape her.

He breathed deeply in and out through his nose. He hadn't raped her! He'd never raped anybody. It had all been a mistake. A misunderstanding.

'What do you want to do now?'

Felicity's voice startled him, and he turned to her. She was dressed now, in leggings and a long blue shirt.

'I don't know,' he said. 'We'll talk, I guess. Make some lunch.'

She nodded. 'Perhaps we can go out again later, if the rain stops.'

'Yeah. Maybe.'

His gaze lingered on her. 'You're really beautiful, Flissie. I...' God, why couldn't he just tell her how much he wanted to fuck her? She wouldn't react well, though. It was too soon. 'I love you,' he said instead.

Felicity

36

I was steeling myself for him to try to touch me, to say he wanted to have sex, but he didn't, and I was almost giddy with relief. Instead, we made our way back to the living room, where I helped him chop vegetables to make soup on the camping stove. We sat on the floor to eat it, while the summer rainstorm continued outside, making the room even drearier. I could imagine that once decorated and furnished this little cottage might be a cosy place for a holiday, but as it was, and under these circumstances, it was dismal. I finished eating and put my bowl down on the floor, while Jay continued to eat slowly, apparently lost in thought.

'The rain isn't getting any better,' I said.

He glanced round at me as though surprised to hear my voice. He shook his head, and quickly polished off the rest of his soup.

'What were you thinking about?' I asked. Although I didn't particularly care, I'd come to the conclusion that my best hope was to try to play along, and hopefully discover Leo's whereabouts. I could try again to force him to tell me, but since Leo was with somebody, Jay would always have the option of contacting them and telling them to move Leo, so I'd never be able to get to him in time. I cursed my stupidity. Why had I let myself be tricked like this?

'Move closer to me,' he said.

My breath caught in my throat, but I did as he asked, shuffling closer to him on the cold stone floor. He put his arm around me, encouraging me closer, until I ended up resting my head awkwardly against his shoulder, and he kissed my hair. 'Sammie used to rest her head on me like this,' he told me.

I didn't answer.

'She used to say how comfortable she felt with me, how safe. We'd stay like this for ages sometimes, just... enjoying being close to each other. I remember the weight of her head, the feel of her hair. But after a while we didn't do it so much. She didn't really want to be close to me any more.'

His words sent chills down my spine. Why on earth was he talking to me about Sammie? How did he think I would react to conversations about his dead ex-girlfriend? 'I... I'm sorry,' I said.

'It's not your fault. It's mine. She didn't want to be near me because she stopped feeling safe with me. I understand that now.'

'She was very young,' I said. In fact, my heart ached for Sammie, who probably hadn't known who to turn to when she'd found herself trapped in such an intense and dangerous relationship. She'd only been a child, really. But he'd been a child too, and yet already filled with so much hate and rage.

'I don't know why it had to end up like it did,' he said. 'I ruined everything. And not just because of Mark, the way he made me think she was cheating. The seeds of doubt were already there. Before he ever told me any of his lies, I still watched her all the time. I never trusted her.'

I let my eyes drift over to the window. The rain was petering out, weak sunlight filtering through the clouds. I couldn't stand having Jay's arm around me. My chest was tightening as my mind raced to all the different, and awful, places this conversation could end up. But he didn't say anything else. He just continued to hold me close to him, until eventually he grew tired of it, and got up to clear away our bowls from lunch and tidy the makeshift kitchen.

...

Somehow the afternoon passed. We ventured out again briefly, but Jay was clearly jumpy about being spotted so we went back inside and he boiled some water to make us cups of tea. Finally, teatime rolled around, and I helped him get the food ready – not too difficult since all he'd brought for our meal was various cheeses, which he took one by one from a cool box, and a pack of crackers.

'I know it's not the fanciest meal,' he said, 'but I thought you'd like it. I wanted something nice for our first proper evening together.'

He placed a bottle of red wine down and I eyed it uncomfortably. I'd have to drink at least some – I couldn't risk Jay realising I was pregnant. Once he'd laid out the food, we sat side by side on the living room floor again. Jay made a toast about our future together so I took a few sips of wine, and I nibbled at the food. Jay kept watching me, and my stomach began to churn. The wine, the fancy cheeses, his talk of our "first proper evening together". It was clear what was going to come next. My hands began to shake while Jay chatted away. I couldn't bear to listen to him. Then he pulled a piece of paper from his pocket and handed it to me. I read it and looked up at him. 'Why are you showing me this?'

'It's how I got by.'

'Man with a van,' I read from the paper. It said he did house removals and clearances. There was a mobile number, and the name Jason Marriot.

'I lived with a girl called Stephanie,' he explained. 'She was a bit younger than me, and she was lonely. She'd just inherited a house from her granddad, and I lived there with her.'

I began to understand. 'So you didn't have your name on anything.'

'She bought me the van, and all the paperwork for everything is in her name. People paid me in cash. I had no bank account–'

'I get the idea.'

'You could do the same. That's how we can be together. Soon – tomorrow, or in a couple of days, maybe, you could tell everyone you've decided to move away, you could buy or rent a little house somewhere, get a new van and I could start up this business again. I didn't earn a lot, but it would be enough to help us get by. Nobody questioned it when I was living with Steph. To the neighbours I was just Steph's boyfriend. They never got suspicious of me.'

The words on the paper swam in front of my eyes. Was he serious? He thought I could just tell everybody I'd decided to move away and that would be that?

'People *would* be suspicious if I said I wanted to move all of a sudden,' I said. 'Especially after Leo going missing. The police would–'

'You'd find a way.'

I swallowed hard, and handed the paper back to him. 'Does Stephanie know what you've done?'

'Not exactly,' he said. He looked pained. *Something's happened to her.* I didn't ask him where she was now. I didn't want to hear the answer.

Stephanie

Several hours earlier

37

Light was shining on her face, disturbing her sleep. She groaned and opened her eyes slowly. She was on the sofa in the living room, and sunlight was coming in through a gap in the old brown curtains, right across her face. What time was it? Early. It must be. The living room got the light in the morning. She felt groggy, and sick, and her head hurt. A lot. Was she hungover? She'd only been hungover a couple of times in her whole life, and she couldn't remember going out the day before. What *had* she been doing the day before? Why wasn't she in bed?

Stephanie swung her legs over the side of the sofa and placed her feet on the carpet, but when she tried to stand it didn't work. Her headache intensified as she fell and slumped down against the cushions again. If the pain in her head wasn't so bad she could almost have laughed at herself; falling about just trying to get off the sofa – how ridiculous. But then, suddenly, she was gripped by fear.

'Granddad?' she called out. 'I'm not feeling well.' The light was on her face again. It was too bright. Way too bright. She managed to sit up. God, she was thirsty. There was a glass of water on the coffee table, and she stretched out her hand towards it. Just that simple action seemed to take forever. It was like she was underwater – all her limbs felt strange, like they weren't really hers. But if she was hungover, she needed to drink some water, and sooner rather than later. She downed the whole glass, and sprawled back against the sofa cushions, exhausted by the effort.

There was a place where her scalp felt odd, like she had something stuck in her hair. She investigated the place gently with her fingers. Her hair was matted and disgusting. Lowering her hand, she stared at the reddish-brown stains on her fingertips. Blood? What on earth?

'Granddad?' she called again. He didn't answer her. Had he gone out to buy a newspaper? It was morning, so that was likely. She should probably go to the bathroom and try to look at her head in the mirror. Placing her feet on the floor again, she took one shaky step. A sudden wave of pain made her cry out, and her legs crumpled.

...

Stephanie woke and looked around slowly, confused by what she saw. The ceiling wasn't right. It was too far away for one thing, and the lampshade wasn't the one that hung above her bed. She blinked. She wasn't on her bed. This wasn't her bedroom, and she wasn't lying on a mattress, she was lying on the carpet. In the living room. She tried to roll over and her arm smacked into the coffee table. What the hell? Why was she in such a weird place? It made no sense. Had she been sleeping on the floor during the day, squashed up next to the coffee table?

She tried to sit up and winced at a blinding pain in her head. 'Granddad?' she called out. 'Granddad, can you hear me?'

No reply.

Shit, she thought, *should I be at work?*

Turning her head, her eyes fell on her phone which was beside her on the carpet. She clumsily reached out her hand for it, but before she grabbed hold of it a wave of pain and nausea made her pause. Forget about work, she needed to have a drink and take some painkillers. There was a glass on the coffee table, but her heart sank as she realised it was empty. She'd have to go to the kitchen.

Getting to her feet seemed to take forever. She staggered down the hall, clutching at the walls. Once she finally reached the kitchen she took some painkillers and drank a glass of water, then she ate a banana, hoping the food would make her feel better. She glanced uneasily around the kitchen as she ate. Where had that big tub of protein powder come from? Where were Granddad's pills, and the tin of biscuits that was usually next to the microwave? Why were there so many vegetables in the fridge? There was a bag of kale, of all things. She wasn't sure she'd ever eaten kale in her life, and it certainly wasn't Granddad's. So why was it there? Something was wrong. Really wrong. Was this not actually her house?

Her scalp itched, so she scratched at it roughly. It hurt. A lot. Lowering her fingers, she cried out at the sight of the blood on them.

Get help. You need to get help. Making her way unsteadily back to the living room, she tried to remember something, anything, to explain her condition. But her mind was blank. She picked up her phone from the carpet, but she couldn't unlock it: she didn't know the pass code.

Emergency call. She needed to press that. This *was* an emergency, after all. But she couldn't do it. Her body just wouldn't respond. Instead she collapsed back down onto the carpet, the phone falling uselessly from her fingers to rest beside her motionless body.

Felicity

38

When Jay got up to go to the bathroom, I was so relieved to have a moment alone that I took great gulps of air and a couple of tears spilt from my eyes. Being with him was so claustrophobic. I had to constantly be on guard, second-guessing how he would react to every word that came out of my mouth. The effort was making me shake, and my legs were like jelly as I quickly took my wineglass over to the kitchen sink and poured most of it away – keeping a little so that he wouldn't be too eager to immediately refill my glass.

When he came back, he was carrying a posh gift box.

'What's this?' I asked him.

'Take a look.'

I put my plate down – I couldn't face eating any more – and took the lid off the box. Inside, nestled amongst tissue paper, was some black, lacy lingerie. I froze in shock. I couldn't form any words. Did he want me to put it on? I was paralysed with fear as memories of the nights I'd spent in the Tatchley house flooded back in, and I involuntarily shoved the box away in a convulsion of horror.

'Don't you like it?'

His words snapped me out of my memories. I couldn't let him see me freaking out. I held up the bra and matching knickers as if I was admiring them, but then I spotted the label on the bra. 'It's not the right size,' I said, trying to hide the relief in my voice.

'It looks okay,' he said.

'My body has changed size and shape a bit since I had Leo. If I put this on I'm not sure it would… it may not look that great.'

'Forget the bra, then. I'll get you a new one once we're away from this place.'

I gave him a fragile smile, which couldn't have been too convincing, and then I looked back down at the lingerie, until he lifted my chin gently.

'We don't have to rush,' he said. 'We've got all night. I know you're nervous. I'm a bit nervous too, but I think it will help us to get to know each other again. It'll remind us how it used to be at the start. We used to be so good together, when it was just simple.'

'Jay... perhaps we should leave it...' I stammered. 'I'm not ready...'

'It's just nerves.'

He stroked my cheek softly with his thumb, and then he moved closer to me, tilting his head to kiss me. 'Don't be afraid,' he said. 'It's not going to be like it was when things were bad. Like it was in Tatchley. We'll take it really slowly.'

He kissed me gently, and I didn't respond. Every cell in my body was screaming. This couldn't be happening. If I opened my eyes I'd realise it had all been a nightmare. But my eyes were already open. It was real. He was expecting me to sleep with him. I'd known it was coming, but now the moment was here, my body shut down. I couldn't kiss him back. I just couldn't. *It's for Leo. Do it for Leo.* But my body simply wouldn't respond, and Jay moved away.

'Once our relationship is healed, we can be a family again,' he whispered. My blood ran cold. He might have said it in pretty-sounding words, but his meaning was clear. He was testing me. If I wanted to see my son, I would have to have sex with him, and I'd have to try to make him believe it was real, that my feelings for him were coming back.

Felicity

39

We perched on the end of the airbed. I let him kiss me again, and this time I dug deep into some hidden reserve of strength inside me, and I kissed him back. I had one single thought in my mind. Leo.

'I've waited so long for this,' he said. 'Too long. Way too long.'

He started to unbutton my shirt, his fingers brushing my bare skin, sending a chill down my spine. Once my shirt was open he slipped it off my shoulders and ran his fingers just above the lace at the top of my bra, following the curve of my breasts, apparently with great interest.

'They are bigger,' he said.

I nodded.

'I like it.'

'I'm glad,' I said, my voice quivering. He watched my face, his head cocked a little to one side. I had an unnerving sense that he was carefully planning his course of action, as if he'd been presented with an exciting plate of food and was deciding where to begin. Finally, he reached behind my back and undid my bra, slipping it from my body, and then he took off his own t-shirt. My skin was like ice when he touched me again, cupping one of my breasts in his hand and stroking my nipple with his thumb.

Tentatively, I placed my hand on his chest, and he looked down at it. 'You never used to be so cold like this,' he said. 'We used to have so much fun together, Flissie. Don't you remember?'

I did remember. But I couldn't reconcile those memories with the man that was in front of me now. How could he imagine it was possible for me to have fun with him now? Any kind of fun, let alone sex.

'What was your favourite time with me?' he asked.

'What do you mean?'

149

'In bed. There must be times that have stayed with you. Times it was particularly good.'

'I don't... I don't know.'

He shook his head. 'That's what's so sad.'

'What are yours then?' I asked, playing along. 'What times do you remember most?'

He leant close to me, whispering some of his memories in my ear, focusing in particular on some of our more daring exploits. It made me wince, but when he moved away from my ear I tried to smile. I *had* enjoyed those things, at the time. Now the reminiscing made me ill.

'I don't see why it couldn't be like that again,' he told me. 'We just have to take it one step at a time.'

He moved his hand from my chest down to my stomach, until his fingertips began to slip under the waistband of my leggings.

'Jay–' I began, my nerves getting the better of me, but he had clearly guessed I would try to protest. Despite what he'd said about taking things slowly, he shoved me down onto the bed and started pulling my leggings down roughly, my underwear along with it.

I froze, and then I found my voice. 'This isn't... this isn't slow...' I said stupidly, trying to twist my body away from him. He kept me pinned down with one arm, quickly undoing his jeans with his other hand.

'I can't go slow any more,' he told me. 'Not after waiting so long. I'm going crazy.'

A tearing sensation filled my mind. I couldn't do it. I couldn't do it! It was as if I was back in the room where he'd held me prisoner, listening to that same sound of a buckle, a zip, knowing what was going to come next, and in that instant I forgot all about trying to get Leo back. I forgot that I was out here alone, at his mercy, and instead I was consumed with more rage than I had ever felt before. It was a wild, animal feeling, where I turned into a thing made of teeth and claws and fury. I cried out and pushed him hard. I tore at his face with my nails, reopening the cut along his cheek that I'd made the day before while I was in his van, and the ferocity of my unexpected attack made him back away from me. For a split second he didn't appear to understand what was happening, but then he tried to pin me down so I went for him again, scraping at his arms with my nails, a strangled screeching noise escaping from me. I took another slash at his face, and this time it was too much for him.

In his hurry to escape he scrambled away from the bed, but it took him only a few seconds to recover. He made a grab for me as I pulled my leggings back up and snatched my shirt from the floor. Darting away towards the bedroom door, I willed myself to run faster, but he was too quick for me. He caught me and shoved me against the wall, and panic filled my body. What the hell had I done? I'd made things a million times worse! He cupped my chin in his hand, squeezing my face and pressing my head back hard. A drop of blood spilt from the scratch across his cheek.

'Why?' he shouted in my face. 'Why are you determined to ruin everything? Why won't you even *try*?'

I didn't answer and he used his hand gripping my chin to pull my face forward and slam it back into the wall. 'I am your *boyfriend*. I am Leo's real dad! I'm desperate for the chance to support you! I'd do anything for you! And you throw it all back in my face.'

'Jay, I'm sorry,' I said in desperation. 'I just got nervous. I didn't mean to…'

'All I'm trying to do is love you!'

'It happened too fast! I got scared, Jay–'

'It's just sex, Felicity,' he spat at me. 'It's what couples do. Do you make this much fuss with Scott? No, I bet you don't. I bet you don't give a second's thought to opening your legs for him. Is he better than me, is that it?'

'No,' I said desperately, 'Jay, please–'

'But you're still happy enough to let him fuck you, though. You must be, or you wouldn't have got pregnant.' He smiled nastily. 'When I heard you'd lost his baby I was so relieved. So

151

happy. But I don't know if I can ever forgive you for letting him get you in that state in the first place. And agreeing to marry him.'

My head was spinning. What had he just said? Surely I had misheard. How hard had he slammed my head back?

'How do you–' I caught myself. He couldn't possibly know I was pregnant again, could he?

'How do I what?' His smugness was unbearable as he taunted me. 'How do I know you had a miscarriage?'

I drew a silent breath of relief, trying not to let him see. *Thank God he doesn't know.* If he realised I was pregnant right now, who knows what he would do.

'I know everything about you, Fliss,' he said, pushing me harder against the wall. 'You can't hide anything from me. I'm the one who knows you inside out.' He leaned in close to me, his mouth at my ear. 'I know all your secrets.'

I barely heard him. My relief at him not knowing I was currently pregnant was now eclipsed as I frantically tried to work out how he knew about the miscarriage. For one terrible moment, I wondered if he really could see inside my mind, as he apparently believed he could do. But, no. That was impossible. There had to be some explanation – but my miscarriage wasn't public knowledge, only a handful of people knew. *One of them being him.* My blood turned to ice. Had somebody *told* him? Somebody close to me? I could count the people who knew about it on my fingers. Scott. Martin. Scott's parents. Natasha and Zack. Leanne. Vicky. *Vicky!* Surely she hadn't… How would she ever have met Jay? It was impossible. But she was the only person who had any reason to hurt me.

Felicity

40

I stared at Jay. 'Who told you–' I began.

'Forget about that,' he said. 'I'm more worried about what happened in bed just then. You were supposed to *try* at least. Don't you care about Leo? Don't you care that he would want his mum and dad to be together?'

'Yes!' I said. Right now, I'd say anything. I just wanted him to let go of me. I just wanted to be safe.

'You don't understand, do you? You don't care about family. Sometimes I think I'm the only person in the world who *does* care about family.'

'I do understand. I do care–'

'No, you don't!' he yelled at me, consumed with anger again. He gripped me harder. 'I am Leo's dad!' he said into my face. 'Don't pretend I'm not.'

My body turned to jelly. It was like I was back in the past again, my every moment, my safety, my *life*, dictated by his mood, and I trembled. 'Don't hurt me,' I told him. 'Please don't hurt me. I'm sorry.'

'Stop snivelling. Stop trying to get me to feel sorry for you. I'm the one who's been wronged here. Have you got any idea what it's been like for me these past couple of years, trying to find you? It's been hell, Felicity! *Hell!*'

'I just want Leo,' I said, my voice cracking. *Don't cry. Don't cry in front of him!*

'It's more than that, though, isn't it. You want *Scott* to be Leo's dad, right? You want Scott to be the man taking you to bed at night. You want to pretend none of this with me ever happened.'

I couldn't speak. My eyes filled with tears. 'Let go of me, Jay. Please.'

He did as I asked and relief flooded through me now that his hands were no longer on me. 'We can try again another time,' he said, his mood different all of a sudden, lighter. 'I suppose there's no rush. There's nothing else for you now, after all. Scott's dead.'

I stared at him. Scott was dead? No. He was making it up to manipulate me. I couldn't believe it. I refused to believe it.

'I'm sorry,' he said, though his face wasn't sorry at all. He looked extremely pleased with himself. 'I didn't want you to find out like this. But... you know, one day you might realise it's all for the best.'

A strange, floating sensation filled my body. This wasn't real. This couldn't be real. 'No,' I said. 'No, you're lying.'

'There was a message from Natasha on your phone. It said they found Scott's body. He'd fallen. They reckon he would have died instantly.'

'I don't... I don't believe you.' The words caught in my throat and I had to force them out, my voice high and scratchy.

'She was starting to get worried about you. She wanted you to go back to her house. She was concerned I might have contacted you.'

I met his gaze. Was he telling the truth? His grey-blue eyes were inscrutable. He could have just made up all that stuff about Natasha, but somehow it didn't sound like it. My stomach clenched. He really had heard a message from her. He'd taken my phone, and there was no question that Natasha would have left me messages. Did that mean Scott was really – my knees buckled. Suddenly, I was on the floor. Jay knelt down beside me. 'He wouldn't have suffered. Take some comfort in that, at least...'

'You're pleased!' I shouted at him. 'You're pleased!'

He started putting his arm around me, and I pushed him away as hard as I could. 'I hate you!' I screamed. 'I hate you, I fucking hate you! I wish *you* were dead! Why can't you be dead? You *deserve* to die, not Scott, not Scott...' A fit of hysterical crying stole my words away. Jay sat on the floor beside me, watching me. 'If he loved you so much,' he said at length, 'why'd he go off and do something as dangerous as climbing mountains, anyway? *I* would never go off and leave you. I care about you too much.'

. . .

It was a long while before I came to my senses again. I was in bed. I couldn't remember how I'd got there, though I knew I'd been awake the whole time I'd been lying here. My face was wet with tears, my body hurt, and I stared up at the ceiling. *Dead. Scott is dead.* A convulsion of pain ripped through me and I curled up in a ball. It was as though I was hollow inside and being crushed from the outside. *I can't bear it. I can't bear it!* I sat up straight in bed, scratching at my wrist as my rage grew, until abruptly I let out a cry of pain and threw the bedding and pillows across the room, screaming blindly until Jay ran in and put his arms around me to restrain me. 'No!' I yelled at him. 'No! No! Leave me alone! Leave me alone!'

He let go of me. 'I'm making some tea,' he said. 'You need to calm down.'

I hit out at him wildly and he moved out of my reach.

'Take it out on me if you want,' he said. 'But Scott is dead. Nothing you do is going to change that.'

I threw myself back down on the bed and buried my face in the sheet – the only piece of bedding I hadn't torn off and hurled away from me. When Jay turned up with a mug of tea, I took it from him and threw it at the wall, and then I curled into a ball again and was still.

Felicity

41

'Fliss? Felicity?'

I sat bolt upright. Scott! I could hear him, he was outside. I leapt out of bed, following the sound of his voice, my heart racing. He was alive! He'd been okay this whole time, looking for me, and now he'd found me! Sun was streaming through the windows and I made my way to the front door, where he was still saying my name. The door was unlocked and I threw it open without a moment's hesitation. There he was, right there in front of me, holding Leo's hand. They both beamed at me.

'It's time to go home,' Scott said.

I threw myself out of the door and into his arms, revelling in his warm and comforting embrace. Reaching out an arm to draw Leo in close to me as well, I said to Scott, 'I thought you were dead.'

'Dead? How could I be dead when I have you and Leo and Dennis?'

He started to laugh, and I laughed too, because he was right. Of course it was ridiculous. He couldn't be dead, it would be too awful. And I'd had enough of awful for one lifetime.

He pulled me in closer to him, and he started to kiss me. I kissed him back, but then things went wrong. Why was there still a voice saying my name? Other thoughts crowded in. *Jay knew about the miscarriage. Vicky must have told him. Vicky would do anything to get Scott to herself. Scott's dead. He would have died instantly. Instantly. Instantly.* My eyes snapped open. The room was pitch black, not full of bright sunshine as it had been in my dream. My present situation came back to me in a series of painful blows, and I let out a long groan and curled up on my side.

'Are you okay?' Jay asked. 'I was trying to wake you. You were talking. You seemed agitated.'

I closed my eyes tight, tears squeezing out from behind my eyelids. I should have known it was a dream. Or at least, it was a vivid daydream, maybe even some sort of hallucination, as my mind was far too broken to enter a state of genuine, restful sleep. I moaned loudly and Jay rubbed my back. 'I'm still grieving for Sammie,' he said. 'I've never stopped.'

I didn't reply. I couldn't find any words.

'The pain never goes away, but you have to carry on living. You're lucky, Fliss, because you have me. You're not alone.'

I ignored him. All I could think about was Scott. The way he laughed, the way he'd looked when he asked me to marry him, the way he held me when my nightmares woke me, his smile; that big, daft, infectious grin he had, especially when he was playing with Leo or Dennis. *Leo!* A fresh wave of pain washed through me. How would I ever explain to Leo what had happened? *If you ever get him back.*

My breath caught in my throat. I wanted to hold my little sandy-haired boy in my arms. I missed him desperately, as though a part of my body was missing. I wanted to cuddle him close, but I didn't even know where he was. Fresh tears spilt out. I couldn't live without Leo and Scott. I just couldn't.

. . .

Jay continued to try to comfort me as the night wore on, his embraces and dreadful attempts at sympathy increasingly unbearable. Finally, with the first light of dawn beginning to spill in through the window, I reached my limits of endurance and I pushed him away, and he snapped at me. 'Fliss, you're going to have to figure out a way through this. You are here, with me. Stop behaving like a spoilt brat, and start appreciating what I'm trying to do for you.'

I sat up. 'What you've *done* for me,' I said slowly, anger bubbling dangerously away inside me. 'What you've *done?* I'll tell you what you've done for me. You held my face over a gas burner. You let me think you were going to burn my face if I didn't apologise to you for going on a night out with my friends! You strangled me and raped me at my friends' wedding because I was taking contraceptive pills when you didn't want me to! You've beaten me, you've yelled at me, you took me prisoner. What part of that am I supposed to appreciate? Do you know what it is you've given me, really?'

He watched me silently, his eyes uncaring.

'You've given me nightmares. Panic attacks. Flashbacks. Anxiety so bad that some days I can barely face going out into the world at all. Even after I got away from you, I had to give birth to your son, *your* son, and look at his face and see you staring back at me! I didn't even want him to begin with. I didn't love him. I was so depressed I wanted to walk out of the hospital and leave him there. Is that what I should appreciate? How you made me feel about my son when he was first born? How you make me feel about *myself*? How you turned my life into one huge fucking nightmare? Well, thank you, Jay. Thank you. And I can honestly say, nobody else could have done for me the things you have done. Because nobody else in the *world* is as fucked up in the head as you are!' I screamed the last few words at him, and once they were out of my mouth I burst into tears of grief and rage. 'Get away from me!' I yelled at him. 'Go away!'

Instead of going away, he pulled me roughly back down onto the bed beside him, his hands quickly finding my throat. His face filled my vision, as his hands began to grip harder around my neck. 'Don't *ever* talk to me like that again,' he said. 'Do you hear me?'

I nodded, terrified as he squeezed tighter and tighter, until my breath caught, but then he released his grip. My emotions overtook me, and I sobbed so hard my body shook.

But then something changed, some survival instinct kicked in, and I stopped crying. I took some deep breaths, and put my hand on my stomach, on Scott's baby. What was I doing? I couldn't just curl up on this bed crying. I had to survive! I'd done my screaming, my rage, and my sorrow. There would be more to come, later, but now I didn't have time for it. Right now, I had to keep Scott's baby safe, and I had to find Leo. When I had Leo back, and Scott's son or daughter in my arms, I'd have Scott too, because he'd live on in my children. If he was here, if he could talk to me, that's what he'd want. He'd want for me to survive. Whatever it took.

So a few minutes later, when Jay got out of the bed, and wandered off down the corridor with the camping lantern, I decided I would follow him. Whatever way I looked at it, playing things right with him had to be my best chance of getting through this. The door to the living room was half open, and I crept towards it, peeking into the room to see what Jay was up to.

I don't know what I expected, but it certainly wasn't what I saw. Jay was sitting with his face buried in his knees, and although he made little sound, his back was shuddering. He was crying. I frowned. What should I do? Perhaps it would be better to leave him alone, but on the other hand, maybe if I comforted him I could start to reason with him. I took a couple of steps into the room and he looked around briefly, swiping his hand roughly across his face to get rid of his tears, but then he gave up and put his face into his knees again. Crouching down beside him, I gently placed my hand on his back. 'Talk to me, Jay,' I said softly. 'It doesn't have to be this way. Let's work out a way through this, together.'

Jay

42

Startled from his miserable stupor, Jay slowly raised his head. Did Felicity mean together like *properly* together? Or did she just mean that they had to decide what they were going to do next? She sat down beside him. 'I can see how much you're hurting,' she said. 'But no matter how it might feel, I'm not *trying* to hurt you.'

'You slashed my face open and screamed at me that you hate me and wish I was dead. Besides, all you care about is Scott. You've made that perfectly clear. Why are you out of bed, anyway? Shouldn't you still be in there wailing and tearing your hair out, if you *love* him so much?'

She didn't reply straight away. But then her words surprised him. 'It's like you said. Scott's dead. I can't change that. All I can change is what's happening right now.'

'And what is happening right now?'

'Well, that's up to us, isn't it?'

He buried his face in his knees again. 'I know you don't love me.'

She stroked his back gently. 'Jay, you must understand that I can't forget what has happened in the past. I know you're offended that I'm frightened of you, but you know why, surely?'

He raised his head a little. 'I've told you I'm sorry. How many times can I say it?'

'I know that you're sorry. I know, Jay. I do.' She put her hand on his knee, and he stared at her fingers. She'd made him fail. He wanted to show her he was different now, and then he'd ended up hurting her almost as soon as he'd been reunited with her. But it was her own fault! She pushed him beyond the limits of endurance, beyond anybody's endurance. 'Don't pretend you care,' he said flatly. 'You don't care about me. You don't care what I've done to find you again, or the plans I've made for our future. All you care about is a man who obviously didn't even treat you as a priority. You and Leo are *all* I care about.'

She sat down beside him and spoke softly. 'And perhaps that's the problem. Jay, you can't only live for other people. You have to live for yourself as well. You say you don't understand why Scott went rock climbing, and really, the fact you don't understand is the whole problem. Scott did it because it's important to *him*. Because he loved doing it.'

'Then he never loved you like I love you.'

'You're right. He has *other* things to live for too—'

'He's not alive,' he snapped. 'He's dead.'

'Yes, I know. But when he *was* alive, his life was full of lots of different things, not just me. And that's okay. It's healthy. Listen to me, Jay, if me and you got back together, it would never work. If Leo and I are the only reason you have to live, then we'll never meet your expectations. You'll squeeze the life out of us. We'll hurt you when we're not even meaning to, because we care about other things too, and you'll always be jealous of that.'

'Scott only wanted to be with you so you could help him look after that kid he already has.'

'You don't know him. You don't know what was going on in his mind.'

Jay tore her hand away from his leg. 'You're *still* defending him? How many times do I have to say it? He's fucking dead, Fliss! I'm the one who's here, and all you do is rip my heart out.'

She was silent for a long time. Jay stared across the room at the wall, a cold, dreary colour in the white light from the lantern. Outside the dawn was grey, the sun struggling to make it through the thick cloud.

'I…' she started. 'I'm not trying to rip your heart out. Is that really how it feels?'

'Yes.'

'And you think I do it deliberately?'

Why was she asking such stupid questions? Of course she did

it deliberately. She'd probably loved coming in here and seeing him in tears – seeing how weak and pathetic she made him.

'I'm asking you to help me,' he said. 'Give me a second chance. I know there's something wrong with me, but you can help me get better. What reason do I have to even try if I don't have you and Leo?'

'Don't you want to feel less hurt and… angry… for your own sake?'

'I already told you I don't care about myself.'

Christ. Why was she drawing it out like this, needling him with her little remarks and suggestions when he already felt bad enough? Why couldn't she just say she'd give him a chance?

'Jay, I… you must realise that me and you are not going to have a relationship again. I don't love you any more. And I'm never going to be able to love you again.'

He looked round at her face. Her eyes were wide, willing him to understand and agree. God, he wanted to wipe that look off her face. His fingers itched to hit her. It would make him feel euphoric to teach her a lesson, make her hurt too, as much as he hurt. But it would only make him feel better briefly. Then he'd just end up feeling even worse.

'Jay?' she pressed him. 'I'm not saying this to be cruel. But this whole thing is spiralling out of control. You're getting in more and more trouble. Sooner or later, you're going to get caught. You must see that. Even if I wanted to, Leo and I couldn't have a life with you because we would always be looking over our shoulders. I want you to be rational about this—'

He couldn't listen to any more of it. The self-control he'd had a moment before evaporated and he lunged towards her, pushing her down onto the floor. A buzzing, roaring sound filled his head. He ripped at her clothes, trying to tear them from her body. He'd remind her who she belonged to. She was trying to push him away, she was saying things – pleading with him. He covered her body with his, pinning her to the floor. He'd never wanted to fuck anyone as badly as he wanted to fuck her now. He managed to keep her held down as he undid his jeans, but she just wouldn't shut up. She kept saying things. Stupid, stupid things that he tried not to care about, but then some of the words got through. 'You said you wanted to change!' she said. 'You said you wanted to be better. You can make a different choice—'

He slapped her and the words paused, but then they started again. 'Think of Leo!' she said. 'What would he say, if he was old enough to understand what you're trying to do?'

He stared at her. God, he fucking hated her. She was a selfish, manipulative little bitch. Trying to use Leo to control him. She made him sick! For a second his desire to hurt her grew even stronger and he lifted her from the floor by her shoulders and slammed her back down, her head thudding on the hard floor. 'Shut up!' he yelled at her. 'Just shut up! Shut up! Shut up!'

Eventually, he realised that she had done as he asked. She wasn't talking now. Her eyes were open but they were unfocused. She was dazed from the knock to her head. Abruptly, all the fight went out of him. He wasn't aroused or angry any more; instead he was left cold, and strangely frightened. What the fuck was he doing? He'd failed. He'd lost. There was nothing left now; it was hopeless. He moved away from her, and she sat up unsteadily, pulling her torn clothes around her body. Her eyes glittered with fear as she stole glances at him. Becoming fed up with it, he shoved her so that she fell back onto the floor again. 'I didn't say you could sit up,' he told her. She stayed down, but it was a small victory.

. . .

He watched her for several minutes. She stayed curled in a ball on her side, scratching mindlessly at the stone floor with her nails. Grief and fear were beginning to make her lose her grip. But when she spoke, her voice was steady. 'Let me go, Jay.'

'No.'

She sat up slowly, and this time he didn't shove her back down. 'Would you rather I died here than let me go to my son?'

she asked him.

'Our son,' he corrected her automatically. Then he processed her words. Was it true? *Would* he rather she died here in this house than went off to get Leo, leaving him behind?

'You're being silly,' he told her, without answering his silent question to himself. 'Look, I'll help you to bed. Let's have a rest, at least until it's a bit lighter. Things will seem better when it's daytime.'

'Jay, I need to be with Leo,' she said. 'If you give him back to me, I'll make sure you don't get in trouble for taking him. I'll say whatever I can—'

He glared at her. She was trying to manipulate him and he wasn't going to let her. 'And will you stop me from being wanted for Mark's murder as well?' he spat, 'and Sammie's? And take back all the fucking nonsense you've come out with about being "falsely imprisoned" in that house in Tatchley?'

She shook her head. 'I can't. Even if I wanted to, the police have evidence. If I tried to change my statement, I don't know how much it would help.'

'Well then, what difference does it make?'

'The difference is that I can tell them you gave Leo back to me willingly. I can say you didn't hurt me while we were here, that you're sorry for everything that has happened. That will count for something. Jay, you're not going to be able to just walk away from this. You're going to be caught, sooner or later. This is about damage limitation now. Let me help you. Tell me where Leo is, and I will do everything I can to show you in a positive light. I promise.'

His skin prickled with fear. *Prison.* It couldn't come to that. He couldn't let it come to that.

'Fliss, we can be together. We *can*. All you have to do is try. I only want to be your partner and Leo's father. It's not that much to ask. That's all I wanted before. I just went about it all wrong. But I can be there for you now. I've grown up, I've got my head straight. I can look after you.'

'You can't, Jay,' she whispered. 'You just can't.'

Felicity

43

I knew better than to push him too far. Jay was in the most volatile of moods. But no matter what I said, I couldn't win – declaring that I cared about him or loved him would make him accuse me of lying and manipulating him, while arguing with him would inflame the situation. My earlier resolve to get through this and survive was beginning to weaken. I couldn't think straight and the state of constant fear was driving me to exhaustion. I was beginning to break down, my mind coming apart at the seams. *Think of the baby,* I told myself, *and think of Leo. They're relying on me, nobody else can help them.* I took a deep breath. 'I'm tired,' I told him. 'Let's go to bed. We both need some sleep.'

After splashing cold water on my face and changing out of my torn clothes into the pyjamas Jay had bought for me, I lay down beside him on the airbed. He put his arm around me and I let him, and after a long time he drifted off to sleep. My thoughts were far too dark and hopeless for me to get any real rest, though I must have drifted off for a few brief seconds, as I woke, sweating and shaking, from a nightmare where I dreamt that I had lost Scott's baby. I sat up and put my head in my hands, rocking back and forth. This was hell. I was in a living hell.

It must be almost mid-morning now. Daylight filled the room. Jay was still asleep, and I lay quietly for a long time, thinking, then not thinking, despairing, then trying to find solutions. Time didn't seem to pass normally any more, but at some point I got up, quietly got dressed, and crept into the kitchen. There was a knife on the draining board. I picked it up and tiptoed back to the bedroom. What I was doing was potentially suicide. I wasn't a violent person; I didn't know how to threaten someone convincingly with a knife, and for all I knew Jay might get it out of my hand and use it on me. But he was asleep, and vulnerable, and if I could get him to tell me where Leo was I had no reason to stay in this godforsaken house. I could stab Jay if I had to, to make sure he didn't pursue me. But most importantly, I had to find out where he'd hidden Leo. At all costs.

Jay was stirring as I made my way towards him. Then he opened his eyes. My stomach dropped to the floor, but I'd come too far to back out now. I raised the knife and pointed it towards him. 'Tell me where Leo is,' I said firmly. 'I'm not messing around. Tell me now, Jay, or I swear to God, I will use this on you.'

Scott

44

After many hours of drifting in and out of consciousness, Scott woke properly, at last a bit more lucid. As his eyes adjusted to the hospital surroundings, he was surprised to find Natasha sitting quietly at his side.

'Oh,' she said when she noticed his eyes were open. She smiled. 'You're awake.'

'Natasha?' he said, confused. 'Where's Martin?'

'I told him he should go home. I…' He looked at her closely. Her smile had evaporated, leaving her face drawn and worried. There was a strange look in her eye, one that made him deeply uneasy. He tried to sit up, wincing at a pain in his elbow. God, it hurt. But he needed to focus. Something was wrong. Badly wrong.

'What is it?' he pressed her. 'Has something happened to Felicity?'

'You need to rest,' she reassured him, but he knew her too well for her to pull the wool over his eyes. Natasha was tough. She was the one who propped people up, who kept things going, but now she looked as though she was about to crumble.

'Just tell me,' he said firmly. 'I know there's something, so don't try to spare me, please. I just need to know.'

By the time she'd finished, the lingering nausea he'd already been feeling had intensified a hundredfold. 'DI Miller has it under control,' Natasha told him. 'She says you should stay in hospital, there's nothing you can really do–'

'Are you joking?' he said. 'Under control? They don't know where the hell Felicity is! Leo was found wandering in the street by a neighbour! I'm going back to Alstercombe right now.' He moved towards the edge of the bed, the pain in his arm making him shudder.

'Scott, you're not in any fit state to do anything back home—'

'I can help! A broken elbow isn't going to stop me.'

'It's not just your elbow,' she told him. 'The doctors want you to stay a little longer because you hurt your head and lost a lot of blood. They just want to check—'

'I don't care! I'll sign anything they need me to sign, but I'm leaving now.'

She paused briefly, and then she nodded, resigned. 'I knew that's what you were going to say.'

Scott glared at the cast on his arm. Felicity needed him more than she ever had, and he was in no shape to be much physical help. How could he have ended up injuring himself at a time like this? He should never have gone away. He'd been too distracted to enjoy himself anyway, and he'd frustrated the hell out of Martin with his worrying.

'You're lucky you weren't hurt more badly,' Natasha said. 'You're lucky you're *alive*. We've been worried sick about you.'

'Where's Leo?' he said, ignoring her comment.

'Mum, Dad and Zack are looking after him between them – I flew here straight away. He's been really good by the sound of it – confused, but he's coping well. We haven't told him the truth about where Felicity is, he wouldn't understand anyway. But we told him Daddy is in hospital, and he seemed to get that. I left Felicity messages, to tell her you and Leo are okay, but we don't know if she ever heard them. Her phone has gone dead now.'

Scott closed his eyes. So Felicity may well believe he was dead. She was alone with Jay, probably terrified for her life, and with no idea what had happened to her son or fiancé. She was bound to fear the worst. It was unbearable to imagine her in that state.

Natasha must have guessed what his thoughts were. 'Scott, try not to—'

'Where the hell am I, anyway?' he said, to stop Natasha saying anything further. 'Am I still in France?'

She nodded.

'Are they going to let me on a plane if I've discharged myself from hospital?'

She shrugged. 'Who's going to know?'

'Let's get going, then.'

...

Even though they got moving straight away, it was as though time was slowed down. Alstercombe might as well be the other side of the world, Scott felt, as he waited at the airport. He managed to speak to DI Miller on the phone, but she didn't say much that reassured him. He threw his phone down onto his lap in frustration, and Natasha glanced at him. 'They're doing everything they can,' she said. 'The police have been going to door-to-door all over Alstercombe–'

'How did Felicity manage to leave?' he said, his frustration spilling over. 'Why weren't there police at the house?'

'There were. They think she must have climbed over the fence into the neighbours' garden.'

Scott fell silent. Their plane was delayed, and he felt more frustrated, hopeless and useless than he ever had in his life. His arm was hurting, the pain becoming more and more overwhelming. He must be due for some painkillers. Natasha was busy checking messages on her phone so he fumbled to open the painkillers with one hand, but they were slipping from his grasp. Instinctively he tried to catch the packet, sending a spasm of movement into his broken arm that made him cry out. 'For fuck's sake!' he said, startling Natasha. 'How did this happen? How did he manage to take Felicity while I'm in another fucking country!'

Some people looked round at them, but he didn't care.

He scrabbled around on the floor with his good arm for the painkillers, and Natasha reached down to get them. 'Let me help you,' she said. She handed him a couple of pills and a teardrop splashed onto his hand as he lifted them to his mouth. He sat back in his seat, desperate not to break down when there were so many people around. 'Jay's a murderer, Tash,' he said quietly, though she already knew.

'I know what he is, Scott. Listen, I understand how helpless you feel, but we'll be on the plane in no time. It's only a short flight. We'll have a bit of a drive after but we'll be in Alstercombe later today, easily. To be honest, there's not much more you could be doing in Alstercombe right now than you can do here.'

'I need to be there if they find her. I need to be there for Leo.'

'Leo is doing fine,' she said calmly. 'I told you, he doesn't really know what's going on.'

'You don't understand! He…' Scott took a breath. 'Jay might have hurt Felicity. Surely you realise that? He probably *has* hurt her. He could be hurting her right now. If he knows where she lives, he probably knows all about her relationship with me, doesn't he? He probably *wants* to punish her for being with me.'

'Don't do this to yourself.'

'Why not? I went away and left her. It's my own fault. And she's… she's everything to me, Tash. If I lose her…'

'There's no reason to think you've lost her. Look, I know this sounds harsh, but if he wanted her dead, and he's known where she is for a while, he probably would have killed her already. If he wanted to kill her, why stage this thing with Leo and get her to go to him? I think he wants to get back together with her, and that's what the police think too.'

'Yeah, and what happens when he realises she doesn't want to be with him?'

'We just need to hope she can either act well, or talk some sense into him. She's survived him before. We have to take some hope from that.'

Scott shook his head. 'I want to kill him. I really want to kill him, Tash.'

'I know.'

'How does he keep getting away with it? Why don't they just catch him?'

'They will. Jay was seen taking Leo. His face is plastered all over the news. It's only a matter of time before he slips up, or before somebody spots him. He won't get away again. Just have faith. Stay hopeful. Somebody, somewhere, is going to see something.'

Keith Vinney

45

Keith Vinney stared at the TV screen, frowning heavily. The image disappeared, but it was still there in the back of his mind. That face. There was something about that face. Ordinarily, he'd try to draw out the mug of tea he'd ordered at Chrissie's Kitchen for most of the morning – sitting in the cheap-and-cheerful little café was a good way to pass the time. It was that or the library, where he could pass a few hours reading at one of the quiet tables upstairs, hidden away amongst the non-fiction books.

Today, he decided he would stay in the café even longer than usual, long enough that he bought himself a second mug of tea. He needed to sit and think. And ideally he needed to wait until the news channel playing from the small TV in the corner rolled round to the story about Jay Kilburn again.

After nearly forty-five minutes of going back and forth in his mind, Keith was still not convinced one way or another about whether Jay Kilburn was, or was not, the man who'd opened the door to him when he'd tried to go and see his daughter Stephanie. That man had had dark hair, he'd worn glasses. But then, on the news they had mentioned Jay Kilburn might have altered his appearance, or be using a different name. Jason was the name they suggested. Had the man at Stephanie's house given his name? He couldn't remember. He drained the last of his tea, and took his empty mug over to the counter, where the café owner, Chrissie, was busy restocking a glass cabinet with canned drinks.

'You look like you've got a lot on your mind, love,' she said when she stood up and looked at him, adjusting the floral headscarf that held back a cascade of tight red curls. 'What's up?'

'You been watching the news?'

She shrugged.

'That Kilburn fella. The one they keep showing, saying he's dangerous and that.'

'Yeah, I know the one,' she said, as she finished one shelf of the drinks cabinet and started work on the second, moving the older cans to the front and refilling it from the back. 'Makes me shudder, him taking that little lad to lure the poor woman back.' She shook her head, and then smiled at Keith sympathetically. 'I knew you were a big softie at heart. You can't start worrying about all the world's problems, you'll drive yourself mad.'

Keith was silent for a moment. Chrissie would indeed think he was mad when he voiced his suspicions. But he needed to talk to somebody, and Chrissie was as good as anyone. He'd been going to the café since he'd been back in Wrexton, and he'd told Chrissie a bit about his life, and his desire to reconnect with his daughter. When he'd first gone to Stephanie's house, he'd been full of hope that her boyfriend would pass on his address, but he'd quickly grown impatient, and he'd lost his flat when he'd started drinking again. Chrissie had been an unexpected source of support, and they'd become something like friends. At least, she didn't seem to mind that he spent a lot of time and yet very little money in her establishment.

He took a breath. He'd started the conversation now; he might as well cut to the chase. 'Thing is, I keep thinking I saw him – Kilburn, that is – when I went round Steph's a few months back.'

Chrissie stared at him. Then her face changed - from surprise to a smirk, as she concluded he was joking. She rolled her eyes. 'Oh, behave,' she said.

'No, Chrissie, I'm serious.'

She shook her head. 'Stop it.'

'Listen!' he insisted. 'When I went round Steph's, something weren't right. I shoulda seen it at the time.'

Chrissie stopped restocking the drinks to look at him properly. 'You're not having me on?'

'No.'

'He can't be that man off the news, surely,' she said slowly. 'Why would he come here? Besides, your Steph would have more sense than to get involved with a wrong 'un like him, wouldn't she?'

'How would I know? I ain't seen her for twenty years.'

Chrissie drummed her long red nails on the countertop. 'It's a bit of a stretch, love.'

'It weren't right, when I went to the house. *He* weren't right. He wanted rid of me.'

Chrissie thought for a long while. 'Then you should call the police,' she said finally. 'You can use my phone. See what they think. They can go check it out, see if your Steph's okay. Or you could go down the station, if you'd rather, and talk to them face to face. It's not far to walk from here.'

'I should go round Steph's house meself.'

'No, you shouldn't.'

'If I go down the station the police'd take one look at me and think I'm some old drunk who don't know his arse from his elbow. They won't take me seriously.'

'Yes, they would. They're desperate to find him. They *want* information.'

'I know what folk think when they see me.'

'Well, I don't want you going round Steph's on your own. Just say you're right, and that man really is there, I don't want to wake up tomorrow to hear your name on the news—'

'I ain't scared of him. Steph's my girl. I'm the one who should check on her.'

Some customers came up to the counter. Chrissie gave them a smile and nod, saying, 'Be with you in a tick,' before reaching across and giving Keith's arm a squeeze. 'If I can't talk you out of it, at least come and see me after. So's I know you're all right.'

...

He got a bus part of the way, and walked the rest. The closer he

174

got, the more sure he became. Why would he feel so strongly he'd seen the man if he hadn't? But on the other hand, his memory wasn't always so good nowadays. Perhaps if he went round there, he'd just seem like a blundering old fool to his daughter and her other half.

As he drew near to the house, he grew increasingly nervous. He'd love to see his little girl – not that she was little, now – but what if she slammed the door in his face? What if the man answered it, and he was completely wrong about his suspicions, or even worse, what if he was right? Keith hesitated. It would be easier to turn around. He could head for the library, or for anywhere other than here. He actually began to turn, and then he stopped himself. He might have spent most of his life trying to put thoughts of Stephanie out of his mind – they would stir up his guilt, and he'd never known what to do to make it right – but since he'd come back to Wrexton, she was all he wanted. She was the reason he'd come back here in the first place, because although he wasn't sure he could ever make things right, he wanted to at least let Stephanie know that she wasn't forgotten. That she'd never been forgotten.

It was mid-morning now – the time of day, probably, when one or both of them would be at work – but he continued anyway. He'd come too far to turn back now, and if nobody was in, well, he'd just sit down on the pavement and wait until one of them did turn up.

Sure enough, when he knocked on the door, there was no response. He'd half expected the house to be empty, but still he couldn't shake a growing sense of unease. The man who answered the door to him *had* been Jay Kilburn. He was convinced of it. He knocked again, mentally going through the conversation he'd had with the man. It had been an odd exchange, and the man had certainly been keen to put him off from coming back again. He'd said it was because Stephanie was hurt and needed space, and Keith had believed that, at the time. But was it all a lie? Was it just because the man didn't want anyone poking around in his business? Had he even told

Stephanie that her father had come looking for her?

Keith made his way over to the front window. There was a lacy net curtain, with heavier curtains behind it, but he could get a vague view of the living room beyond through a gap where the curtains didn't quite meet. He stepped into the front garden to get a closer look, standing nose-to-nose with the glass and peeping through holes in the lace net curtain. Nothing.

Wait! He squinted, trying to make sense of what he was seeing. There was a shape on the carpet. Legs, and then the rest of the body was obscured behind the coffee table. Somebody was lying on the floor inside the house! That wasn't right. He knocked again on the front door, and called through the letterbox. In desperation he tried the door handle, and when he pushed down on it the door simply opened.

He rushed into the living room, not even pausing to close the front door behind him. On the patterned brown-and-yellow carpet a young woman was slumped face down. Her hair was caked with blood. There was a large patch on the sofa, too, and a heavy lamp with blood on it was lying on the floor.

Keith quickly knelt down beside her, turning her onto her side and sweeping hair out of her face. Her eyes were closed, her hand had been stretched out towards her phone which was beside her on the carpet. It looked as though she had woken at some stage, tried to call for help, and collapsed. He shook her lightly but her body was a dead weight, and when he put his fingers against her wrist, there was no obvious pulse. 'No,' he said, squeezing her hand tightly, 'you're not allowed to be dead. You're not allowed to be dead, Steph. You're my little girl. You're not allowed...' He took a deep breath and tried to pull himself together. Her body wasn't cold. She wasn't showing any response to him, but he felt stirrings of hope. He held her wrist again. Was there a little whisper of a pulse? He couldn't be sure, and he quickly grabbed her phone to call for an ambulance, and then sat holding her hand.

'You're going to make it, Steph,' he told her gently. 'You're a survivor, like me.' Of course, he had no idea what sort of a

176

person she was, not having seen her since she was a child. But he vowed that if she pulled through this, he would make sure he got to know exactly who she was now. And if this had been done by Jay Kilburn – and he was certain now that it had been – then God help the man if Keith ever managed to get his hands on him.

His body surged with relief as Stephanie's eyes flickered open. She was utterly bewildered. 'Granddad?' she said vaguely. Then she fixed her gaze on him. 'Who are you?' she asked, frightened.

'I…' What should he say? 'I'm Keith Vinney. Your… your dad.'

Her eyes closed again. Had she even heard him? It didn't matter, not right now. What mattered was that she was alive.

Scott

46

'It's good news, isn't it?' Natasha said.

'That Jay smacked some poor girl over the head? He nearly killed her, by the sound of it.'

Natasha sat down next to him and handed him a mug of tea. He'd never been so sick of tea. It was like people thought they could fill the void of Felicity's disappearance by giving him enough cups.

'No,' Natasha said patiently, 'I mean it's good that they know where he was.'

Scott sighed. He'd just been given an update from the police on the progress of the search for Felicity. Although it was undoubtedly a step in the right direction that the police had now discovered where Jay had been staying, the fact he'd left for dead the woman who had been sheltering him for years didn't fill him with hope about what state Felicity would be in. And they still didn't know where he was now.

'They'll make a breakthrough soon, I know it,' Natasha said. 'Finding somewhere he's lived, someone he's had a relationship with… they might not be able to ask her any questions just yet, but who knows what they'll be able to find from her phone, from neighbours, or what they'll turn up in the house.'

'I know, Tash,' he said. 'I know it's progress, but I'm just… I'm so…'

'You're scared about what might have already happened to Fliss.'

He studied her face. She had an odd look about her again, like she knew something. She was fiddling with her ponytail and trying not to meet his eye.

'What is it, Tash?'

He thought she was about to protest, but she sighed instead. 'Look, I wasn't sure when would be the right time to tell you about this. I don't want to give you more to worry about.'

'Tash, please, just tell me,' he said. 'Don't try to keep secrets, not at a time like this.'

'I'm not trying to keep it secret. It's just... after what happened the last time she was pregnant, having the miscarriage after all that stress with Vicky...'

His heart skipped a beat. 'Fliss is pregnant again? Is that what you're telling me?' Worries immediately crowded in. Would Jay realise she was pregnant? And even if he didn't, if he treated her the way he had in the past, it wouldn't only be Felicity whose life was in danger now.

Natasha nodded. 'She did a test just after we heard from Martin about your fall. She–'

'So she found out she's pregnant and she thinks I'm probably dead?'

'I don't know. Like I told you before, I tried to call her. I left messages, but... I'm sorry, Scott. I should have kept a better eye on her.'

Scott put his hand up to his head. This was too much to take. He pressed his palm against his skull for a moment then lowered it when his initial wave of horror had subsided. 'It's not your fault,' he told her gently. 'I just... when's it going to end, Tash?'

She put her hand over his. 'I don't know.'

'I mean, even before Jay came and took Leo, she had all those "pranks" of Vicky's to deal with. In fact, if Vicky hadn't been messing with our heads so much, perhaps we would have been better able to notice signs that Jay was watching her. Maybe we would have been more alert.'

'It's impossible to know now.'

Suddenly, an idea grew in Scott's mind. An awful idea. But one that began to seem frighteningly plausible. Vicky. Why *had* she put that rose on Felicity's car? She'd acted so weird about it afterwards, as though she considered their anger utterly unjustified. Could she... could she have been trying to warn

179

them? Did she do something that attracted Jay here? Just before the rose incident he'd told her that Tim had been on the point of breaking up with her. She'd been crushed. Had she somehow managed to contact Jay in the heat of the moment, then regretted it and tried to warn Felicity he'd found her?

Then there was the garden ornament through the window. She'd taken the blame for that, but she'd been in their house when it happened. Had she really got a friend to throw it, or had she known that Jay was coming? Was she trying to hide the fact that Jay had found Felicity, perhaps so that he could do something worse, something more carefully planned?

Then there were the conversations he'd had with her about his trip to Chamonix, how keen she had been for him to go, and how, almost as soon as he'd gone, Jay had turned up.

He stood up abruptly, startling Natasha. 'What is it?' she asked. 'What's wrong?'

'I just thought of something.'

'Something that could help find Felicity?'

'Maybe.'

'Then call Detective Miller—'

'Not yet.'

'Scott, you—'

'I need to go and talk to somebody first.'

Scott

47

Scott didn't go straight to Vicky. First he walked to Martin's house. If he was just being paranoid and letting his thoughts run away from him, Martin would put him straight. He watched Martin's face carefully as he explained his suspicions about Vicky, and at the end Martin said, 'It's a bit of a leap, isn't it? I mean, I know this stuff with the rose, and your window, it's pretty messed up, but would she really try to help Jay? How would she even have crossed paths with him?'

'I don't know. But the way she's been behaving has been all over the place. And she really was keen for me to go away this week. When has she ever been keen for me to have my own life in the past?'

'Her behaviour has always been all over the place. You know how it was with Tim: she'd have those crazy conspiracy theories that he was cheating on her and we were covering it up for him, and then the next minute she'd be apologising to him for being so suspicious. She does the same with you – you've never known where you are with her. But helping Jay is going to extreme lengths, even for her. She could get in serious trouble herself.'

'Perhaps she didn't fully understand what she was getting herself into, though. She didn't know all the facts about him to start with. Maybe she had some kind of contact with him, just online or something, but when she realised exactly what he'd done, she got frightened and warned us with the rose.'

'And then what? Did a u-turn and decided to help him take Felicity prisoner?'

'Perhaps me and Fliss getting engaged tipped her over the edge. I think she's always hoped I'll make a go of it with her, even though half the time she hates me.'

Martin sat quietly for a while. They were in the living room of his small house, just off of Alstercombe high street, and every few minutes snatches of conversation from people walking by outside would drift in through the window. It was a warm day, and the heat was claustrophobic in the small room, making Scott's head swim, despite the rotating desk fan on top of a cupboard in the corner.

'Have you told the police your suspicions?' Martin asked eventually.

'No. I know how it sounds. I don't want to say it out loud to anybody else.'

'So, what are you going to do?'

'I'm going to go and ask her.'

Martin shook his head. 'Look, if you're wrong, you're going to mess up whatever shreds of a civilised relationship you've got left with the mother of your child.'

'And if I'm right, she might know something that can help us find Felicity. She... Felicity's pregnant again. I just found out from Tash.'

Martin paused. Scott waited impatiently as he thought it over. 'All right,' Martin said finally. 'Did you walk here?'

Scott gestured at his broken elbow with his free hand. 'Can't drive like this. And it didn't take long to walk here.' The last bit wasn't strictly true, and even as he said the words a wave of exhaustion washed over him. The pain in his elbow was still very bad, too. It took everything he had just to concentrate. He tried to stand, but slumped back down and shook his head.

'You don't look like you're in great shape, Scott. I'm driving you back to Natasha's–'

'No!' he said, his voice so loud Martin was taken aback. 'No,' he repeated, more quietly. 'I can't rest until I've got the truth out of Vicky. I have to know. I want her to look me in the eye and say she had nothing to do with it.'

'And you really don't think it would be better to leave it to the police?'

'That's too slow. If Vicky knows something, I'll get it out of her. I know I will.'

'Okay,' Martin said with a sigh. 'I'll drive you to Vicky's if you're determined to talk to her, but I'm taking you straight home after. You need to rest.'

...

Vicky didn't answer the doorbell. After knocking a couple of times, Scott looked round at Martin, who sat waiting in the car. Martin shrugged. Determined not to give up, Scott made his way over to the gate at the side of the house, beyond which was a paved path down to the back garden. Sounds of Dennis playing reached him from the garden, so he quickly opened the gate and hurried down the path.

Vicky was laid out on a sun-lounger on the small patio overlooking the grass. Dressed in shorts and a bikini top, she was busy looking at her phone through a pair of large, showy sunglasses.

'Jesus!' she said, sitting bolt upright when he said hello. 'You scared the shit out of me, Scott.' She sat up on the edge of the sun-lounger, and Dennis ran over. 'Daddy, Daddy!'

He gave Dennis a one-armed hug, and Dennis looked curiously at the sling around his other arm. 'Is it ouchy?'

'Yeah, it's pretty ouchy. But it's nothing to worry about.'

Dennis ran back over to his toys, and Scott fixed his eyes on Vicky, as she pushed her sunglasses up into her hair. 'I need to talk to you,' he said.

Vicky

48

Her stomach flip-flopped. Ever since she'd dropped Leo back near Natasha's house, she'd been terrified of who might come knocking at the door asking questions.

'What do you need to talk to me about?' she asked casually, though her mind was racing. What the hell was he doing here? What did he know? She hadn't even realised he was back in Alstercombe. 'If you've come to tell me you're alive, then you could have saved yourself a journey, I already knew. Martin told me you were in hospital.' She frowned at him. 'Are you sure you shouldn't *still* be in hospital? You look like crap.'

'The only thing I care about right now is whether Felicity is alive.'

Vicky's blood turned to ice. 'How would I know anything about that?'

Scott gave her a long look. She met his gaze. She had to front this out. If he suspected, he'd be looking for signs of weakness.

'Why were you so keen for me to go away with Martin?' he asked.

'I wanted a bit of time where I didn't have to see you. Or think about you. Or speak to you.'

Scott nodded. 'Vix, tell me the truth. I know you hate Felicity. You told her once that you hoped her ex found her.'

'I don't know what you're talking about,' she said, though her mind was in turmoil. He knew! How had he found out? Could he prove it, or was he just suspicious? 'I don't think we should be having this conversation in front of Dennis,' she told him.

'All right,' Scott said, 'Martin drove me here. I'll ask him to keep an eye on Dennis and we can talk inside, if that's what you'd prefer.'

'I'd rather not talk about this at all. I feel like you're accusing me of something. I've already had the police round here, asking if I've seen anything, because they know what I did with that rose. I don't deserve this, Scott. I've done nothing wrong!'

'I hope that's true,' he said. 'Because if I find out you had something to do with this...'

Her head began to pound. She'd barely slept since Jay had turned up at her house; she couldn't get her thoughts straight. 'I want you to leave,' she said. 'This conversation is over.'

'I'll just tell the police to come and have another chat with you then, shall I?'

'They're not going to come here just because you ask them to. They'll only come here if they have a good reason, and they won't get a good reason, because this is nothing to do with me. I mean, what do you think you're doing, showing up and coming out with these wild theories? Has your spell in hospital pickled your brain or something? Or did you hit your head harder than you thought when you fell? Because this is harassment—'

'So you're not glad Felicity is out of the way, then? Because that's what you wanted, isn't it?'

'I don't care enough about her to get myself into trouble!' she shouted. Dennis looked round at them. Until this point they'd been keeping their voices hushed, but now Dennis came over. 'Why are you arguing?'

'We're not, sweetie,' Vicky said. 'But your daddy is upsetting me, so I think he should go.'

Dennis frowned at Scott. 'Say sorry to Mummy.'

'Vicky, listen to me, if you know anything, for God's sake just tell me. Even if you had some involvement, do the right thing now.'

'You're always so willing to see the worst in me! It's not even a stretch for you to believe I'd do something to get rid of Felicity, is it?'

And he's right. You're such an idiot, Vicky. He knows. He knows, and you're going to prison.

She took a deep breath, trying to focus on what Scott was

saying.

'I know that me being with Felicity hurts you. Some odd things have happened, Vicky, you can't deny that–'

'I've never tried to deny anything. I've made mistakes, but so have you. Why are you always trying to blame me for everything?'

Scott swayed a little. He was so pale. 'Go and play with your toys,' he told Dennis, who was standing on the lawn watching them warily. 'I'll come and join you in a minute, maybe.'

Dennis ran off, and she pointed a finger at Scott. 'You need to get out of here, now,' she said. 'For one thing, you look like you're about to keel over, and for a second thing, you do not get to come and threaten me just because your *precious* Felicity has gone back to her ex. Maybe she's exactly where she wants to be.'

'She has not *gone back*. He took Leo–'

'Yeah, yeah, whatever.'

Scott narrowed his eyes at her. 'You honestly don't care, do you?'

'About Felicity? No.' She leaned close to him. 'And you're only so upset because you know that if she's gone to him, it's because she still loves him, and she just can't help herself.'

'What are you saying?' Scott asked, his voice full of disgust. 'She doesn't *like* how Jay treats her.'

Vicky raised her eyebrows. 'All right. If believing that helps you sleep at night.' She started to turn away and Scott caught her arm. 'I have tried and tried, Vicky. I try to tell myself that you don't mean all this stuff you say, but it… this is too much. I can't live this way any more. I'll go now, but if I find out you had *anything* to do with all this, I am going to go for full custody of Dennis.'

'Like hell you are!' she yelled at him, wrenching her arm away. 'You wouldn't have a leg to stand on.'

'And what makes you say that?' His eyes flashed. 'Is it because he isn't really mine?'

Vicky's mouth dropped open. How long had he known? He'd never said anything before. He was watching her, shocked. 'I'm

right, aren't I?' he said slowly. 'Dennis really isn't mine? You...
you *cheated* on Tim?'

'How can you ask me that?' she exploded, and then she
slapped him. Hard.

He took a couple of steps backwards. 'I'll do a paternity test,
then, shall I?'

'Do what you want.'

He shook his head. 'I can't believe it,' he said. 'I suspected,
but... I can't believe it.'

'Really? It seems like you're willing to believe a lot of other
nasty things about me, so why not that?'

'You always say how much you loved Tim.'

'I did. I do.'

He didn't reply. He was looking at her like she was something
on the bottom of his shoe. He'd never understand. He didn't
know what it was like to be that scared of losing somebody –
although, perhaps now, with Felicity gone, he was finally getting
an idea. And that was exactly what he deserved.

'How did it happen?' he asked her. 'Who was it?'

'Who was who?'

'Dennis's father!' he insisted. 'Who is Dennis's biological
father?'

Vicky

4 YEARS AND 4 MONTHS AGO

49

Vicky quickly pulled her clothes back on while the man slept. Her eyes drifted over to him, and then she quickly looked away again. The man. She knew his name, his first name, anyway, but she willed herself to forget it. It was better if he was just "the man". Any man, a stranger. Anonymous.

She slipped out of his house onto the street, and her agoraphobia hit her, the way it still did sometimes, when she was stressed or upset. She stepped back towards the front door, eyes flicking nervously here and there. *Pull yourself together,* she said to herself harshly. *You need to get home before Tim starts wondering where you've got to.*

She'd told him she was out with some friends. He was expecting her back late, but it was getting *really* late. She could phone for a taxi, but that would mean hanging around waiting. She didn't want to go back inside the man's house, and she didn't want to wait around on the street. Walking was preferable. She'd keep her head down, walk fast. It would probably only take twenty minutes or so to get back home.

She set off at a brisk pace. *I was out with some girls from work…* She repeated it silently, making sure she got her story straight in her head. *It ended up a bit of a crazy night. We went to Kiki's, that new bar just off the high street…* She sighed. She didn't need to think of a good story. The way Tim had been with her recently, he probably wouldn't even ask how her night had been.

Sure enough, when she got inside he was in bed asleep, and the next morning he apparently had no memory, or no interest, in the fact that she'd been out the night before.

'I had a great night, thanks for asking,' she said sarcastically as she poured herself some cereal. He looked up from his phone. 'Oh... yeah. Sorry, Vix, I for–'

'–You don't care,' she said, finishing his sentence for him. 'Don't say you forgot.'

'I *did* forget. I... there's lots on at work, I'm not–'

'Lots on *at work?*' she said. 'Give me a break, Tim. You teach guitar, you're not a bloody brain surgeon.'

He shook his head. 'I can't talk to you when you're like this.'

'No,' she said. 'No. Don't turn this around on me! Just admit you don't give a shit where I was last night. You probably wouldn't have noticed if I hadn't come home at all!'

As she sat down at the table to eat her breakfast, he got up to leave the room. She shovelled food into her mouth and chewed angrily. It better bloody work this time. She'd better be pregnant.

PRESENT DAY

'It was a good plan,' she said.

'What was a good plan?' Scott watched her closely.

'I did it to save our relationship. I won't let you say I was cheating on Tim, and that I didn't love him. I did it *because* I loved him.'

'But you had sex with somebody else?'

'I had to.'

Scott shook his head. 'This is so fucked up, Vicky. This is *beyond* fucked up.'

'The other men...' She quickly stopped herself. Too late. Scott had heard the word "men", and he was about to speak so she cut him off before he could start. 'They... *he*... was just a sperm donor as far as I was concerned. I had no attachment to him. I don't remember his name. I wouldn't be able to track him down even if I wanted to. Tim *wanted* to have kids, he told me that earlier on in our relationship, before things started going bad. Before *you* interfered. He was never going to be able to get me pregnant, so I did the next best thing I could. We both wanted a baby. If he hadn't died, he would have stayed with me so that he could have a family. He would have thanked me in the end.'

'For having sex with other guys? He would have *thanked* you. Really?'

'I just told you! The baby would have healed everything–'

'Babies don't heal relationships. You throw a baby into a relationship that's already broken and it won't fix it, Vix. It'll blow it apart.'

'You don't know what you're talking about.'

'If you'd both wanted to have a family, you could have worked something out together. There were other routes you could have explored. You didn't have to do what you did.' His eyes widened as if something had occurred to him. 'Except you *knew*. That's why you tried to do it behind his back. Because you knew he was going to break up with you.'

4 YEARS AND 4 MONTHS AGO

Daylight was streaming in through the curtains when Vicky woke, and she rolled onto her side to look at Tim. He was just waking up, his straw-coloured hair all messy, and when his eyes fell on hers a little crease formed between his eyebrows, as though instead of being pleased that her face was the first thing he laid eyes on, he was disappointed and fed up. Though a week had passed since their argument after her night out, the atmosphere in the house was still frosty.

'It's a nice day,' she said. 'Why don't we go for a walk or something?'

'Vix, you know I'm going climbing with Scott today.' He paused, and then added unconvincingly, 'We'll do something tomorrow.'

'We won't, though, will we?'

Tim rubbed his face with his hands. 'It's too early for this. I only just woke up.'

'You never want to talk to me, Tim.'

He sighed and swung his legs over the side of the bed. 'I'm going to have a shower.'

She reached across and caught his arm. 'Why won't you talk to me? I've got things I want to say–'

'You never have anything new to say, though, Vix. It's just the same thing, round and round in circles. We can't have a proper conversation, you're always so suspicious of me. The trust... I'm not sure there is any, is there?'

'I want to talk about having a baby.'

Tim turned and stared at her. 'Are you joking?'

He sat down on the edge of the bed, and touched her arm gently.

'Vix, you know I can't–'

'There are ways, though. If we wanted to do it, we could look into our options...' At the look in Tim's eyes she trailed off. He hated the idea – it was written all over his face.

Her period wasn't due for another week yet, so it was too early to do a test to see if her latest attempt to get pregnant had been successful, but the thought there could be a new little life inside her frequently filled her stomach with butterflies. There were no butterflies now, though. Now she just felt sick, and her head was beginning to hurt. If he didn't like the idea at all, not even in principle, how would he react if she did have to tell him in a week's time that she was going to have a baby?

You're so stupid, Vicky. What were you thinking? He doesn't want you. He never wanted you.

'Well?' she demanded. 'Are we going to talk about it?'

'I don't know,' he said vaguely. 'Maybe. But we should have this conversation another time.'

'That's not an answer!'

'Vix, I can't... I just can't talk about this now. It's not that long till I'm meeting Scott. We need to sit down and discuss this properly–'

'No,' she said, 'you always just dismiss me! You can say right now whether you want a baby or not, it's not that complicated a question.'

'All right. Fine. I think that our relationship is nowhere near in the right place for a baby.'

'That's because we don't spend enough time together! Do you really have to go out with Scott today? Why don't you stay so we can talk now?'

'Because I need some space!' he snapped. 'All we do is talk, and argue, the whole time I'm here–'

'I'm just trying to make things better! When you're out you just ignore me–'

'I don't ignore you!' he said, his face reddening. 'I just don't reply to every text within ten seconds. I sometimes have other things going on! And I'm sorry you can't handle that, but you have to...' He paused and took her hands in his. 'You have to let me breathe, Vicky. Look, I'll be back later tonight. We'll talk more then.'

'Yeah, after Scott's been dripping poison about me in your ear all day.'

'Believe it or not, Scott talks about other things besides you. You're so... I don't know. I'm not trying to blame you. I'm not perfect either, I know that. But this house, you, us, it's like some sort of pressure cooker. We need some time out. I need some perspective. I think... I think you do too. Then we can talk once we've had a chance to clear our heads.'

Vicky's eyes prickled with tears as he walked out of the room. It was painfully obvious what he really wanted to talk about, and it wasn't new beginnings and babies. She dug her nails into her palms so hard that she drew blood.

Told you, the little voice said. *He doesn't love you. You've driven him away. You drive everybody away.*

PRESENT DAY

'It was fine, until you messed everything up for me,' Vicky said quietly. 'My whole life. It would have been okay, if you just hadn't messed it up.'

'*I* messed up *your* life?' Scott kept his voice low, and they both glanced across at Dennis, playing at the other end of the garden, oblivious to their argument as he busied himself with his toys. 'You knowingly lied to me about me being Dennis's dad! Yes, I love him. Yes, I wouldn't have it any other way, not now, but that is one hell of a way to interfere in somebody's life, Vicky! To make me think—'

'You had to be pretty deluded too,' she snapped. 'Either you missed all your sex ed classes, or you must genuinely not be able to remember that night we were together.'

'What do you mean?'

'Well, I'll give you some credit, you managed to actually get it in. But you weren't in a fit state to make any babies, Scott. You passed out on top of me. I pushed you off me and we both went to sleep. *That* is all that happened.'

Scott

50

Scott couldn't bring himself to speak. His elbow throbbed. His head throbbed. He'd never been able to remember that night clearly – he had a fuzzy recollection of kissing Vicky, and touching her, and when he'd woken up in the morning they were both semi-naked. He had always believed that night had happened because they were trying to comfort one another after Tim's death, but now he realised that Vicky had been playing him all along.

'You wanted somebody to be your baby's dad,' he said slowly. 'Tim was gone. It was supposed to be him, but without him, you just needed someone else–'

'You,' she said. 'I wanted it to be you.'

'Why?'

'Because you were the one who took Tim away!'

'If… if you hate me so much, why did you tell me something that would mean I'd be in your life forever?'

She shrugged. 'To make you pay.'

'Dennis isn't a punishment! He's one of the best things that ever happened to me. He gave my life meaning–'

'Don't be so ridiculous. Meaning? No. He gave you *responsibility*. Something you've never shown any of before.'

'I don't know why you have this obsession with me,' Scott said. 'I've never purposefully done anything to hurt you. I never meant for our paths to even cross, if I'm honest–'

'And that,' she said, 'is the biggest problem.'

'What?'

'You weren't interested. None of you were, not back then.'

'When?'

'That party. The night I wanted you to walk me home.'

194

Scott's frustration boiled over. 'That was years and years ago! What the hell does that have to do—'

'Everything, really,' she said. 'It made me who I am. It made me the person who is standing in front of you now. So it couldn't be more relevant, could it?'

Vicky

18 YEARS AGO

51

'Where are you going dressed like that?' Sandra asked.

Vicky turned at the sound of her mum's voice. 'To a party,' she said simply.

Sandra burst out laughing, and Vicky tried to block it out. Every time her mum laughed at her, it hurt more. It was like having broken glass pushed into her ears. 'Don't laugh like that!' she shouted in desperation. Immediately she regretted it. It was better with bullies not to let them know they were hurting you. *Just ignore them and they'll get bored,* wasn't that what people said?

Sandra held her hands up, as if Vicky's reaction had been completely over the top. 'Woah,' she said, 'calm down. For God's sake, Vix.'

Watching her mother, Vicky tried to keep a lid on her emotions. She couldn't remember when Mum had got so mean. It hadn't always been that way, but when Vicky looked now at the mass of fifty-something-year-old woman filling the old armchair in front of the TV, she couldn't feel anything apart from resentment and, to put it bluntly, contempt. Even though it was only the two of them in the house and her mum was hardly likely to go out anywhere with her health the way it was, she was dressed in a sparkly purple top and her face was fully made up, her hair styled. She was watching a cooking show on TV. It was absurd. She hadn't cooked a proper meal in the kitchen for years now.

'Look,' Sandra said, 'stop pretending you have somewhere to go.'

'I *do* have somewhere to go!'

'So you were invited, were you? Whose party is it?'

Vicky twisted her hands around in front of her. She hadn't been invited. She'd overheard Scott, Martin and Tim talking about it, and was determined to go along too.

'I thought as much,' Sandra said. 'Come and sit down–'

'No!' Vicky said. 'I'm going out.'

Sandra narrowed her eyes. 'Is this about a boy?'

'No,' Vicky said quietly.

'It is, isn't it?' Sandra leaned forward in her armchair, the cookery show forgotten now that she'd found something much more entertaining to focus on. 'What's his name?'

'I'm not telling you.'

'Because he doesn't exist?'

'He does exist.'

'So, he must have a name, then.'

Vicky stopped twisting her hands around and dug her nails into her palm. She wanted to run away from this conversation, from her mum's voice that wormed its way into her mind until it taunted her even when she was away from the house. But even if she ran away from Mum's questions tonight, she'd have to come back home sooner or later. She'd have to go and pick up her mum's prescription tomorrow, help her with the grocery shopping, make sure she was fed and kept swimming in cups of tea. She couldn't avoid these conversations. If she didn't have this one now, she'd only have to have it later. 'Scott,' Vicky said, 'his name is Scott.'

'And he likes you, does he?'

'I don't know. I think so.'

Sandra laughed again, and Vicky snapped. 'He does like me! Why is it so hard to believe?'

'Have you looked in a mirror? Tottering about in heels with those shapeless legs and fat feet of yours, I'll be surprised if you don't fall flat on your face. You look ridiculous. And I don't know what on earth you've done with your face; you look like a toddler who's been playing with Mummy's make-up! You know, when I was your age I used to have boys queuing round the block, but you're about as appealing as a wet flannel. With a personality to match.' Sandra pealed with laughter again, and Vicky saw red. There was a half-empty mug of tea on the table, one that Vicky had made several hours earlier, and she picked it up and threw the cold liquid at her mum's face. For a moment, there was silence. Neither of them could believe what had just happened.

Sandra tried to leap up from the armchair – something that was never going to happen. Instead she flopped back down again, and then began to lever herself up more carefully with the help of the armrests. 'Mum, I'm sorry...' Vicky started.

'You ungrateful little cow,' Sandra snarled. 'When I think how much easier my life could have been if I hadn't had you–'

'You'd have nobody to look after you if it wasn't for me.'

'Do you think I *like* having to rely on you all the time? I hate it! If I could have it any other way–'

Vicky didn't hear the rest. She fled from the house, determined not to return until she absolutely had to. Or at least to try and arrive home with one of the boys, preferably Scott. *That* would give her mum something to chew on, if she managed to get a boy to walk home with her. Maybe it would wipe the smug smile off her face for a day or two at least.

Scott

PRESENT DAY

52

'I had no idea,' Scott said. 'I didn't know your mum treated you like that–'

'Yes, you did. You knew what she was like when the agoraphobia was really bad, how she used to try to "cure" me by kicking me out of her car in the middle of town, among all the people, because she was so angry I couldn't help her out with things like I used to. That's why I had to move out. And you know the funny thing? When I did move out, she managed surprisingly well on her own.'

'I knew what she was like about your agoraphobia,' Scott said, 'but I didn't know she used to laugh at you like that–'

Vicky shrugged. 'Everyone used to laugh at me, and criticise me. You know, she got so far under my skin that I can still hear her now, droning on, putting me down. And she's not even here any more. She's been dead for fucking years now, and I can still hear her.'

Scott was silent for a while. Vicky had had problems with her mum for most of her life, but he genuinely hadn't realised it had been quite so bad. 'So you wanted me to walk you home that night to prove a point to your mum?'

'I thought it would shut her up. And I knew she'd still be angry with me, so I was scared to go home alone. And I...' Vicky's voice trembled, but she quickly got herself back under control. 'I just wanted to feel like I had friends. And for somebody to like me. You know, really like me.'

'I didn't know you felt that way about me.'

'I don't any more. I didn't carry on fancying somebody who got me stabbed.'

'I didn't get you stabbed—'

'You did! I didn't want to go straight home after I realised you had no interest in me, and I didn't want to stay at the party either. I wandered around the streets for ages. I got soaking wet. I was freezing cold. I thought a man had started to follow me, and you know, for a split second, I wasn't sure I even cared what happened to me. Once I realised he really was after me, though, then I got scared. I didn't want to die, even if nobody else in the world gave a shit whether I was alive or dead.'

'We did give a shit—'

'Don't lie to me. None of you were interested in me. I just hung around like a bad smell. I knew I irritated you. But I hoped... you were the only people who seemed to be able to tolerate me, so I thought that was a place to start.'

Scott tried to make sense of it all. Vicky had been very awkward when she was younger, though as an adult she was popular enough. Once she'd got out of her mum's clutches. But how could he forget the way she'd treated Tim, and now him and Felicity? If anything, shouldn't she have known how horrible it was to be bullied and controlled, and not want to inflict it on anybody else? His heart hardened towards her again.

'Vicky, do you know anything about what has happened to Felicity?'

Vicky looked like she'd been slapped. She watched him, speechless, and then she took a step towards him. 'You *still* don't give a shit, do you?' she shouted. 'I just told you all that about me, and all you ask is where your precious Felicity is! Well, I'm not telling you, Scott. You and her, you can both go to hell!'

'You're telling me that you *do* know where she is?'

'Yeah. I do,' she spat, furious. 'But you can't prove anything. I'm not going to help you find her—'

'I'm calling the police,' he said.

Vicky flew at him, and he dodged away from her, shielding his broken arm. He tried to get his phone out but a wave of nausea and exhaustion washed over him and he plonked down onto the edge of the sun-lounger, scared his legs were about to give way. The pain in his elbow was becoming unbearable again; he must be due more painkillers. 'Tell me where she is!' he said desperately to Vicky, but the scrape of iron on concrete distracted her, and she looked round behind her at the garden gate. Martin came into the garden first, followed by two police officers. Vicky stared at Scott, her eyes huge and glassy with fear.

'Vicky, tell me where she is,' Scott said as calmly as he could, while he struggled to get to his feet. 'If you try and cover this up, you're going to make everything so much worse.'

'It can't get any worse,' Vicky said.

Scott

53

'So they *arrested* Vicky?' Natasha said again, even though they'd already gone through it all with her.

'She told me that she knows where Felicity is,' Scott said, because he couldn't think about anything else. 'She *knows* where she is!'

'Don't get worked up again,' Natasha said calmly, 'you—'

'She knows what Jay is capable of!' Scott shouted, 'and yet she's happy to let Felicity be raped, and beaten, and most likely murdered, just to make some stupid fucking point to me!'

'Scott—'

'She's lucky the police came when they did! I wouldn't be responsible for my actions if I'd been left with her much longer!'

They both looked round as Martin came in, carrying a couple of mugs of tea. He handed one to each of them. Scott stared down at the brown liquid. 'How does this help?' he said.

'I've put four sugars in it. Since you won't eat anything—'

'I can't eat right now! All I can think about is Felicity, and Vicky, and what she's done—'

Natasha touched his arm. 'None of us can believe it, Scott,' she said softly. 'And as for what she said about Dennis not being yours, I... I'm so sorry.'

Scott tried to calm down, and he took a few sips of the sweet tea. 'It makes no difference to me whose Den really is,' he said finally. 'A part of me always suspected, but it doesn't matter Dennis is my son, and I love him. It's as simple as that.'

'Yes,' Natasha said, 'you're right. And you've always been a fantastic dad, and you've tried to help Vicky too.' Her face contorted with disgust. 'Not that she deserved it.'

'The police will get her to talk,' Martin said. 'I'm sure she won't make things even worse for herself trying to cover for Jay.'

'I don't know,' Scott said. 'I just don't know anything any more.'

Suddenly, his emotion overtook him. He thrust the hateful mug of tea back into Martin's hands. 'I can't... I can't take all of this. I can't take it!' He ran out of the room, and out of the house.

...

He wandered aimlessly for a while, not thinking where he was going, until eventually he ended up on Alstercombe beach. Kicking up sprays of shingle, he walked angrily across the bay, finally throwing himself down and glaring out at the sea. After about half an hour had passed, a hand on his back made him jump, and then Martin sat down beside him. 'I guessed you would come here.'

'Yeah.'

'You left your phone at the house.' He held it out and Scott took it. 'There's good news,' Martin said.

'There is?'

'They've got an address in Scotland. They think that's where Jay has taken Felicity.'

Scott stared at him, a surge of hope filling his body. 'Vicky told them?'

'I don't know. But they seem pretty confident. The local police have got cars on their way there now. It's remote, but it still won't be long.'

Scott tried to stand. 'We need to go there!'

'Let's... let's not be too hasty just yet.'

Scott glared at Martin. 'Just say it,' he said. 'The police think she might be dead. Or that Jay might have moved her somewhere else.'

Martin didn't reply.

Scott's mind was racing. What should he do? What would Felicity need from him? 'Let's get back to the house,' he said quickly. 'Help me up. I still feel kind of… bad.'

'That's because you discharged yourself from hospital and spent most of today marching around Alstercombe without eating.'

'Yeah, I… I've been an idiot. I know you and Tash are trying to help me. I'll eat something back at the house, I promise. I need to be strong for when they find Fliss.' He held out his good arm, and Martin helped him to his feet.

Felicity

54

Jay sat up in bed, staring at me. He didn't seem scared. Instead, when his eyes flicked from the knife in my hand to my face, he just looked disappointed in me.

'Come on, then,' he said. 'If you want to stab me, then stab me. You couldn't hurt me any more than you already have. I'm not scared of dying.'

I took a step closer. 'I'm serious, Jay.'

'I know you are. So am I.'

I faltered. What was I supposed to do? He wasn't afraid of me, but surely he was afraid of dying, no matter what he'd just said. He just didn't think I'd actually hurt him. I stood still, my eyes fixed on him. He had Leo somewhere. He was hiding my son from me, and he was never going to tell me where he was. I lunged towards him, and he didn't even flinch.

'Tell me where he is!' I yelled, holding the knife inches from his throat. My hand was shaking. I had no idea what I was doing, but I was desperate.

'Fliss, you're not going to stab me,' he said, though I thought I saw a flicker of fear in his eyes. 'If I die, I definitely won't be able to tell you where Leo is.'

'Just tell me!' I screamed.

Before I knew it, he'd grabbed my wrist with both of his hands, and I was fighting to hold on to the knife. Fear overtook me and I clung desperately, but he was pushing the knife back towards me. My eyes fixed on the blade, and as Jay forced it in my direction I released my grip on it in a desperate bid to try to make it go away. He immediately snatched it up.

'You're a very stupid girl, Fliss,' he said, gripping the knife. 'How did you think that was going to end?'

NEVER LET HER GO

'I just want my son. I want Leo. Please… I wasn't going to hurt you. I don't want to hurt you, I just want Leo.'

Jay nodded. He lowered the knife, but he was still holding it in his lap. 'You know, my dad always told me that women were bad news.'

'What do you mean?' I asked shakily.

'That they lie. Cheat. Betray you. Hurt you. Make you feel weak and hopeless.'

I didn't reply.

'I wanted to believe he was wrong. But life has taught me otherwise. Apart from Sammie, of course. Sammie was the only good one.'

I kept watching the knife in his lap. He was holding the handle firmly, but the blade was resting harmlessly against the duvet. God, why had I done this? One wrong word now and he could slash my skin open with that knife. Or kill me with it. *He hates blood, though.* Would that be enough to stop him? I had to hope so. And I had to pick my words carefully.

'I… I'm sorry about what happened with Sammie,' I stammered. 'I know how much you loved her—'

'Love,' he corrected me.

An idea suddenly struck me. 'Would Sammie want you to do this?' I asked. 'Would she want you to separate me from Leo? To keep me in this house?'

'She'd think you were an ungrateful little bitch for turning away someone who wants so badly to be with you.'

I swallowed hard. 'Sammie loved you so much, Jay. I know she did. She'd want you to be with somebody who deserves you.'

Jay's mouth twisted into an unpleasant smile. 'Don't try to be clever.'

'What can I do? What can I do to make things better?'

'Nothing. There's nothing you can do now. You don't want to be a family, fine. I accept that now. But you don't get to be a family with anyone else.'

...

Seconds ticked by. He wasn't looking at me, he was looking down at the knife. Was he considering attacking me with it? Was he planning his next moves? Terrified, I leapt up and ran from the room, but in the hall I didn't know where to go. The front door was locked, and I was suddenly overcome with nausea so I fled into the bathroom, where I threw up, and then I tried to open the small window behind the toilet. It was locked too. I looked around for something to smash it with, but the bathroom was bare; there was nothing apart from our towels, our toothbrushes and a couple of other toiletries. I was sick again, and then I collapsed exhausted against the bath. I couldn't get out.

Jay was in the hall, and he came slowly into the room, and took a long look at me. The pieces clicked into place in his mind – I saw the moment he figured it out. There was nothing I could do to stop it. 'Are you… are you *pregnant?*' he asked.

I shook my head.

'You're a terrible liar, you know that, Flissie.'

'I'm not!' I said, 'I swear I'm not–'

Jay crouched down in front of me and I cowered against the bath. He was still holding the knife. I had nowhere to go. There was nothing I could do.

I'm going to die.

Jay

55

It hurt to think, but the voice in his head wouldn't stop talking. *She has a baby inside her. Scott's baby, growing and swelling in there, like a disgusting little parasite. Growing because she spent so much time fucking Scott. Every night, probably. Over and over, with him, when she should have been with me…* He put his hand up to his head. He was losing the plot. Felicity's eyes were huge, and she was pressing herself so hard against the bath in a bid to get away from him that he could almost imagine her disappearing into it. 'You could have had everything, you know,' Jay said slowly. 'But instead you push me and push me and push me. It's like you want to see me break!'

'I don't. I'm sorry, Jay. I'm sorry I've hurt you so much. I didn't mean to, I just—'

Swiftly, he raised the knife, holding it against her cheek, and she squealed with fear. 'No! Not my face, not my face—'

'Why not your face? What does it matter what your face looks like, hm? Unless you want men to want you. *Is* that what you care about?'

A tear fell from the corner of her eye onto the knife blade and trickled down the metal. She was shaking uncontrollably, trying to back away, but she had nowhere to go.

'Do you think Scott ever loved you the way I do?' he asked.

'No… Yes…' she sobbed, confused. 'I mean no… I don't know.'

'*Scott* was only interested in you because you're so easy. You're a slut, Fliss. You always have been, and you always will be. I wish I'd realised it sooner.'

'I'm sorry! I'm sorry. Please, please—'

'Don't beg like that! It's not endearing! It's pathetic. It makes me sick to even look at you.'

She stopped talking, but her eyes were still silently pleading. Was this really what he'd come to? Threatening to cut the face of a terrified pregnant woman? He pressed the knife harder, and it began to cut into her skin. She whimpered, but didn't speak. He wasn't the monster here. He wasn't doing this because he enjoyed it. He was doing it because she'd betrayed him, over and over again. He was justified.

'No one will want you any more, you know that?' he told her. 'You're dirty. You're used. No other man will ever be able to love you.'

'You... you're right,' she said. She didn't mean it, though. That was obvious. She was just trying to calm him down.

'I don't understand why you won't even give me a chance!' he said. 'It never had to end up like this. This is your own fault!'

He pushed her back against the bath, but to his surprise she kicked out at him hard with her legs, knocking him off balance. The knife slashed across her cheek as he fell, and thick drops of blood began to leak from the wound. His eyes fixed on it. He couldn't look away, though it horrified him. *Blood! Dirt.* Why had she decided to bring a knife into things? He hated knives. He'd only use them as a last resort, like when he'd needed to get information from Vicky, fast.

While he was distracted, Felicity took her opportunity to strike. She shoved him hard while he was still off balance, and he toppled to the floor. She scrambled to her feet, and then turned and kicked him in the groin.

Pain exploded in his body and for a time he was incapacitated, curled up on the floor while she sprinted through to the living room. She was going to run away. She'd obviously given up on getting answers from him about Leo, and was only interested now in preserving her own life. Hot anger flooded his body as he listened to the sounds of her making her escape, and as soon as he was able, he pulled himself to his feet. He ran after her, reaching the living room just in time to see her disappearing through the open window. He quickly followed, catching up with her as she raced down the grass towards the narrow track, and he wrestled her to the ground. Before he knew what he was doing, his hands were around her throat, and he squeezed, and squeezed, while Felicity grabbed desperately at his arms, trying to push him away.

. . .

Moments ticked by. Felicity's struggles, initially frantic, grew weaker. Jay stared down at her face, her short blonde hair splayed around her against the scrubby grass, her blue eyes losing their light and life, the cut on her cheek, steadily oozing blood. Suddenly, it was as though he was no longer looking at Felicity. Instead he saw Sammie: her panicked face as he pinned her against the wall in her family's home, squeezing and squeezing her throat because he believed she'd been cheating on him. He released his hands from her throat, his eyes filling with tears. 'Sammie, no,' he said, 'I'm sorry. I didn't mean to! I didn't mean to.'

The woman's face turned back to Felicity's again. She rolled over to her side, coughing and straining to get her breath back, but Jay carried on kneeling, transfixed by his memories. Sammie when he'd hit her, with blood on her lip. Sammie when he'd attacked her in Tatchley wood, her clothes and face all messed up with bits of leaves and mud, Sammie trying to reason with him, telling him over and over that Mark was trying to mess with his head, and he hadn't believed her. Tears rolled down his cheeks. He thought of Stephanie, blood in her hair, lying dead in the living room of her house, and his eyes fell to Felicity again, still gasping for air. What had he done? What had he *done?*

Felicity

56

As soon as I could breathe again I tried to run, but Jay grabbed me by the ankle and I stumbled. 'Let go!' I screamed at him. 'Let me go!'

'I can't let you go,' he said. He was crying, and his voice was oddly low and soft. 'I can't let you go, Flissie. I love you. We have to be together.'

I tried to shake his hand from my leg but he was hanging on with all his strength. 'Get off me!' I said. 'Get the fuck off me!'

'Everyone who ever cared about me is dead,' he said. 'You're the only one left.'

I cried out in frustration, and turned to look down at him. 'Then tell me where Leo is.'

'I... I will. I will tell you.'

I crouched down beside him, though it took every ounce of my willpower. All I wanted was to run. After all, was he really likely to tell me now? Probably not, but I had to take the chance. 'Go on, then.'

He didn't speak straight away, and then he said, 'I'm sorry about your face. Come back inside and I'll clean it for you. It's not a deep cut, but it's bleeding a fair bit.'

I reached up to my face, and when I lowered my fingers they were smeared with blood. 'I'm not going inside with you.'

'Fliss, please. I didn't mean to hurt you. I never meant to hurt anyone. Not you. Not... not Sammie.' His eyes went misty. 'Especially not Sammie. I never meant to hurt her. I was a kid! I didn't know what the fuck I was doing. I couldn't... I couldn't deal with it. With what... I...'

He couldn't finish his sentence. I stared at him. Was this him being reasonable for a moment? I spoke gently. 'You mean that you couldn't deal with what you felt?'

'Don't pretend you understand.'

I forced myself to touch his arm, and he looked at me in surprise. 'I *do* understand,' I said softly. 'I know how much you want to feel like part of a family. I know how much it hurts you when people let you down. You and Sammie both wanted to feel like you belonged, I get that. But sixteen is so young to have a relationship that intense, and nobody realised you were having trouble dealing with it. *Somebody* should have realised, Jay. I wish somebody had. You could have got help before it was too late.'

'I didn't need help. I just needed Mark to not fuck things up.'

I took a deep breath. I had to try to get through to him. 'Jay, how old was your mum when she had you?'

He didn't seem to hear my question. Instead, his eyes were wide, wild. 'I don't want to go to prison, Fliss,' he said. 'I can't go to prison. I'm not… I never meant to do any of this!'

'I know that. But Jay, please, listen to me. You're suffering, I can see that. You're lashing out because you hurt so much and you've driven everybody away.'

'Not you, not yet.'

'I'm here because I want Leo.'

'Then you're a selfish bitch!' he shouted.

'Jay, listen to me. I know you love me, and I believe you love Leo too, don't you?'

He nodded.

'Leo is just a little boy who needs his mummy. I'm sure you of all people understand that.'

He glared at me. 'You think that's why I'm like this? Because I have *mummy issues?* Is that why you started asking me about her?'

'I'm trying to understand. Just talk to me, Jay. You obviously need to talk to somebody.'

I thought he was going to shout at me, then he said, 'She was sixteen.'

I nodded. 'Like Sammie would have been, if she'd had your baby.'

He gave me a warning look.

'And how old was your dad when you were born?'

'I don't know. Early twenties, I guess. What the hell does this have to do with anything?'

'Jay, did your mum ever tell you why she left you?'

'I don't want to talk about this. It's not important.'

'Please, Jay.'

He shrugged angrily. 'I don't know. I never really listened to her. It was just noise.'

'I don't believe that you didn't listen.'

'I don't give a fuck what you believe.'

'Isn't it possible that you want a family so much now because you feel like you didn't have one when you were a child? That you're so set on everything being perfect that you're trying to control everything? But people don't like being controlled. Jay, I loved you, but you trapped me. You frightened me. Whether you truly meant to or not. And, I mean, you say you love me and Leo, and I'm not saying you don't, but since I've been here you haven't even asked anything about us. You haven't asked me what Leo likes doing, what his personality is like. And you haven't so much as asked me how I am. Maybe you love the *idea* of us, more than anything else. And you can't make us fit your ideal. People don't fit nicely into moulds, Jay, and when you try to force us, all we do is break.'

'I never did anything to you that you didn't bring on yourself!'

'Okay, well–'

'And my mum brought everything on herself, too! She used to drive Dad mad, wanting to go out partying with her friends all the time. She had a baby! She had responsibilities! He said he couldn't trust her to do anything, not even to go back and try to get her exams, because if he let her out of his sight she'd be gone. He said she didn't love us.'

'I bet you anything in the world that that wasn't true,' I said. 'She may not have loved your dad, but I'm sure she loved you.'

'She was really fucking great at showing it.'

'Yes, she left. But she came back, didn't she? When you needed her. Look, I don't want to start speaking against your

213

dad, but doesn't what happened between your parents sound a little bit like what happened between you and Sammie? Between you and me?'

Jay didn't answer. He'd shut down again. 'Let me clean your face,' he said.

. . .

Reluctantly, I followed him back towards the building, but I refused to go inside. I sat on the grass near his van, and after a few minutes Jay came out, dressed in jeans and a t-shirt instead of the shorts he'd been wearing when I'd woken him in bed – and carrying a little first aid kit. He sat beside me and cleaned my face, covering the cut with a large dressing. 'We could still go,' he said. 'Just get in the van and drive somewhere. Start again. I told you how Steph and I made things work. It's still not too late. You could do the same, we won't get caught.'

'That's no life for any of us.'

He was silent for a time. 'This is your last chance, Fliss,' he said.

'What do you mean, my last chance?'

'I'm not going to let you walk away from this. You do not get to go back to your life – back to Scott. Back to Leo.'

I stared at him. Back to Scott? What was he talking about?

He smiled nastily. 'Scott's alive,' he said, as if it was no big deal. 'And Leo's fine too, by the way. You know how much it hurts me, that you think I would put our son in danger? He was never in danger. He was with that ex of Scott's. Only she got scared and left him near Natasha's house. That's who has Leo now.'

My mind was racing. Scott was alive? Leo was with Natasha and Zack? Vicky really had been involved? *The miscarriage. That was how Jay knew, just as I suspected.* I tried to stand. My heart was crying out to be with Scott and Leo, my body surging with emotion now I knew that they were both safe, that Scott was alive. Alive! But Jay pulled me back down. 'Last chance,' he said again.

Fear began to seep through me. 'Last chance before what?'

Jay

57

Deep down, he'd suspected it would come to this. That was why he'd brought the tape out with him. She would never go with him willingly. He'd never get her to do anything willingly. She struggled when he grabbed her and taped her wrists behind her back, but he managed to do it, and then he bound her ankles too. 'Jay, don't do this!' she cried. 'Let me go, let me go!'

'I'm not going to let you go,' he said calmly. 'I haven't decided what I'm going to do with you yet. But I have decided what I'm going to do about Scott.'

She stared at him with her eyes wide. 'Jay...'

'There's really no other way,' he said. 'I can't let you be with him, Fliss. I can't let him bring up my son.'

'I won't go back to him!' she said. 'I'll leave him, if that's what it takes.'

'I have no way of knowing you'll stay true to your word, do I? As soon as you're away from me, you're just going to do whatever the fuck you want. So, you see, I'm going to have to kill him, Felicity.'

'Jay, think about it,' she pleaded, struggling against the tape that bound her. 'You said you don't want to go to prison—'

'I'm going to end up there anyway. I've got no way out of this, you've told me that yourself.'

'But you can make it less bad for yourself. Jay, please. Just let me go, and leave Scott alone. Not for my sake, for Leo's. How do you think he'd feel if he knew you'd killed Scott? The only father he's ever known.'

He slammed his fist down next to her head and she gasped, trying to wriggle away. 'It's not my fault Scott's the only father he's ever known!' he shouted. 'That's *your* fault!'

'Yes,' she said, 'yes, it's *my* fault. It's not *Leo's* fault. So don't hurt him like this. Don't make it so I have to tell him what you've done. Make it so I can tell him you let me go. Make it so I can tell him that you love him, because I *will* tell him, I promise. Maybe... I could even bring him to see you, in prison. I'll make sure he knows who you are, once he's old enough to understand. I'll tell him all about you. The good stuff, I mean. Because there *is* good stuff. You're not a psycho, Jay, I know that. You don't do this stuff because you don't have feelings, you do it because you lose control. You can get help. I'm sure you could get help in prison, if you can just take a step back and think about what you're doing.'

Jay considered it, briefly. But what the fuck did it matter any more? He would never have a relationship with Leo. Felicity would probably never tell Leo that he loved him. She was just saying whatever she could think of to save Scott's life. That was all she cared about.

He picked up the tape, and though Felicity protested and tried to squirm away, he tore off a strip and stuck it over her mouth. He smiled. 'Yes,' he said, 'I'll go and kill Scott. But first, I need to lure him out.'

Taking his phone from his pocket, he turned it on and snapped a picture of Felicity. It made him a little nervous to turn his phone on – he'd kept it off since he'd left Alstercombe – but he needed to contact Scott, and this was the only way. Then he dragged Felicity over to the van and locked her in the back. He sighed. He had done almost exactly the same thing when he took her to the house in Tatchley. But this time there was no point driving her anywhere else. He'd reached the end of the road with her. In fact, there wasn't much reason to take her with him at all, but he couldn't face the idea of leaving her behind. He needed her near him, he needed *somebody* near him. Somebody who had loved him once.

He had to drive for a few minutes before his phone got any signal, and when it did he quickly pulled over. First off, he checked the news. A few quick searches revealed something

217

damning. He'd read things about himself in the past – notices urging the public to look out for him, but now there were fresh ones: appeals for information, for witnesses, dire warnings that he was dangerous and to not approach him. None of that mattered. What did matter, was one small sentence.

Kilburn has connections with the towns of Coalton, Tatchley, Alstercombe and Wrexton.

His heart skipped a beat. Wrexton. They had found Stephanie. That's surely what it meant. They'd found her, that's how they knew he'd been in Wrexton, and if they'd found her they would have gone through her mobile. Jay stared at the phone in his hand as if he was holding a live grenade. Could the police tell where he was from his phone? He needed to get rid of it!

Scott. Focus on Scott.

Yes. He'd gone too far to back out now. He'd get rid of his phone as soon as he could, but he had work to do first. He quickly found a social media page about Scott's furniture business, and since he had no other way of contacting him, he sent him a private message containing the image of Felicity bound and gagged. *I'll give her back to you,* he typed, *come to me alone. No police. Wait for me to tell you where.*

Now, he just had to find somewhere to meet him. Somewhere quiet, with a good opportunity to ambush Scott. He'd drive around until he found somewhere. Hopefully it wouldn't take too long to discover a good spot.

Scott

58

'No,' Martin said, when Scott showed him the photo, and read out the message. 'Don't even think about it. You need to tell the police.'

They were driving up to Scotland. Scott had gone back to Natasha's house briefly, forced down a sandwich, and then insisted that they get on the road so they'd be close by if the police found Felicity.

Abruptly, Martin pulled over in a lay-by and gave Scott a stern look. 'If you won't call the police, I will.'

He took out his phone, and Scott grabbed it from his hand. 'You saw what he said. He's got Felicity–'

'Don't be so stupid!' Martin said. 'Do you really think he's going to hand her over to you? It's a trap, Scott. He's going to make you meet him somewhere with promises that Felicity will be there, but she won't be. It'll just be him.'

'I'm not scared of him.'

'Well, you should be! I'm not taking you anywhere to meet him. You need to call the police, right now.'

Scott's mind was racing. Martin was probably right, but that photo of Felicity was overwhelming. He couldn't get it out of his head. She was tied up, her eyes terrified. A plaster covered her cheek and a huge bruise bloomed around her nose. His emotions boiled over.

'Just carry on driving!' he said. 'He's probably still in Scotland somewhere–'

'No way.'

'Then I'll do it myself!'

He started to open his door, and Martin said, 'For God's sake, Scott. Stop. Think. This is fucking crazy.'

'That animal has done who knows what to her. She needed me, and I was halfway up a mountain with you! I'm not abandoning her now.'

'He got her to go to him by making her think Leo was in danger. He's doing the same with you, surely you can see that.'

Scott took several deep breaths.

'Martin,' he said firmly, 'we've known each other since we were kids. I've helped you out before… nothing quite like this, but we've got each other's backs. That's how it's supposed to be, isn't it?'

'You're not going to talk me into this.'

'Listen.'

'No.'

'Listen!' Scott insisted. 'Felicity is the love of my life, and that man *terrorised* her. I'm not going to let him think he's won. I can't… I've got to face him.'

Martin gave him a long look. 'What do you care what he thinks? Are you seriously going to risk your life out of some sort of pride? It's ridiculous. You won't be able to look after Felicity if you're dead.'

'I'm not going to die.'

'No? Even at the best of times this would be a terrible idea, but look at you now. You've got a broken arm! Let's just say, for one crazy moment, that I took you to meet him. What are you going to do if he attacks you? Give him a little kick in the shins?'

'I've only broken one arm, not both of them.'

'What if he has a knife? Or a gun?'

'He doesn't have a bloody *gun*, Martin. He's not some sort of gangster, he's just a coward who bullies women.'

'And beat a man to death.'

'Are you going to help me, or not? Because if you won't, I'll just get myself a taxi, and then I'll be in even more danger.'

Martin shook his head. 'This is such a bad idea.'

'Does that mean you'll do it?'

Martin didn't reply.

'Will you do it?' Scott pressed him.

'I'll go in with you, to wherever he tells you to go,' Martin said finally. 'I'm not going to sit in the car while you go and get yourself killed.'

'He'll freak out if he sees you.'

'Then it's a no.'

Scott sighed in exasperation. He held out his phone with the photo of Felicity. 'Look at what he's done to her!'

'I know. It's sickening. Scott, I understand you want to beat the crap out of him, I would too if I was you. In fact, I want to just because of what he's done to you and Fliss.'

'There you are, then.'

'Felicity would not want you to fall for this. She'd tell you to call the police.'

Scott was silent for a long time. 'When he tells me where to meet him, take me there, Martin. Please. If I don't come back with Felicity within a couple of minutes of getting out of the car, call the police. Or come in after me. Both.'

'I am one hundred per cent sure that Felicity is not going to be there.'

'Fine. That's up to you. But even if she isn't, I… I just want to look him in the eye. I want to face him. I need to.'

'I must have lost my mind,' Martin said, as he started the engine. The second he started to pull away, the phone bleeped again. There was an address. And the words: *This is where I will leave her. How long will it take you to get here?*

Felicity

59

Jay started driving almost as soon as he had thrown me into the van. But to my surprise, he pulled over almost straight away. What was he doing? Immediately, I understood. He was sending a message to Scott. Depending on how quickly he found a way to contact him, I might have a few minutes. If he was distracted enough, could I let myself out of the van without him even realising I was gone? I didn't have time to try to cut my bonds, and it was pitch black in the van, so it would be hard to find anything to use. But perhaps I could get to the rear doors and let myself out. If I did it without him noticing, he would simply drive away. I'd have plenty of time then to try to cut the tape, and once free I could run down the track until I found civilisation.

It wasn't likely to work, though. In fact, it was pretty crazy. Jay would have to be very distracted. But it was worth a try. So, while the van was stationary, I rolled around, trying to lever myself up. Instead, I flopped around like a dying fish, ending up on my stomach, nearly crying in frustration. *Focus. Stay calm.*

I rolled slowly onto my side. Then I managed to use my hands behind my back to push myself upright into a sitting position. Good. I took a deep breath and let it out slowly. From there, I got up onto my knees, and rose steadily to my feet. My ankles were tied so tightly I could barely move my feet at all, but with an effort I jumped towards the door. It made a loud noise. Would Jay assume I was just innocently moving about? He'd expect me to struggle, surely. A couple of bangs wouldn't worry him unduly, would they? I prepared myself for another jump, and the van pulled away, fast. I fell hard, my head colliding with something heavy and solid, and then the darkness inside the van became even blacker.

Scott

60

Martin found the house easily enough, and parked a little distance away so they could scope it out before Scott committed to going inside.

'So, this is it,' Scott said, casting his eye over the street. It was deserted. The address Jay had given them was an abandoned building project on a run-down street. It was fenced off, but one of the graffitied fence panels was loose. That must be how Jay had got in. Scott shuddered. It was as uninviting a place as he could imagine.

'I don't like this at all,' Martin said.

'I know you don't. Look, we stick to the plan. There's a chance he's telling the truth. He might genuinely want me to go and get Felicity.'

'The hell he does.'

'I know what you think about it, but my mind is made up. We'll park a bit of a way away, and I'll walk back down.'

They parked just around the corner, near a block of garages where a couple of old cars sat rusting. Scott got out and made his way back down the street, slipping through the gap in the fence into the building site, where the half-finished house took up most of the plot. It was boarded up, but there was a way in through one of the windows at the back, where the board had been torn away.

Inside, he stood in a large, dim, apparently empty space, lit only by the small amount of sunlight making it in through the one window. Before he'd taken two steps, the back of his thighs exploded with pain and he crashed to the floor, only narrowly avoiding landing on his broken arm. The movement still jarred his arm, though, and he cried out in pain as he rolled and tried to look up at his attacker, but there was nobody there. Then a figure appeared behind him.

Scott just about managed to jerk himself out of the way as a metal bar swung towards him, but his movement was limited. He wouldn't be able to keep dodging the attacks for long. If nothing else, he'd grow exhausted. Adrenalin wasn't enough – he was still too weak after his accident. Martin had been right. What the fuck had he been thinking? Expecting more blows, he curled up on the floor, his elbow still screaming with pain after the jolt it had just received. He couldn't even look up at Jay. Finally, the pain subsided enough that he could speak. 'Where… where is she?' he asked. He raised his head, and Jay crouched down beside him.

'She's not here,' he said.

Scott tried to stay calm, focused. He had expected this, after all. Jay was rotating the metal bar menacingly in his hand, and Scott couldn't help but start to panic. But he couldn't let his fear show. 'Why do you want me, then?' he asked.

'I would have thought that was obvious.'

Scott felt weak and helpless, his exhausted body pushed to its limit. But he fixed his eyes on Jay. 'Killing me won't make Felicity love you.'

Jay smiled. 'Perhaps not. But it'll make me feel better knowing that you're never going to get your hands on her again.'

'So,' Scott said, 'why are you waiting? You've got a pretty effective weapon there, why not just crack on?'

'Oh, I will. I wanted to tell you a few things first. Like who it was who helped me to take Felicity. I thought you'd be interested to know.' Jay took out his phone, and started to play a recording he'd made of himself and Vicky talking. Arguing, in fact. She was angry that Jay had brought Leo to her house, she was saying he was supposed to take them both; Felicity and Leo. It made Scott feel sick. Jay was clearly enjoying his reaction. 'Bet you didn't expect that,' he said. 'The mother of your child, hating you so much that–'

'I know it was Vicky,' Scott said. 'I worked it out myself.'

Jay stopped the recording. He looked disappointed, but he

quickly rallied, putting the phone away and getting a firm grip on the metal bar again. Scott's heart was pounding. How was he going to get out of this? Martin would have called the police by now, surely. And Martin would come to find him soon, once he got worried about how much time had passed. He only needed to make sure Jay stayed talking a few minutes more. But he was so angry, and he couldn't think straight.

'You know, I'm glad I've met you,' he said. 'I always wondered what sort of lowlife would treat women like you do, and now I know.'

Jay slammed the metal bar down on the floor, inches from Scott's face. But then he went back to holding the bar in his hands, a contemplative expression on his face. 'Sometimes I wonder, if I could count them all up, how many times I've fucked Felicity over the years. I mean, I've known her quite a while now, and although we had a little... break... she was pretty wild when I first knew her. I don't think I've ever known a woman who loves fucking as much as she does.'

He gave Scott a scathing look. 'Oh, your experience with her is different, is it?' he said, though Scott hadn't made any reply. Jay moved closer to him. 'Maybe it's because, no matter what she tries to tell herself, she *likes* someone to take control. To show her who's in charge.'

Scott was overcome by a surge of rage so intense that he lurched across the floor towards Jay, punching him in the face with his free arm. Then he collapsed to the floor in a heap, while Jay laughed and wiped some blood from his lip.

'I'll let you have that one,' he said, 'I know it's not nice finding out about who Felicity was in the past.'

'I don't blame her for anything that happened to her. I blame *you.*'

Jay smiled. 'You can tell yourself whatever you want. I wonder, Scott, why did you come here? You must have known I wouldn't give Felicity to you. I imagine you're telling yourself you came here to help her, and to teach me a lesson. But it's not true. I know what the truth is. You came here because you don't like the fact that I know every inch of her body. That *I'm* Leo's father. That I'm always going to be inside her head, every day, for the rest of her life. You came here because you're *jealous* of me.'

Scott swallowed hard. He couldn't let Jay play mind games with him like this, but he found himself yelling, '*I'm* Leo's dad. Felicity wants to be with *me*!'

Jay raised the metal bar, and Scott cowered against the floor. But then the sound of sirens made them both pause. The effect on Jay was instant. He froze, terrified. Scott braced himself, expecting the metal bar to come crashing down, but it didn't. Jay dropped it, his face a mask of panic. He scurried off towards the window, and disappeared.

Martin

61

Martin didn't wait for even a couple of minutes to call the police. He did it as soon as Scott was out of the car, and then he got out himself, intending to follow Scott down the road. But then something caught his eye. At the end of the block of garages was a patch of waste land, with tufts of grass growing up between cracked concrete, an old sofa and a few black bin bags that had torn and spilt their contents. That wasn't what had caught his eye, though. Round the side of the garage block, almost behind it, was a white van. And unless he was very much mistaken, it had just moved, as though something alive was moving around inside it. He frowned, squinting at the van. There! It did it again.

He approached it cautiously. Could it be Jay's van? Probably not, really. For all he knew there might be a couple having sex in it, or something stupid like that. He was about to turn away and rush after Scott, but then it hit him. Scott had said Jay used to drive a white van. And Jay had Felicity somewhere. His mind made up, he ran over to it.

'Felicity?' he called out. 'Felicity? It's Martin. Are you in there?'

He put his ear up against the door. Was that a moaning sound inside? 'Felicity? Are you in there? It's Martin. Can you answer me and let me know if you're okay?'

There was a feeble banging sound from within. He tried to open the doors, but the van was locked. 'Felicity, you're going to be okay,' he said. 'The police are coming. Scott is here–'

He heard a squealing noise. She banged again, more urgently this time.

'Is Scott in danger?' he asked, though it was a stupid question.

They both knew the answer. 'Has Jay come to hurt him?'

More banging.

Martin turned, intending to sprint back towards the house, but he stopped in his tracks. There was a man standing motionless at the other end of the garage block, with blood on his face. Martin peered closely. Was it Jay?

Unsure what to do, Martin stayed frozen on the spot. But when the sounds of sirens filled the air the man made a dash for the van. It *was* Jay. It had to be. Martin tried to stand in his way, but Jay was like a man possessed. He slammed into Martin, practically throwing him out of the way, and scrambled into the van. Martin turned to see Scott, half-running, half-limping.

'Felicity is in the van!' Martin yelled. 'She's in the van!'

They rushed to stand in the way of Jay's escape, but he drove the van at them full pelt, and they were forced to jump out of its path. 'In the car!' Scott said. 'After him, quickly!'

Felicity

62

My heart was racing. I'd only just come round, and before Martin's words had truly sunk in, the van had started moving again. Fast. Very fast. What had Martin said? Scott was here somewhere? He'd come to meet Jay? There had been some yelling before the van moved; Martin had been calling to somebody that I was inside the van. Scott? Had he been telling Scott?

The van swung round a corner, and I slammed into a hard plastic object. I rolled over, so that I could touch it with my bound hands. Was it what I thought it was? Torturously slowly, I moved my fingers over the plastic toolbox, finding the catch where a metal bar hooked over a clip to keep it closed. I tried to keep my breathing slow and calm as I tried once, twice, three times to lift the bar away from the clip. Finally, I did it. I pushed the lid back, and felt around inside. There were screwdrivers, a hammer, pliers. I was making sounds in my throat, desperate moans and cries of frustration, useless sounds, drowned out by the van and the sirens.

My fingers closed around cold metal. This was what I was looking for; at least, it certainly felt like it. I gripped it with difficulty, crying out in frustration as my bound wrists made everything so difficult. But this was my only hope. I wouldn't be able to stand up with the van moving like this. I had to cut the tape to stand a chance of making it to the door. If I could get the blade on this Stanley knife to come out, then I could turn it and bring the knife edge against the tape. I pressed and poked at the handle. Jay was driving fast. There were sirens everywhere. Perhaps they'd manage to stop the van and rescue me, but I couldn't take any chances. I cried out in frustration yet again, but at the same moment I obviously did something right. The blade popped out. I turned the knife in my hands, fumbling and awkward, and it cut into one of my fingers. Tears spilt from my eyes, but I had to carry on. I had to save myself.

Jay

The sound of the sirens filled his mind. He drove madly, blindly, panicking at the police cars behind him. This couldn't be real. This couldn't be happening to him.

Some tears splashed onto his cheeks and he wiped them away. He couldn't go to prison. He couldn't bear it – trapped in there, with nothing to think about but what he'd done, with no hope of ever being with his family.

You have no hope of that anyway, his mind nagged him. Felicity hates you. She'll never let you be a part of her life. She'll never let you be a part of Leo's life.

'Fuck!' he yelled out loud. He'd lost everything. It was all gone, everything gone.

Police cars filled his rear-view mirror. Would they block the road ahead? He looked around wildly. There had to be a way out of this. There had to be.

A way out to what? What have you got left?

His tears were flowing freely now. How had he fucked everything up so badly? Why was his life like this?

Panicking, he took a turn to the left, into an industrial estate. He didn't slow his speed for a second, and he was sobbing as he set his sights on the side of a large, pale grey warehouse.

Felicity

After a sharp turn, Jay began to drive very fast in a straight line, just as I finished slicing through the tape around my wrists. I brought the knife to my ankles, hacking madly at the tape, and I tore away the piece that was covering my mouth. I ran across the floor of the van, legs unsteady, and my hand closed around the handle on the door. To begin with, I was in such a blind panic I couldn't open it. But I was sure the door was supposed to open if someone tried the handle from the inside. I pushed down again, harder. It was stiff, but finally the door swung open, and there was tarmac speeding by beneath the van. We weren't on a normal road. It was a car park. Jay was no longer trying to escape, that was clear. He was driving towards something; a building, a vertical drop, I didn't know what. But instantly it hit me that he was trying to kill himself, and his efforts would likely kill me too. The tarmac was moving so fast beneath the van. I screamed, and I jumped.

Jay

He pressed the accelerator pedal to the floor, and the warehouse wall grew bigger, closer. He closed his eyes. 'Sammie,' he whispered. 'Sammie, I'm coming. Sammie, I love–'

He opened his eyes a crack. '–you,' he said. His vision was all wall now. Then, it was as if the wall and the van exploded; a smashing, cracking, apocalyptic sound. Then, nothing.

Felicity

63

From the darkness inside the van, there was suddenly so much light, so much activity, so many people. I was being asked if I was injured. Told an ambulance was coming. I tried to speak, but I couldn't. I felt cold, and dazed. I closed my eyes, and then I opened them again. Where was Jay? Where was the van? Out of all the figures of people I didn't know – police, a small crowd of onlookers – a figure came forwards. He seemed familiar, though his face was bruised and grazed, and he had his arm in a sling.

'Scott,' I mouthed silently. Then my voice returned. 'Scott!'

He rushed over to me, crouching beside me where I lay on the ground. I tried to sit up.

'No, don't move,' he said. 'The ambulance will be here soon, you need to stay still.'

He turned to the two police officers closest to him. 'She's pregnant,' he told them.

I wondered vaguely how he knew. *Natasha, that's how he knows.* I remembered Jay had said Leo was with Natasha and Zack. I needed to know if it was true. 'L–L...' I started to say. My words had escaped me again. How hard had I fallen? I felt like I'd been hit by a bus. 'Leo!' I said finally, desperately.

'He's safe,' Scott said quickly. 'He's with Natasha and Zack–'

Suddenly, I burst into tears. People were talking comfortingly to me, but I couldn't hear them, I just kept crying.

Martin appeared close beside Scott, and when he spoke, his words got through to me. Words I would never forget. 'Jay is dead,' he said.

'Are you sure?' Scott asked him.

'I just heard one of the police officers say it,' Martin said. 'He's dead.'

Scott looked me in the eye. 'He's dead, Felicity. He's gone. He's never going to come near you again.'

I stared at him. I couldn't reply. Dead. Jay was dead. Relief washed through me, and tears overwhelmed me again.

'It's over,' Scott said. 'It's truly, truly over.'

I closed my eyes. I felt weak, cold, shocked. But in another way, I felt alive. I knew I wouldn't feel free straight away. Maybe I wouldn't feel truly free for a long time. His lasting legacy would be my fear, but my lasting rebellion against him would be my survival. And now he was dead, that was something he would never be able to take from me.

Epilogue

Stephanie

She blinked a couple of times after opening her eyes, and her now familiar hospital surroundings came into focus. When she'd first woken and seen the hospital, she'd been disoriented, confused, terrified. But now that some time had passed, she was more used to the place, the quiet rhythm of life that went on around her bed. Sitting up against a pile of pillows, she yawned hugely. She still couldn't remember anything about what had happened to her. They said Jason had hit her with a lamp. Except it was weird because they'd called him Jay. In fact, it was her finding out his identity that had led to the attack – at least, that's what the police thought.

The door to her room opened, and her dad came inside. She smiled at him. Of all the mysterious things that had happened since she'd woken in hospital, the sudden appearance of her father had been the most surprising, and the most wonderful.

'There's a young man out there for you,' her dad said, somewhat mischievously.

'What "young man"?' Stephanie asked. 'What are you talking about?'

She looked around at a little knock on the door.

'Well, are you going to tell him to come in?'

'I don't know…'

Her dad got up and opened the door, and a nervous, dark-haired man clutching a box of chocolates edged into the room.

'I… your dad wasn't sure if you'd recognise me. I know we've only talked online a few times…'

The pieces clicked. 'Xavier!' she said. 'I remember. Yes, I remember!'

She looked from her dad, to Xavier, and back to her dad

again, warm butterflies fluttering in her stomach. Then she glanced at the box of chocolates in Xavier's hand. 'So, are you going to give me those, or what?' she said with a laugh.

Xavier handed them to her, and his hand brushed hers. It felt tingly, like the tests the doctors did to check she had feeling in her fingers, except nice. More than nice. It felt... right.

Felicity

Four months later

'I can see your bump!' Leanne squealed, when the wind blowing off the ocean flattened my top against my body. 'Can I touch it?'

I nodded and she put her hands on me. 'Oh, it's so lovely, Fliss!' She let go of me to try, without success, to wrangle her windswept red hair into a ponytail. 'You must be so excited!'

'I am.'

'Good job you're getting married in a few weeks, or you'd struggle to fit into your dress.'

'Yeah.'

She turned serious. 'It's all happening fast, though, isn't it? Are you sure you're okay?'

I nodded. 'I have good days and bad days.'

We walked along Alstercombe beach in silence for a time, the blustery wind snatching at my breath, and turning my cheeks pink.

'You know what gets me?' Leanne said.

'What's that?'

'Vicky. I mean, what the hell was going on in her head?'

'I don't know.'

'So Dennis really isn't Scott's?'

'No.' Scott had done a paternity test. He'd been upset, though he said it made no difference to him. It had still been a shock, however, to see it in black and white.

'But does she love him or hate him?'

'I don't think she ever decided. With some people, I don't think there's much distinction between the two.'

I found it hard to think about Vicky. She'd been the reason Jay had managed to do what he did. 'They found a picture in her house,' I told Leanne. 'It was a big canvas print – a photo of her with Scott and Dennis.'

'Creepy.'

'She'd scratched Scott's face out.'

'My God, Fliss. You must be glad she's in prison.'

'I feel bad for Dennis. He's got me and Scott, but he doesn't have his mum. Well, one of Vicky's friends takes Dennis to visit her regularly, but it's not the same, is it? And none of it is his fault.'

'And it's certainly not yours! She chose to do what she did. She could have gone to the police much, much earlier. As soon as she saw Jay in Alstercombe. But she tried to help him. She covered up for him. There's no excuse.'

'I just...' I sighed. 'It seems like people hurt the most the ones they want to be with the most. How can that make any sense?'

'You and Scott got super unlucky with Jay and Vicky. That's all it is, Fliss. Don't read any more into it than that.'

I plonked down onto the shingle. A young family were down near the water, battling with a kite. I smiled at their efforts, and Leanne said, 'I tried to go kite-flying with Kayleigh once. We were both bored to tears.'

I laughed. 'Scott's come down here with Leo and Den a few times to fly kites. They seemed to enjoy it.'

'You've really fallen on your feet with Scott, you know that?'

'I do.'

I watched the young family. Behind them, the sea was a dark grey-blue, and the waves had an angry, foamy look to them.

'You know the weirdest thing with Jay?' I said after a while.

'Everything about that man was weird.'

'Seriously, though.'

Leanne cocked her head to the side. 'I'm listening.'

I took a deep breath, and let it out slowly. 'It's just... all he wanted was Sammie. All along. I'm not sure any of it was ever about me, not really.'

'You mean the teenage girl he and Mark killed?'

'Yeah. I don't think he ever moved on. Not a single day.

think in his mind he's still back there.'

She shivered. 'Thank God he's gone.'

'They said he would have died instantly.'

'Well, I'm glad,' Leanne said. 'Though I wouldn't have minded him suffering a bit before he snuffed it.'

I didn't answer her. I stared intently ahead, at the angry waves. I couldn't be sure if Jay had truly been intending to kill me as well as himself that day in the van, and to be honest, I was glad I would never find out. By the end he'd grown so absorbed in a world of delusion and obsession that I doubt he'd really known himself what he was trying to achieve. I sighed, and Leanne reached out her hand for mine.

'The important thing is that now you'll never have to look over your shoulder again,' she said, giving my hand a squeeze. I smiled at her, but she didn't really understand. I wasn't sure there would ever be a time when I never felt I had to look over my shoulder. But hopefully those times would grow fewer, and further apart. Perhaps, at some point, I'd go a whole day without needing to look. Maybe a whole week, two. I squeezed Leanne's hand back. I'd get there, someday.

Jay

They said he died instantly. But he hadn't. He'd died quickly, that was for sure. But it hadn't been immediate. Before he died, he'd seen something.

He'd felt some pain. He'd heard sounds. He knew he was dying, and he'd stopped seeing what was really in front of him, and found himself looking at something else entirely. He was in a room, a dark grey, empty room. Wait. It wasn't empty. Sammie was here! And in her arms, a baby. Warmth spread through him. Sammie was glowing, her light brightening the dull space, and the baby was glowing too – her son, their son. He tried to rush towards her. He felt light, free, the happiest he had ever been. He was desperate to touch her, smell her hair, hold her in his arms.

He tried to run closer, but he was still too far away. Why wouldn't she come towards him? Why didn't she smile, or reach out to embrace him? Wasn't she glad to see him?

Her face was expressionless; it was as though she couldn't see him at all. Then she changed. Instead of looking angelic, with the glowing, perfect baby in her arms, she seemed to darken. The baby shrivelled, and disappeared. The skin around Sammie's throat turned purple and bruised. Her eyes were bloodshot, and suddenly she was naked. There was blood on her, bruises on her chest, her stomach. He tried to cry out that he'd help her, but he couldn't speak. Her eyes were fixed on his now, and her mouth moved but he couldn't understand her words.

Finally, his fingers were close enough to touch her, but instead of feeling warm and soft, she was as cold as death, her skin like marble. Her eyes stayed fixed on his, pleading, desperate, and then her body dissolved, turning into a cloud of grey ash that fell through his fingers, and disappeared.

Author Note

Thank you for reading my No Escape series. I hope you enjoyed reading it as much as I enjoyed writing it!

A few words about the journey that brought me to writing the No Escape series…

Anything For Him, the first book in the No Escape series, was such an important book for me because it was when my writing changed from something that felt like a hobby into a career, since people were actually buying my book!

I self-published my first novel, a sci-fi thriller called Networked, in 2014, and it was a steep learning curve. I originally used a self-publishing company, who went bust not long after, so I never even found out my sales figures or received any royalties. I found myself in the position of starting again, and this time I self-published completely from scratch, learning how to do everything from formatting the e-book and paperback and writing the blurb to marketing and promotion, building my website, and making a new cover for Networked with the help of my husband!

At the same time, I began working on Anything For Him, a completely different genre, which I started writing without any fixed idea on where I was trying to go with it. I knew I wanted to write about a love triangle with a revenge element to it – that idea had been floating around in the back of my mind for years – but the direction Anything For Him ended up taking was a surprise to me, as the terrifyingly insecure and possessive character of Jay was born.

I have to say, there were a few dark days when it was difficult to keep going with writing Anything For Him. Not because I wasn't engaged with the story or the characters, but because it is very, very difficult to get self-published books noticed, and at times I would start to wonder what the point was in writing something that nobody would ever discover or read.

But how wrong I was.

After being invited by one of my readers to join an online book club, THE Book Club (TBC) on Facebook, everything changed for me. Thanks to the support and recommendations from members of this wonderful group, people were actually buying my book! Soon, it began travelling up the bestseller lists on Amazon, making it easier for even more people to find it. It was a wonderfully exciting time, giving me a huge boost and encouraging me to write my third novel, The Stories She Tells, published in 2017.

It must have been some time towards the end of working on The Stories She Tells that the idea of growing Anything For Him into a series occurred to me, and now, a couple of years later, here I am, with five novels self-published. One even has an audiobook edition, after I sold the audio rights to Anything For Him in 2018.

It's been a real rollercoaster ride becoming an author: unpredictable, wonderful, frustrating, thrilling, scary and inspiring. Without readers, though, I wouldn't have got anywhere. I am so grateful to my readers, who have taken a chance on a new author, and in many cases gone on to review and recommend my books, which means the world to me.

It's been an incredible few years, and most exciting of all I don't know where my journey as an author will take me next!

Make sure you hear about new releases from LK Chapman!

If you liked the No Escape series and you're keen to read more of my books in the future, I invite you to join the LK Chapman Reading Group. I send only occasional emails with information about new releases, offers and giveaways – no spam. You will also be able to download a free copy of my short story about a one night stand gone wrong, 'Worth Pursuing' (a prequel to the No Escape series that's now available exclusively to Reading Group subscribers) when you sign up!

Visit my website, www.lkchapman.com or any of my social media pages to sign up to the reading group.

Thank you so much for supporting me by buying my book, it means a lot to me, and I hope you enjoyed reading Never Let Her Go.

Help and support for issues covered in Never Let Her Go

UK

Refuge
Support for those who have experienced violence and abuse
www.refuge.org.uk
Call 0808 2000 247

Respect Phoneline
Help for people who inflict violence
www.respectphoneline.org.uk
Call 0808 802 4040

US

The National Domestic Violence Hotline
www.thehotline.org
Call 1-800-799-SAFE (7233)

Also by LK Chapman

No Escape series:

Worth Pursuing (short story)

Anything For Him

Found You

Never Let Her Go

Psychological Suspense:

The Stories She Tells

Sci-Fi:

Networked

Too Good for This World (short story)

Acknowledgements

It has taken the best part of two years for me to write my two sequels to Anything For Him; in fact, if you add on the time it took me to write Anything For Him as well, the whole No Escape series has taken just over three years of work! Through all of that, my husband Ashley has been there for me, supporting me at every stage. I am so grateful to him for doing everything from reading through drafts of my books, helping me with formatting e-books and paperbacks, to listening to my frustrated outbursts when I got stuck on some aspect of the story! I couldn't have done it without you.

I would also like to thank my wonderful editor Carrie O'Grady for her work on Never Let Her Go, your suggestions and advice have been invaluable. For my fabulous cover thank you to Stuart Bache at Books Covered.

A huge thank you to the lovely people who helped me with my research. Having people to turn to for help with my research makes such a difference, and I'm so grateful to all those who assisted me. I hope I have done justice to all your advice, and if any there are any mistakes or inaccuracies in Never Let Her Go, I take full responsibility.

Last but not least, thank you to my readers, and to all my family and friends who support me. It means such a lot to me to have people believe in me and in my books.

About the author

My full name is Louise Katherine Chapman, and I am a psychological thriller author (although I've also written a sci-fi novel!) I have always been fascinated by the strength, peculiarities and extremes of human nature, and the way that no matter how strange, cruel or unfathomable the actions of other people can sometimes be, there is always a reason for it, some sequence of events to be unravelled.

After graduating from the University of Southampton in 2008 with a first class degree in psychology, I worked for a year as a psychologist at a consultancy company. In 2009 I had to give up work after developing chronic fatigue syndrome (CFS) – a long term health condition that causes debilitating physical and mental exhaustion. After a few years I thankfully managed to regain enough energy to spend some time volunteering for the mental health charity Mind, and eventually to begin writing. Although my energy levels are still limited, I am mostly recovered from CFS and I am so grateful to be able to write and for the support of my readers.

Mental health is a topic I often explore in my books. I suffer from bipolar disorder and OCD myself, and I find writing very helpful and therapeutic.

I live in Somerset with my husband and son. When I'm not writing I enjoy walks in the woods, video games, and spending time with family and friends.

You can find out more about me and my books by visiting my website: **www.lkchapman.com**.

Connect with LK Chapman

Keep up to date with the latest news and new releases from LK Chapman:

Twitter: **@LK_Chapman**

Facebook: **www.facebook.com/lkchapmanbooks**

Subscribe to the LK Chapman newsletter by visiting **www.lkchapman.com**

The Stories She Tells

A psychological page-turner by LK Chapman

A heartbreaking secret. A lifetime of lies.

When Michael decides to track down ex-girlfriend Rae, who disappeared ten years ago while pregnant with his baby, he knows it could change his life forever. His search for her takes unexpected turns as he unearths multiple changes of identity and a childhood she tried to pretend never happened, but nothing could prepare him for what awaits when he finally finds her.

Rae appears to be happily married with a brand new baby daughter. But she is cagey about what happened to Michael's child, and starts to say alarming things: that her husband is trying to force her to give up her new baby for adoption, that he's attempting to undermine the bond between her and her child, and deliberately making her doubt her own sanity.

As Michael is drawn in deeper to her disturbing claims, he begins to doubt the truth of what she is saying. But is she really making it all up, or is there a shocking and heartbreaking secret at the root of the stories she tells?

Lightning Source UK Ltd.
Milton Keynes UK
UKHW010809211120
373821UK00001B/98